WHEN THE WAR IS OVER

WHEN THE WAR IS OVER

martha attema

ORCA BOOK PUBLISHERS

National Library of Canada Cataloguing in Publication Data
Attema, Martha, 1949 -

When the war is over

ISBN 1-55143-240-4

1. World War, 1939-1945 – Netherlands – Juvenile fiction. 2. World War, 1939-1945 – Underground movements – Juvenile fiction. I. Title.

PS8551.T74W43 2002   jC813'.54   C2002-910998-1

PZ7. A8664Wh 2002

First published in the United States, 2003

Library of Congress Control Number: 2002111247

Summary: In occupied Holland during WWII, a young girl's work for the resistance becomes dangerously complicated when she falls in love with a German soldier.

Orca Book Publishers gratefully acknowledges the support for its publishing programs provided by the following agencies: the Government of Canada through the Book Publishing Industry Development Program (BPIDP), the Canada Council for the Arts, and the British Columbia Arts Council.

Cover design: Christine Toller
Cover illustration: James Bentley
Printed and bound in Canada

IN CANADA:
Orca Book Publishers
PO Box 5626, Station B
Victoria, BC Canada
V8R 6S4

IN THE UNITED STATES:
Orca Book Publishers
PO Box 468
Custer, WA USA
98240-0468

04 03 02 • 5 4 3 2 1

This book is dedicated to all the courageous girls and women who risked their lives working for the resistance to help liberate my homeland.

Pronunciation Guide

Alie	Al-ee
Afke	Augh-ke
Baukje	Bow-ke
de Bruin	de Brew-in
de Groot	de Hroat
de Wit	de Vit
Dijkstra	Dyke-straw
Douwe	Dow-e
Enkhuizen	Ank-husen
Freerk	Fray-urk
Friesland	Frees-land
Jan	Yon
Janke	Yan-ke
Japp	Yaa-p
Jeltsje	Yell-chye
Kees	Kase
Klaas	Klass
Klaske	Klass-ke
Leeuwarden	Lay-oo-varden
Piet	Peet
Pieter	Peet-er
Sietske	Seets-ke
Thea	Tee-ya
Tine	Teen-e
van Echten	van Ach-ten
Verbeek	Vur-bake
Visser	Vis-er

1.

"ATTENTION!"

In the pitch darkness Janke Visser jumped from her bed. Outside her window, engines blared. Voices barked orders. Doors slammed. Startled out of a deep sleep, she grabbed the pillow and pressed it over her head. Her heart pounded. The shouts of a German officer forced Janke back to the harsh present of November 1943. She groaned and fell back onto the bed.

For the past two and a half years Janke had often woken to the commands of German officers, the sound of army trucks, the slamming of doors. Even though she couldn't see them, she knew their routine. She could see the soldiers, lining up to mount the back of the trucks, their boots shiny, their rifles gleaming. She could see them marching, stiff legged, single file, double file and in rows of four.

This ritual had become part of daily life in Bishopville, a town of eight thousand in Friesland, in the northern part of the Netherlands. German soldiers had taken over her country and her town and made it their home. They behaved as if they owned every building, every street corner, every piece of land, but, most of all, every citizen.

In the darkness, she pushed away the pillow and stretched. She stuck her tongue out at the wall and the enemy outside her bedroom. Though she understood the futility of the gesture, she felt better for her small rebellion.

The sound of engines grew louder. Without seeing them, she counted the trucks as they drove down the street in front of her house. At least ten. The soldiers were housed next door, in the building that used to be her school. The school where her father had been the headmaster. Most of the school buildings in her town had been taken over by the enemy. Only the agricultural college had been allowed to remain open.

The blackout curtains kept her room pitch-dark. Since the occupation, the whole world had turned black at night. Not a single lamp could be visible for fear it might attract the attention of Allied bombers. Every night, planes flew over Friesland to drop their bombs on German targets. But only two weeks earlier, a family of five had been killed when a bomb had hit their home. Despite these casualties, Janke applauded the Allied attacks and imagined how hard it would be for the pilots to find the right targets in the black night.

"Janke! Time to get up!" Mother slipped into her room and switched on the light. "It's cold today." She closed the door behind her. "You need to take a package to Aunt Anna." Her voice had dropped to a whisper.

Mother stroked the short, dark curls away from Janke's forehead. She pulled back the covers. "Come on, you need to leave soon." Her hands straightened the blankets. "It's a long ride. As soon as it gets light I want you to be on your way."

Janke's feet landed with a thud on the wooden floor.

"Ssh." Her mother pushed her towards the wash basin. "Not so loud. Your father is still asleep. He didn't get back till five this morning. And Jan stayed with Harm."

Janke turned, her dark eyes big. "Do you know where they went?"

Mother shrugged her shoulders.

At least her father and brother were safe. For now. Otherwise Father wouldn't have risked coming home during curfew. He would have gone into hiding. If the operation had gone wrong, her brother wouldn't have found a safe hiding spot at his friend's farm.

Janke felt the cold penetrate her skin.

Mother's lip quivered. "I don't know what they did, Janke." She wrung her hands together. "Your father never tells me. He says, 'What you don't know, you can't tell'."

In the mirror above the basin, Janke looked at her mother's reflection. She caught her breath as she realized how her mother had aged so suddenly. The short curls framing that face had turned from shiny brown to a dull gray with streaks of white. Her red cheeks had lost their firmness and glow. The sparkle in her brown eyes had dimmed, and the smiling, full lips had turned into a straight line with deep groves etched on either side. Janke looked at her own face. Before the war, Janke used to look like a younger version of her mother. People had often commented on their similarities. Now these similarities had gone.

Janke balled her fists. The war had taken her once lively mother and replaced her with this person who spoke softly and whose hands trembled. With her eyes alert, Mother was always watching the windows. Like a skittish horse, her ears were tuned to every sound from outside.

"The war has to stop, Janke. How long can your father go on doing all these dangerous things without being caught? How long will it take for our neighbors to find out that Jan and you are involved in the resistance?"

"What about you, Mother?" Janke asked. "Why aren't you doing more for the resistance?"

"Janke, stop! You know I don't want to know details about the resistance." Her arms went up. "It scares me. Especially with the soldiers living next door to us."

"You can't just stand by and do nothing." Janke's voice rose.

Mother placed her finger on her lips. "I wish you would feel the same way. I wish you weren't involved. You're too young."

"*You* got me up." Janke's eyes darkened. "*You* told me there was a package for Aunt Anna."

Her mother wiped her eyes. "I keep telling myself that they'd let you go. They don't arrest young girls."

Janke sighed. "You're fooling yourself, Mother. I *am* risking my life," she whispered. "Do you know what will happen when they stop me and find I'm carrying false identity cards?"

"No! No!" Mother covered her ears. "I don't want to know."

"You're hiding from reality." The muscles in her chest tightened. Turning away from the mirror, she grabbed her clothes from the bedside chair, opened the door and bolted down the stairs, forgetting about being quiet.

"Janke! Janke, listen to me!"

Janke stormed into the kitchen, where she halted in front of the stove.

Spreading out her arms, she let the heat embrace her trembling body and took a deep breath, wishing for the anger to leave her. She didn't turn when her mother entered, but stripped off her pajamas and stuck her feet in black, woollen stockings. Over her knit camisole she pulled a green sweater, a hand-me-down from Jan, and a gray flannel skirt. She rolled her pajamas into a tight ball and threw them in the corner.

"Janke! Watch your temper." Mother grabbed her arm. "I can't stand it when you behave like a stubborn child."

Janke struggled.

Mother released her arm, grabbed a kitchen chair and eased herself down. For an instant, Janke felt sorry for her; then she shrugged her shoulders to shake off the feeling.

"*You* live in an imaginary world, Mother," she spoke softly. "You're pretending that if you don't do anything this war will go away." Janke's breath quickened. "But you give me packages to deliver halfway across the province. Do you know how many checkpoints I have to pass? No! You never go anywhere. You hide in your little house while your husband and children are fighting the Nazis." She took a deep breath and looked at her mother's angry face. "Why don't you bike the forty-five kilometers to Aunt Anna and deliver the package yourself?"

Now she'd said it. Her body shook as she sat down and placed a piece of dry rye bread on her plate. She looked at the butter dish, topped with creamy, yellow butter which she had churned last night. She wished she could swallow those last words instead. No matter what she said, her mother wouldn't change, wouldn't become the brave resistance fighter Janke wished her to be.

Across the table, she met her mother's eyes. They glared at her with a coldness Janke didn't often see. She shivered. This was the mother she feared, the dark, unpredictable woman. The mother who could lash out for no reason.

"Don't you ever talk to me like that again," Mother's strained voice whispered. "You don't tell me what I should do or how I should feel!"

Janke took a bite. The piece of bread stuck in her mouth. She couldn't swallow it.

The grandfather clock ticked. A chunk of wood inside the stove fell, *clunk*, followed by a hissing sound. Unable to bear the tension in the room, Janke sprang up from the table, her hand upsetting her plate. It fell to the floor and broke. For a moment she looked at the china fragments. Her eyes met her mother's. Then she snatched her winter coat off the hook, grabbed the brown paper-wrapped package from the sideboard and went out through the door into the shed.

With the package stowed in her saddlebags, she pushed her bicycle into the pre-dawn light. She went out through the back yard, where they had made a small path through the willows and alders. On the left a thick elderberry bush and a beech hedge hid the headmaster's house from the school building and the fields behind it. If they rode their bikes out front, the Germans would be able to track the comings and goings of every member of the Visser family.

The path ran behind the row of houses. A two-meter hawthorn hedge, the back yards, sheds and houses sheltered Janke along the bumpy route and made her invisible to anyone who journeyed down School Street. Between house numbers sixteen and eighteen, the path turned right onto School Street.

Janke waited and listened. The stillness of the early morning encouraged her. She mounted her bike, crossed School Street and turned right onto Cornflower Street. Not many people were out yet. Most factories had been closed, except for the dairy. Men between the ages of eighteen and thirty-five were sent as forced laborers to the weapon factories in Germany instead. She worried about her brother, who would turn eighteen in January. Just before the summer, her best friend's brother had been sent to work in Germany. She knew that Alie and her family feared for his life.

Janke followed Cornflower Street. On one side gabled houses lined the street. The dark water in the canal was empty of summer boats. Just three houseboats were permanently moored on the south quay.

At the corner of Cornflower and Main Street, Janke dismounted. Across the street stood city hall, the center of local government. Now the historic building housed a foreign invader. Behind city hall stood the police station. There ordinary citizens were often detained. She looked both ways and turned left. She passed Hotel Canal View. Two soldiers guarded the majestic front entrance. The rooms of the hotel were now occupied by high-ranking German officials. The large ballroom was still in use. Once a month a grand orchestra entertained the Germans.

Janke biked across the drawbridge over the South Deep, a canal which enclosed the city and had once protected the town from invaders. She passed the German checkpoint at the outskirts of the town. The soldier on duty casually waved her through as he continued reading his book.

But that was just the first of many checkpoints she had to cross. If they were all this easy to pass, Janke thought, she wouldn't have any problems getting her package to Aunt Anna.

Dark clouds rolled in from the west. Pollard trees bent, lining the road on either side, whirled the last of their brown leaves towards her. Neat rectangular fields, sprinkled with farm buildings, reached as far as she could see. Her eyes spotted a flock of seagulls diving down behind a horse-drawn plow. Two black horses pulled the blades deep through the heavy sea clay, bringing worms to the surface. On the horizon to the south, the steeples and buildings of Leeuwarden stood out firm and strong. Janke now left behind the winding ribbon of the dike that protected the low-lying land from the high waves of the Wadden Sea.

Soon a light rain started falling. Janke silently cursed the dampness seeping through her clothing, gradually chilling her skin. A military truck honked its horn and passed. She met a few more cyclists and an army jeep, as well as a farmer's wagon pulled by a horse.

As she pedaled through picturesque villages with their proud steeples surrounded by clusters of houses, her thoughts escaped to memories of better times. It seemed so long ago that Janke and her best friend Alie had looked forward to dances in the ballroom of Hotel Canal View. They had imagined themselves wearing lovely dresses with flowing skirts of shiny fabric.

Janke had always dreamed of dancing in the arms of Harm, her brother's best friend. Since she was twelve, she'd had a crush on the tall, blond boy whose brown eyes shone with stars when he smiled. Janke's cheeks still warmed when she remembered the kiss. After the last school dance, Harm had walked her home. In the shadows of the chestnut tree in her front yard they'd stopped. He'd taken her face in his big hands and pressed his lips on her mouth. Janke had relived that kiss a million times.

But since the occupation, large gatherings like dances and theatre plays had been forbidden. They were allowed to go to the movies, but who wanted to when the films only showed how the Germans won at every front?

However, the Germans did invite the local girls to the dances at the hotel. Janke knew that some of her former schoolmates went, but they would never catch her, or Alie, in the arms of a *mof*, the slang name for a Nazi. Never would Janke set one foot in that ballroom until her country was liberated. After the war, she would dance. After this damn war was over and won, she would dance. Dance in the arms of Harm and whirl with him on the smooth, hardwood floor, their steps matching the rhythm of the music, their eyes locked.

But for now Harm had no time for her. No time for romance. He was too busy working on the farm, going to agricultural college three days a week and helping the underground movement. Janke knew that once this war was over, Harm would see her again.

The cold dampness brought Janke out of her revery. At least the rain had stopped. She pedaled harder. Why, she asked herself every time the pedal went around. Why did Hitler have to invade her country? Why did he hate the Jews? Why couldn't people live in peace? The pedals turned in circles. As did her thoughts. But there was no answer. Lately, Janke felt more and more drawn into the resistance. For her, the only answer was to fight the Nazis as much as she could. To do whatever she could to make their stay more difficult. Her work as a courier had started six months ago. Her father had asked her to take a message to the butcher. A few weeks later she was asked to take a box of jewelry from the butcher to Harm's farm. Lately her jobs were more frequent as the need for false identity cards and ration coupons rose. Janke often delivered these papers to various addresses throughout the country. Her father had patched the rubber tires of her bicycle many times.

Since Janke's father had lost his job as headmaster, he had been employed at the office where ration coupons were printed and distributed. This made it easy for him to obtain extra coupons. Janke suspected that the office equipment was secretly used to produce false identity cards. Until now she hadn't minded the biking too much. With the school closed she found it boring to stay home with her mother. Working as a courier for the resistance gave her a feeling that she was helping to defeat the enemy and to save lives, even if her contributions were small.

Her thoughts wandered to Jan and Father, who took part in more dangerous operations. Even though she didn't hear much about it, she knew their actions often involved hiding weapons and ammunition dropped by Allied planes.

As she neared the city, the traffic became heavier. It had taken her two hours to reach the checkpoint at Leeuwarden. All around the capital city the Germans had built a concrete wall, which they called the *Mauer*. This wall could seal the city in case of an attack. The first few times Janke had biked to the city, she had been very nervous. There were even more German soldiers than in Bishopville.

Today the city streets bustled with activity. Janke maneuvered her bicycle through busy intersections. She followed the canal to the city centre and then headed south. She had no trouble at the checkpoints at either end of Leeuwarden, except that she had to wait in a long line of cyclists leaving town.

The landscape changed as she bicycled through dairy country. She passed the entrance lanes of many large farms. This part of the province was rich farmland, more suitable for growing grass than crops. In the summertime, black-and-white Holstein cows dotted the green pastures. Now all animals, except for the odd flock of sheep clumped together around a feed trough, were warm in their stables.

Gateway, where Aunt Anna lived, was smaller than Bishopville, but in the summertime its population swelled with large numbers of tourists who sailed the lakes that surrounded the city on the south and the east sides. Janke followed the canal to downtown. The bells in the church steeple chimed eleven. The dreary weather kept many people inside. Aunt Anna's neighborhood seemed particularly quiet. At 11 Thrush Street, the lace curtains of her aunt's living room were drawn. Janke parked her bike against the side of the house and rang the doorbell. When the door opened, she froze. Instead of Aunt Anna, the tall frame of a German officer greeted her.

2.

Her heart drummed in her ears. Janke tried to swallow the terror that gripped her. She struggled to find something to say, but the words wouldn't come.

Then the German smiled and said with a heavy accent, "You must be looking for Mrs. de Bruin, yes? I'm afraid that we requisitioned her house just this morning. But I can tell you where she lives now."

"Thank . . . thank you." Janke's hands trembled in her pockets.

"It is not far from here. You go down this street," he pointed to the end of Thrush Street, "turn right on Sparrow Street and go to the last house on the right, yes?"

Janke thanked him again. He smiled. As she walked to her bike, he followed her. Her heart skipped. Now he would want to know what was in the saddlebags.

"You have come a long way, yes?" he said. "Your face is red from the wind."

"Yes," Janke nodded as she mounted her bike.

"Have a safe trip." He waved.

Thankful she hadn't taken out her package when she arrived, Janke didn't look back until she reached the end of the deserted street. With her heart still in her mouth, she biked down Sparrow Street. At the last house, she stopped. More cautious, the package hidden beneath her coat, she rang the doorbell.

A sigh escaped her lips when Aunt Anna opened the door. The woman pulled her quickly inside and held her close.

"Thank God, you're safe," she whispered.

"What happened?" Janke struggled out of her still-damp coat. She looked at her aunt closely. Deep lines were etched in the pale face. Her red-rimmed eyes filled as her thin lips managed a faint smile. Taking Janke's coat and hat, Aunt Anna pushed her into an unfamiliar kitchen. She hung the garments over a clothesline which ran overhead from wall to wall.

"Sit down," she said. "I'll make you some tea and something to eat. You must be starving."

Janke studied her aunt's weary face again. In it she saw the resemblance to her father, the high forehead, the brown eyes and the perfectly shaped nose.

As her aunt busied herself with filling a kettle and putting it on the stove, Janke's eyes wandered to the mantel, to the photograph of her cousin. Twenty-year-old Hendrik had been one of the casualties in those first days of war, when the Dutch armies had fought so desperately to defend their country. He'd fought at the Afsluitdijk, the dike that connected Friesland to the province of North Holland and closed the Zuider Zee, which was now called IJssel Meer. On the third day of the battle Hendrik had been killed by a German grenade.

Uncle Piet had vowed to avenge the death of his only child and had been one of the founders of the resistance in Gateway. In the spring, during a raid on one of the distribution offices, he'd been captured and sent to a concentration camp in Germany. Her aunt hadn't heard from him since. Rumors about the horrific conditions in the camps slowly reached the people in occupied countries.

Aunt Anna stayed involved in the resistance. She found safe addresses for many "divers," people in hiding, and was in charge of the distribution of false identity cards and ration coupons in her area. Students, Allied pilots, Jewish men, women and children, as well as young men who had refused to work for the Germans, all needed a place to hide. Aunt Anna found safe addresses, supplied the families who hid divers with extra ration coupons, and provided people in hiding with clothes and false identity cards.

The teacups rattled in their saucers as Aunt Anna placed a small tray on the table. A thick slice of rye bread with cheese covered a small plate. Janke warmed her hands around the steaming cup.

"Why did the Germans take your house?" Janke watched her aunt, who stared at the wall beyond her.

Aunt Anna moistened her lips. "Last night about nine, two Germans came to the door. They told me they were requisitioning my house. I could pack a suitcase, but I had to be out by eight this morning. I was allowed to take only my clothes and personal belongings."

"But were you alone at the time?" Janke knew her aunt often hid divers waiting for false identity papers. She looked at her aunt. Two red spots stained her cheekbones.

"No, I had two boys hidden upstairs in the attic. They were waiting for these papers you've brought." Her bottom lip quivered. "As soon as the Germans left, I sent them off to a farm on the outskirts of town."

"Did they make it?" Janke whispered.

Aunt Anna nodded. "Yes . . . But at four o'clock this morning, the Gestapo raided the farm."

Janke covered her mouth.

"The farmer, his wife, their son and five divers were placed against the wall of the barn and shot. Their bodies are still lying in the rain. The Germans have forbidden anyone to take the bodies for twenty-four hours."

Janke felt cold. Her hands trembled. Her eyes filled.

"I didn't find out until later this morning." Aunt Anna's eyes flooded. "The Germans came knocking on my door at eight. I'd packed my suitcase. They gave me the address and the key to this house." Her eyes looked beyond Janke. "After I moved my few belongings, I went to get some vegetables . . ." Her hands clasped together on the table. "The woman who owns the store had heard what happened." She stood up, her hands balled into fists. "They have no hearts!" Her voice rose. "They think they kill with God on their side!" Her fist hit the table as she collapsed back onto the chair. Dishes and teacups clattered, tea sloshed into the saucers.

Aunt Anna swallowed. Composing herself, she picked up the teacup and the saucer. She poured the tea from the saucer into the cup. Janke trembled. This was the first time she had seen her aunt, a model of self-control and discipline, so outraged.

For a time they drank their tea in silence.

"But why your house?" Janke broke the silence. "If this house was empty already?"

"My house is bigger. I assume that must be the reason." She paused, then continued. "With four bedrooms upstairs and one down, it's big compared to this one. This house," her eyes wandered around the small kitchen, "belonged to a Jewish family that has gone into hiding."

Janke thought about the risk people took when hiding divers.

"So now you don't need the package I brought, do you?" Janke spoke softly.

Her aunt looked up. "No," she said. "I don't need those anymore. Give them to me. I'll burn them in the stove before they get into the wrong hands."

Janke undid the paper wrapping. She pulled out two pairs of knitted socks, stuck her hand inside and took out the identity cards. She looked at the pictures of two young men. Smiling faces, perhaps nineteen or twenty years old.

"They were such nice boys." Aunt Anna sighed. "The handsome one here," she pointed at the darker one, "he wanted to become a pediatrician. The other one was a musician." With her index finger, she caressed both faces. "What a waste." Her eyes wandered to the picture on the mantel. "What a waste," she repeated. She wiped her eyes and with a last glance at the boys' faces, opened the little door in the woodstove and threw the cards into the fire. Janke heard the paper crackling. The flames flared as they consumed the existence of the two young men.

They sat without speaking and drank the tea without tasting it. Janke chewed on the bread, but her hunger had disappeared. She thought instead of the risks her aunt took. And the fear she must face every day. Would the Germans now find the hiding place in her house? And what would they do if they did?

Watching her aunt, Janke's heart filled with overwhelming sadness and anger at the senseless murders. Aunt Anna returned a weak smile. In her eyes, Janke noticed a new determination. Aunt Anna was bracing herself to fight the enemy. She had no more to lose. Her parents had died before the war. Janke had never known the grandparents on her father's side. There was nothing left for Aunt Anna to do, except to fight. Some of her aunt's determination crept into Janke's heart. She would do her bit she vowed to herself.

Janke wished her mother was like Aunt Anna, but a realization struck her — Mother would rather go into hiding. Hide away and wait out the war, that's what her mother wanted to do. A bitter taste came into her mouth. Janke didn't understand her own mother.

"Do you want to come home with me?" Janke felt a tremendous urge to be with her aunt.

"No. No." Aunt Anna waved her hand. "What would I do in Bishopville, Janke? My work is here."

"But you're not even in your own home?"

"I know," Aunt Anna smiled weakly. "But from this place I can keep an eye on my house. And," she paused, "many people here depend on me. The resistance is a secured network. It's like a chain, if you take one link out, the chain is broken and the network won't work anymore."

Janke nodded. She understood that her aunt wanted to continue the work her uncle had started.

"The socks will be worn, don't worry. Your trip was not in vain." Aunt Anna reached for what was left of the package. Her voice sounded stronger. "Out there are many cold feet that will need socks this winter."

Janke stayed till her clothes were dry, but not so long that she couldn't still be home at a reasonable time.

After she closed the large button at the neck of Janke's coat, Aunt Anna hugged her. "Be safe, Janke."

Janke nodded. She threw her arms around the tall woman, who she respected and loved, who radiated that same quiet confidence she admired in her father.

"I hope you come back soon, even though it's a long way to bike."

"I will," Janke promised before the door closed behind her.

She biked past 11 Thrush Street. A German car had parked in front, but nothing else looked different.

November rains once again escorted her on her return journey. But the wind was behind her now and the pedaling easier. Dark clouds raced overhead toward the east. No happy daydreams of dancing with Harm accompanied her on the long way home. Instead, the image of eight bodies lying in the mud haunted every kilometer.

3.

"I'm going to stop by to see Alie before I go to the store."

Mother had her head stuck in the pantry where she was washing the empty shelves.

"You just washed those shelves last week," Janke remarked.

"I know." The sound of her mother's voice was muffled. "Don't stay too long at Alie's. Your father wants his tobacco."

"Where is he? I haven't seen him or Jan this morning."

"They didn't come home." Mother turned and moved out of the pantry. Her eyes blinked. "They're alright. Marie came early this morning and she told me the men had better stay in hiding today. That's why I want you to get me some things from the store. You can take it to Marie after. We need bread, too, and potatoes. Don't forget the ration coupons."

Janke watched her mother dive back into the pantry. She shook her head and took three coupons from the bowl on the sideboard. The words "TOBACCO," "POTATOES" and "BREAD" were printed across the thin paper.

Janke left out the back and followed the path behind the houses on School Street. She didn't want to run into any of the soldiers. During the day, they were always hanging around what used to be the school yard.

The parsonage, where Alie and her family lived, was at the northwest end of town. The front gardens, which consisted of rectangular flower beds and two plum trees, had been prepared for their winter sleep. Janke rang the bell and waited on the slate steps.

Seconds later, the door opened. Alie, her face flushed, stared at Janke.

"Were you expecting someone else?" Janke glanced back at the road and trudged behind her friend into the vestibule.

"We have new people in hiding," she whispered, "and we were just practicing how fast they could get into their shelter when the doorbell rang."

"Oh." Janke hadn't realized that divers had to practice, but it made sense. At her home, they would never risk hiding people. Taking in divers, Janke thought, would be exciting and dangerous at the same time.

"The previous people were able to get into the shelter in two minutes and twenty seconds, but the man and woman we're hiding now are quite old. They have trouble climbing the stairs to the attic."

Janke surveyed the large entrance with the wide, oak staircase in the middle. A large front room and a dining room flanked the hallway. Janke followed Alie towards the kitchen. The smell of fresh-baked bread made her mouth water. "Have the Germans ever searched your house?"

Alie stopped at the kitchen door. "We're lucky. They haven't. Father thinks it's because it's always busy at a parsonage. The Germans don't find it suspicious that many people come and go. Still, we can't take any risks."

Janke nodded.

"Come inside. Mother is baking currant buns."

"Good morning, Mrs. Bergman," Janke greeted the tall woman standing at the sink washing dishes.

"Good morning, Janke." A smiling Mrs. Bergman turned around. "We haven't seen you for a while, but if you stay long enough you can have a taste of these wondrous creations."

Janke smiled. She watched how Alie's mother cleaned away the utensils and pots she'd washed. Her movements were quick and graceful. Her clothes, though worn, still showed the quality of good material and, especially, good taste.

"Have you been busy?" Alie asked.

Janke nodded. "Not as busy as I would like to be." It had been three weeks since Janke made the trip to Aunt Anna's. In the last while she had only made short trips, mainly delivering ration coupons to people who hid divers. "And you?" She noticed how much Alie resembled her mother, except for her lighter hair.

"Yes, very busy." Alie looked at her mother.

"Girls, you need to be careful. You might not think that the work you do is dangerous, but the Germans see you as enemies." Mrs. Bergman wiped her hands on the red-checkered apron. "Lately they have become more aggressive in their actions against people in the underground movement. Since they have established the civilian guards to spy on us, many more people have been arrested. Please don't take any unnecessary risks."

"We won't, Mrs. Bergman." Janke sat down at the table.

Alie poured two glasses of milk. "Should we tell Janke about the executions?" Alie looked at her mother.

"It's terrible news," Mrs. Bergman sat down at the table. Her voice quivered when she said, "My husband knows many people who work in the underground movement. Last week he was notified that three girls who worked for the communist organization had been executed. They were just a little older than you two." Her hands gripped the edge of the table. "They had been arrested and sent to the concentration camp Sachsenhausen in Germany."

"Rumor has it that they sang the national anthem while they were put against the wall," Alie added in a soft voice.

Janke's heart skipped. She couldn't believe it. And just as the image of the farmer's family and the young men's bodies had been etched in her mind, she now visualized the lifeless shapes of three young girls like herself and Alie, lying in the mud.

"I can't help thinking how hard it must be for their parents." Mrs. Bergman's eyes filled. "How could they?" She stood up from the table, picked up a laundry basket and left the kitchen.

The two girls sat silently. Each knew what the other was

thinking — about the possibility that the risks they were taking could lead to the same tragic consequences.

"We can't give up because of what might happen to us," Alie broke the silence.

"I know," Janke agreed.

"I also have some interesting news,"

"What is it?" Janke sipped her milk.

"There's a new one in town."

"A new what?"

"A new girl, working for the resistance. Her name is Dinie van Echten and she's from Amsterdam. She brought two Jewish children with her. One was a baby."

Janke's mouth fell open. "Wow, I wouldn't like to do that. I mean travel with Jewish children. You can't hide them. They're right there for the Germans to see. How did she do it?"

"I don't know, but she did it. I saw her when I had to fill a prescription. She's staying with Doctor de Wit. She's the new assistant, but I think that's just a cover. She's here for other reasons."

"So, did you talk to her?" Janke couldn't believe the girl had brought two children to Friesland.

"Oh, yes." Alie batted her eyes. "She speaks very . . . uh . . . shall we say 'upper class'?"

"Does she speak Frisian?"

"No, of course not. She's from Amsterdam. She speaks Dutch. And she's pretty, with long auburn curls, huge eyes, perfect teeth and full lips." Alie pushed her fine lips out to make them look fuller.

Janke laughed. "Oh, come on, she can't be all perfect."

"Oh, and a body like a model." Alie puffed out her flat chest.

"Oh, yeah, right. I don't believe you. You look pretty perfect yourself, lady, with your flowing, blond hair and your tall, slim body."

"My chest is so flat, there's no difference between my front and my back. And these sixteen-year-old lips have never been kissed, unlike someone else in this room."

Janke blushed and quickly changed the subject. "I have to go shopping. I hate going into the tobacco shop. Do you want to come?"

"Sure. I wouldn't mind trying one of these first." Alie pointed at the currant buns cooling on the counter. "And you should've seen her clothes. No hand-me-downs for that lady. No, siree. Brand-new quality. Latest fashion."

"Boy, you must have stared at her for a long time." Janke burst out laughing. "Or did you take notes? My, the details you observed."

Alie stood in front of her and lifted the hem of her woollen skirt.

"Look at us. When was the last time you had something new?"

Janke shook her head. "The last time I got a new-to-me dress was when Grandmother Janke altered one of hers to fit me." Janke pulled up her nose. "The material, which hadn't faded too much, is of a rich brown, with a fine, white lace collar. It makes me look sixty."

Alie laughed while she spread the buns with butter. She handed one to her friend. "You better take your time eating this. We don't know when we will ever have such a treat again."

Ten minutes later the girls biked down the street towards the center of town.

"I'm glad you're with me. I don't like going into the tobacco shop," Janke said. "I bet you there will be Germans in there. It's like a dungeon, dark, small and smoky."

"Don't worry. Those soldiers have no clue what we do in our secret lives." Alie smiled. Her light blue eyes lit up her whole face.

"I love it when they think we can't understand German," Alie continued. "But thanks to Mr. Verbeek and hours of night classes, we studied their language for almost four years. That might come in handy one of these days."

"Yes, we could become spies," Janke added.

They were still giggling as the bell announced their entrance to the small shop. It took a few seconds for their eyes to adjust. An uncomfortable feeling quickly stopped Janke's chuckles as she noticed four soldiers in the store. Their foreign eyes eagerly observed the new clients.

The tall one closest to Alie spoke in German. "Ooh, pretty girls."

"Let's get out of here," Janke coughed. "I feel choked already."

"Are you kidding?" her friend whispered back. "We'll give them our loveliest smiles." She pushed Janke in front of her and passed the first soldier. Janke held her head high, her lips pressed together. She wasn't going to smile at those rotten soldiers. Arrogant they were. If they thought they could pick up any girl in Bishopville, they were mistaken. She managed to get past the whole lot without looking at them. The tall one had the nerve to whistle softly, which made her want to vomit. Finally she made it to the counter and waited for one of the soldiers to pay Mrs. Abma.

As the soldier put his wallet back into his pocket, he turned and stepped on Janke's foot.

Janke gasped. She tried to pull her foot away, and as he lifted his heavy boot, Janke lost her balance. Her hands automatically grasped at his coat. At the same time, she felt two hands on her shoulders, steadying her.

"I am so sorry." The young man looked at her. "Is your foot hurt?"

He spoke Dutch with a heavy German accent. Janke shook her head, even though she could still feel the pressure of the imprint of his leather boot. His hands stayed on her shoulders.

By now the other soldiers had caught on to what was happening.

"It's clumsy Helmut again," they said in German.

"That's not the way to seduce a pretty girl." Their bold laughter filled the store.

"Janke, you alright?" Alie had never made it past the first soldier and couldn't tell what was going on.

"Yes," Janke answered through clenched teeth. She looked up. The face in front of her had pale skin. He was close. Dark gray eyes looked intently into hers. A sadness radiated from those eyes.

"I am so sorry," he said again.

Janke stood rooted. Their eyes locked. Her face burned. She forgot the store, the jokes and the laughter around her.

"You have to make up for that, Helmut." The tall soldier, followed by Alie, finally made it to the counter. Janke pretended not to hear anything.

"You have to invite her for dinner."

Helmut didn't answer. He let go of her shoulders and moved away to make room for Alie.

Alie looked at Janke's face. She stood between the tall German and the soldier they'd called Helmut.

"What happened?"

"One of them stepped on my foot." Janke nodded in Helmut's direction.

"How stupid." Alie looked at Helmut, then she turned back to Janke. "If the tall one didn't have such a big mouth, he would be kind of handsome," Alie whispered.

"Oh, come on, Alie. You wouldn't . . . "

"Of course not. You look so upset. I just wanted to make a joke."

One by one, the soldiers filed out of the store. Janke let out a long breath.

"They're always in here." Mrs. Abma nodded at the door. She grabbed a rag and wiped the counter. "What can I get you, Janke?"

"Tobacco, please." Janke's hands rummaged through the large pockets of her coat until she felt the coupon.

"Was there anything else?" Mrs. Abma took the coupon from Janke and placed it in a drawer underneath the counter.

Janke scanned the mostly empty shelves. "Nothing else, thank you."

The girls said their goodbyes and left.

A short distance away, Janke noticed the four soldiers leaning against the bridge, smoking. The one named Helmut stared into the water; the others started laughing as soon as they spotted the girls.

"Look at those bastards," Alie said, "especially the one who crushed your foot under his heavy boots. He looks so sad, staring into the canal. He must really miss his mommy."

Somehow, the joke didn't strike Janke as being funny. "Yes," she nodded. The whole incident had shaken her. "I better get my other shopping done," she said. "My mother will have a fit if I stay away too long. I still need to go to the greengrocer's for potatoes and then the bakery."

"Good luck with Mrs. Gossip, I mean Mrs. de Beer from the bakery." Alie took her bicycle. "I need to help my mother, too. And Janke . . . "

"Yes?"

Alie's face flushed. "I haven't seen Jan lately."

Janke smiled. "Too busy. He's working on the farm among other things. Jan and Harm and the other boys who used to be fun are all caught up in underground activities. They have no time for us."

Alie sighed. "They're not interested in girls right now. Their battle is far more exciting."

"We have to wait till the war is over," Janke said.

"It's been more than three and a half years now." Alie bounced the tire of her bicycle on the cobblestones. "How much longer do we have to live this horrible life? We are wasting our best years!"

"We have to fight harder." Janke's eyes shot fire. "I want to be more involved. I'm tired of bicycling around the country with a few false identity cards or a bag full of ration coupons."

"Would you be willing to bring Jewish children to Friesland?"

Alie's eyes questioned her. "Or carry weapons around? Especially now that you know what your punishment will be when you're arrested?"

Janke thought hard. Alie watched her. Janke stared back.

"If I was asked to do that, I would."

"So would I," Alie said.

They looked at each other; then Alie turned her bike and mounted. Janke watched her turn right on the bridge. She heard the whistles of the Germans. Before she mounted her bike, Janke spit on the ground.

The grocer still didn't have any potatoes. At the bakery she had more luck. A fresh batch of milk bread stood cooling on the racks. Mrs. de Beer talked non-stop. "You're lucky. The bread is still warm. And I haven't seen your mother in a while. Is she alright? Or has she gone into hiding too? Ha, ha." Her laugh echoed through the store.

"My mother is fine!" Janke snapped. She couldn't believe how the woman stuck her nose into everybody's business.

She stopped four houses before her home and dropped off the tobacco at Marie's.

"They'll be home tonight," the elderly woman answered Janke's unspoken question.

4.

Alie's parents kept their radio in a secret spot underneath the stairs. In the spring of 1941, the Nazis had required that people hand in their radios. It was forbidden to listen to the news from England. Many people had hidden their radios behind walls and under floorboards. As news came from the British Isles, it was quickly passed on to those who didn't have radios.

When the sound of static and the scratchy voices crossed the Channel, everyone crowded around the box and listened. Sometimes Queen Wilhelmina spoke to the Dutch people. She praised them for their courage and spoke words of encouragement. As hope grew, the members of the resistance grew more bold and took more risks, but the reprisals from the enemy were merciless, too.

Janke's parents had handed over their radio. Mother didn't want to keep it. If ever the Gestapo came to search the house, she would have nothing to hide. Jan and Janke had been really disappointed.

"We don't want to add to her nervousness," Father's voice had been firm. "We will hand in our radio and I don't want to hear about it."

On Sunday afternoons, the BBC broadcast a music program. Janke often went to visit Alie and sit with her family around the radio that was placed on the kitchen counter. This Sunday, after the music, they listened to the news that the Russian army had successfully recaptured Kiev from the Germans and was now preparing for a large offensive in the Ukraine.

"Great," Alie's father said enthusiastically. "With the German defeat in Africa and now these losses on the Eastern front, the Allied troops might finally achieve the breakthrough we've been waiting for."

"Do you still think they'll land in France?" Alie's eyes gleamed. "And what about those American troops who landed in Italy?"

"I believe they will land in France soon. Hopefully the troops in Italy will move north." Mr. Bergman patted his daughter's head. "Let's not give up hope, even though help is coming too late for many."

After the broadcast, the girls went to Alie's room and listened to old records from before the war. Mrs. Bergman had taught them the steps to the foxtrot and the English waltz. In the big bedroom with large Gothic windows that let in a pale December sun, the girls had plenty of space to practice their steps.

"We want to be prepared for the big ball when this country is liberated." Alie twirled around the floor, hugging herself. "I can't wait to go dancing when this war is over."

Janke giggled. "I can guess who the lucky boy is you would like to dance with."

"I hope it's your brother." Alie looked away from Janke, but not fast enough. Janke caught the deep crimson in her friend's face.

"For now, we have to be happy to dance together." Janke laughed and took Alie's hand, placed her arm around her friend's waist and lead her around the bedroom. "We'll dance when the war is over."

A knock on the bedroom door ended their romantic dreams. Alie opened the door.

"Girls." Reverend Bergman walked inside and sat down on the edge of Alie's bed. "I just got a message." His eyes went from his daughter to Janke. "You have to meet at the butcher's house at three-thirty. Go through the back alleys to Market Street. Enter the house behind the shop. Arrive within ten minutes of each other."

"What do we need to do?" Alie sat down beside her father.

"I have no idea. But I want you to be extremely careful."

"We will," both girls answered.

Janke left first. She biked from the parsonage, past the cemetery and through Cabbage Alley. The roads were busy with people biking, enjoying the sun and the mild temperatures. Janke used the back door into the barn. Mr. Dijkstra, the butcher, always wanted his visitors to take their bikes inside, so no one could see how many people came to the house. The butcher's house was sheltered by the shop and a barn where the animals were killed. Janke held her nose as the stench from slaughter and dried blood hit her.

Mrs. Dijkstra met her.

"Hello, Janke," she said as she put down a small bucket filled with what looked like a muddy starch. In her hand she held a paint brush.

"We'll wait for Alie and then I'll explain." Her breathing came in uneven gulps, and Janke watched as Mrs. Dijkstra leaned her heavy frame against the door.

A few moments later the door opened and Alie rushed in. "Hi, Mrs. Dijkstra." She pulled her bike inside and closed the door behind her.

Mrs. Dijkstra pointed at the bucket and explained, "We want you to glue a flyer on every fifth pole on Market Street and down Main Street to the drawbridge. One of you will paint on the glue, the other will stick on the flyer." She indicated a basket of flyers that sat next to the wall.

Janke's mind worked quickly. Market Street didn't seem too dangerous, but Main Street usually crawled with soldiers. Besides, there was city hall, the police station and Hotel Canal View with guards on either side of the entrance. Janke looked intently at Alie. The deep frown in her friend's forehead showed Alie's mind was moving as quickly as her own.

"You'll have to be quick and very careful." Mrs. Dijkstra sighed and wiped her forehead with the tip of her apron. "But be casual

about it and no one will notice you. I have disguises for you too."
She opened the door to the kitchen and pulled two light-colored
raincoats from a hook on the wall beside the door and handed
them to the girls.

Janke and Alie tried on the oversized coats. In the pockets
were large scarves that they tied around their heads. As soon as
both girls were dressed, Mrs. Dijkstra handed Alie the bucket with
glue and the paint brush. She gave Janke the basket with flyers.

"We look like two middle-aged women," Janke smiled at her
friend, but Alie's face stayed serious.

"Go, now." The butcher's wife opened the door. "And be
careful!"

Alie, watching both ways, headed out into the street. She
tried to walk as inconspicuously as possible among the Sunday
strollers. Janke opened the door and followed Alie after about
twenty seconds. She walked behind an elderly couple with a little
boy in a stroller and kept her eyes on Alie.

When Alie approached the fifth pole, she quickly glanced
behind her; then with brisk strokes she painted on the glue and
continued on her way. Janke kept walking until she reached the
pole. In a swift movement she took a flyer from the basket and
stuck it on. She caught up with the couple and the child and
continued walking behind them. The other pedestrians hadn't
noticed anything unusual going on.

Janke's heart beat fast. An oncoming German car drove slowly
down Market Street. Janke held her breath and kept her head
down, trying to keep the basket behind her coat. The car moved
on.

Janke felt like she was playing a part in an old slapstick movie.
First came Alie. She'd look both ways. When the coast was clear,
she would paint glue on the pole and disappear. Next came Janke.
She looked both ways, walked to the pole and quickly stuck on
the sheet of paper.

The people of Bishopville were always eager for news. Especially good news! So it didn't take long for men and women to

begin to gather around to read the news about the murder of the notorious police officer Elzinga, who had been responsible for the transportation and death of many Jews in Friesland.

Suddenly the sound of a German army truck alarmed Janke. She dashed behind a house and watched the crowds scatter as the truck stopped and soldiers jumped off the tailgate. That was all she needed to see. Janke hurried down the alley that parallelled the street. The Germans had caught on quickly. And, of course, the city was full of informers. People were not allowed to gather in groups of more than two.

Janke's feet pounded on the cobblestones as she ran. Her heartbeat matched the pace of her feet, and the basket with flyers banged against her thigh. The alley between the houses would soon end. Janke searched for a place to hide. She stopped in front of a brown gate. She lifted her coat and stepped quickly over it. A door opened and a man, older than her father, motioned her to come inside. He closed the door behind her.

"What were you doing?" His breath came rapidly. "Don't you know what the Nazis do to little girls like you?" He pushed her into the kitchen and grabbed her basket. He threw the remainder of the flyers inside the kitchen stove and hid the basket under a pile of clothes.

"Here. Take off your scarf and coat. Put on this apron and peel the potatoes." His voice was deep, but firm. "They'll be here any minute."

Stunned, Janke followed his orders. With trembling hands, she tied the strings of the apron, while the man placed a bowl with potatoes and a knife on the table in front of her. The man gathered up the coat and scarf and left the room. Her heart pounded. When the man returned he looked nervous. He paced back and forth in the narrow space. The clock on the mantel ticked. The sounds of the street were faint, but soon grew louder.

Boots came running down the cobblestones and orders bounced off the walls in the streets and alleys. The man sat down across from her. He stared out the window which faced another alley behind the row houses. Janke peeled potatoes. She worried and waited for the pounding on the door.

They remained silent until finally the sounds faded in the distance. The soldiers had moved on.

"You better stay for a while." He rose from his chair and went to the door. "I'll check it out first." The man exited and walked into the street.

Janke was left peeling potatoes in a stranger's house. She looked around at the sparsely furnished kitchen. The wooden table was rough and square, with no tablecloth. In the corner was a small, enamel sink. Two long shelves above the sink held the pots and pans.

The door opened and the man returned. "You can go now. They're gone."

"Thank you." Janke got up.

"I have a daughter, Klaske. She worked for the movement." Janke held her breath.

"She took risks. Too many." His eyes misted. He looked away from Janke. "She's in Vught. The women's camp."

As Janke undid the apron and handed it back to the man, she searched his face. His eyes were dark, filled with sorrow and anger. He took the apron and followed her to the door.

"You need a coat." His voice was gruff. "Here, take this one."

He handed Janke a navy, woollen coat with a hood lined with gray fur.

"I can't . . . " It must have been Klaske's, she thought.

"You can keep it," he said. "If my Klaske comes back alive, I'll buy her the warmest coat in the world."

Janke pushed the shiny blue buttons through the holes. Her fingers trembled. She shivered as she thought of the girl in the camp, who probably had no coat for the winter.

"Be careful. They have no mercy. Not even for pretty little girls like you and my Klaske."

Janke took a deep breath. She felt cold despite the warm coat.

"Go right and follow the alley till the last house. There is a small path that will lead you to North Street. From there you can make your way to the harbor, where you should be safe for a while before you find your way home."

The man grabbed the door handle. He opened the door for her.

Janke's head felt dizzy. She hadn't thought of how to get back. Mrs. Dijkstra hadn't told them what to do, just to stay out of sight.

Gently, he pushed her out into the alley. Janke turned right and followed the man's directions. Her eyes and ears on alert, she walked and walked. She waited, letting people pass before she crossed North Street. The wind picked up and sent chills through the warm coat. As she trudged along the North Deep, her hands tucked in the pockets, her mind filled with images of girls, like her, like Klaske and Alie, blindfolded against the wall with a row of soldiers aiming their rifles at them. Tears ran down her face. How could they sing while they were being murdered? Oh, how she hated the war and the rotten Germans.

The sharp cries of seagulls told her she had followed the canal to the harbor. Fishing boats were resting against the quay. Fishermen hurried into the boat houses. As the afternoon moved along, the sun lowered, chilling the air.

Janke scanned the horizon. The sea dike protected the land in the distance. Beyond the dike, the Wadden Sea rolled its waves onto the basalt rocks. How she longed to see the sea. To walk on the dike and smell the salt, feel the wind and watch the birds dive for food. Standing on the dike she would be able to see the islands. Ameland would be the closest. To the east she would see her favorite island of Schiermonnikoog. They used to stay on Schiermonnikoog for a week during the summer holidays.

Janke walked on until she found shelter behind one of the boat houses. She turned an old wooden crate on its side and sat down. The memories of those summers played through her mind. Again she saw her father and Jan put up their tent, while she helped her mother get the cooking stove ready. The campground consisted of thirty small campsites in the dunes. They would bike, fly kites, walk along the beach and swim when the tide was coming in. Her eyes followed the length of the dike. A seagull screamed and made her look up. A soldier walked along the quay toward her. Janke wanted to jump up and run. Would he be after her for the flyers? But she wore a different coat. Alie! They must have caught Alie. She panicked inside.

The soldier came closer. Janke didn't move. No, this one didn't look like he was going to arrest anybody, and they always came by the truckload.

As he came near, he looked at Janke. Their eyes met. Janke gasped. Helmut. The boy from the tobacco shop who'd stepped on her foot. The boy with the sad eyes. Those eyes lit up as soon as Helmut recognized her. "Good afternoon, Janke," he said formally. Janke nodded. She hoped he would walk on. There were no people around, but still she didn't want to be seen talking to a German.

"Do you often sit here?" Helmut leaned against the side of the boat house.

"Sometimes." Janke didn't look at him.

"I like it here. It reminds me of home."

Now, Janke looked up. His eyes traveled beyond the harbor and the sea dike.

"I lived close to the sea when I was a little boy." Helmut watched Janke. "My father often took me fishing." A faint smile marked his memories. Janke sat still and listened.

"When I was thirteen, we moved to Hamburg. I did odd jobs, working in the big harbor, but I did not like it. The city was loud and dirty and too crowded."

"Why did you move?" Janke couldn't help herself.

"My mother wanted to live in the big city so she could get more involved with the Nazi Party." A bitterness shone from his eyes.

Janke rose from the crate. "I have to go," she said. They

stood beside each other. He wasn't much taller than she was.

"I would like to see you again." His words caught her off-guard.

Janke shook her head. That was out of the question. She wasn't going to see a German soldier. She wasn't one of those . . .

"I know it is difficult, but perhaps we could meet here." His voice was gentle, like a caress.

Janke hesitated. "It's not possible," she said.

"I know." The sadness in his eyes returned.

Janke's heart fluttered. "I have to go," she repeated.

"Yes, you have to go," he said. "But I will try to be here every Sunday afternoon at four."

Janke started walking. She didn't want to hear anymore. Did he expect that she would meet him? Surprisingly, she had felt no fear of this soldier. He didn't act as mean as the others. Oh, stop it, she berated herself.

As dusk settled over Bishopville, Janke made her way back to the parsonage. The city had quieted down after the commotion in Market Street. Janke knocked on the back door. Alie opened it and pulled Janke inside.

"Oh, Janke, where were you? We were so worried about you. I thought you had been caught."

Janke smiled weakly. "I was worried that you had been caught as well. A man took me into his house and hid me while the soldiers searched the alley." A sigh escaped her. "I guess I was really lucky."

"I was almost caught," Alie confessed. "When I thought the soldiers would get me, I dove into a doghouse. The dog, a German shepherd, was tied up and stood barking in front of his house while I sat in it."

"Oh, Alie, I know that's not funny, but I can't help it . . . " Before she knew it, Janke was howling with laughter, imagining the scene Alie had described. Alie finally saw the funny side of her action and it didn't take long before both girls were holding their sides, relieving the tension and the fear of the afternoon.

That's how Mrs. Bergman found them.

"Come in the kitchen for some hot cocoa," she said. "If it hadn't been for that generous German shepherd, you two wouldn't be here, laughing."

"I know," they said in unison.

The hot cocoa calmed her down, and Janke felt happy to be alive and to be sitting in the warm kitchen of the parsonage.

"Where did you get the blue coat?" Alie placed her cup on the counter.

"The man gave it to me." Janke stroked the woollen fabric. "It belonged to his daughter. She worked for the resistance and was caught and sent to a women's camp in Vught."

"Oh, that's awful." Mrs. Bergman clasped her hands together. She looked from Alie to Janke and both girls knew what she was thinking.

"Do you know the man's name?" Alie asked.

"No." Janke shook her head. "But his daughter's name is Klaske."

Mrs. Bergman did not recognize the family.

"Did you stay with him all afternoon?"

"No." Janke's face grew hot. "He told me to go to the harbor and stay there for a while until things had calmed down." Janke looked away. She felt awkward. Something stopped her from talking about Helmut.

"It's only two weeks till Christmas." Alie looked at Janke's red face. "Will you come to the service?"

Janke nodded.

"And bring your mother," Mrs. Bergman added. "It would be good for her to get out of the house."

On her way home, Janke thought of Mrs. Bergman's request. She hoped her mother would agree to attend the Christmas service. Her other thoughts were of a soldier with a pale face, sad eyes and a gentle voice, who had sounded so bitter when he talked about his mother being involved in the Nazi Party.

5.

"I don't like it when people gawk at me." Mother took her winter coat from the wooden hanger in the front hall.

"They won't, Mother," Janke sighed. They'd been over this many times. "You will enjoy talking to Nel and Baukje and Pietsje from the Ladies' store."

"Yes, but Wietske de Beer from the bakery will have something to say about me. Only because I don't leave the house as much as I used to do. Because I'm scared and everybody else pretends not to be afraid of the Nazis, but they don't have to live beside them." Mother buttoned her coat and sniffed. She took her green woollen hat, with the cluster of pheasant feathers, from the shelf and pressed it on her head.

"We'll stay away from Wietske." Janke opened the front door. She watched as her mother took a lipstick from her purse and painted her lips in the oval mirror. Before the war her mother had always enjoyed using powder and blush and a pencil to trace her eyebrows, but today was the first time in a long time that Janke saw her use lipstick.

"Don't worry about church yet." Janke buttoned her worn coat and stuck her head in a toque knitted from yarn especially twined for socks. "We will have a great meal with Grandmother Janke and Grandfather Pieter."

"A nice Christmas meal on food ration coupons," Mother snorted.

Janke swallowed a response. She knew her grandmother well enough that she was convinced the Christmas dinner would be special, despite the food rations. Relieved that she didn't have to spend Christmas Day alone with her mother, Janke decided they would walk down School Street to her grandparents' house in the southwest part of town. They had nothing to hide, and many people would be out on the street today to visit with family and friends and to attend the special Christmas services and mass.

Janke waved at the Ademas next door. Mother and four sons stood in the window. They must miss their father, Janke thought. He had been in hiding since the beginning of the war.

"I wish your father and Jan could come with us." Mother pulled up the collar of her tweed coat. "They can't leave the war alone, not even on Christmas Day. And you want me to listen to Alie's father, who will be preaching about peace this afternoon."

Janke was also upset that her father and Jan were involved in an operation on the holiday, but at the same time she knew that most of the Germans were stuffing themselves with big Christmas dinners, so the risk of getting caught today was less, and for that she was thankful.

A strong northwest wind blew. Janke, her arm hooked through her mother's, felt the cold through her coat. She should have put on Klaske's, but she couldn't bear the thought of wearing that coat in church. What if someone recognized it? Someone who knew Klaske.

Mother didn't talk much and Janke tried to keep up a conversation about everyone's hope that this would be the last Christmas under enemy rule. Surely next year by this time the Allied troops would have managed to defeat the Nazis.

"That's why it's so important that the resistance works very hard to help the Allies." Janke looked sideways at her mother.

Marie waved at them from her front room window. She was alone as well. Janke knew that Marie's husband was probably involved in the same operation as her father and Jan. He often worked with them.

"The Allied troops promised to liberate us before," Mother's voice was angry. "I'll believe it when I see them."

When they crossed Market Street, Janke noticed a group of six soldiers standing near the greengrocer's on the corner. Her eyes settled automatically on the one who stood a little off to one side. Her heart skipped when she saw it was Helmut. Embarrassed, she bent her head. She didn't want him to recognize her, but as the two women walked past the group, she felt his eyes on her face. Just for an instant she looked up, and in that moment she saw a smile in his eyes. Quickly she returned her gaze to the cobblestones. What would he think of her, wearing a worn coat on Christmas Day when she had been wearing a beautiful, blue woollen coat that Sunday at the harbor?

In silence Janke and her mother walked the rest of the way to Java Street in an old section of town where the streets were all named after the Dutch East Indian colonies. It was no use trying to convince Mother about the importance of the underground movement, Janke thought. She left the topic alone and her mind wandered to the soldier, who somehow didn't fit his uniform.

On Java Street, the door of the eighteenth-century gabled house opened as soon as Janke lifted the latch on the small garden gate. Before she walked inside to embrace her grandfather, Janke noticed the lace curtains move in the side window of the neighboring house. Janke shivered. A family of Nazi sympathizers lived next door to her grandparents.

The smell of coffee, "real" coffee, floated from the kitchen as Janke and her mother took off their coats and hats.

"You brought a nasty wind with you." Grandfather Pieter winked at her. His white hair was combed to one side to cover his bald spot. His red cheeks shone like apples. He smiled, but in his eyes Janke read the disappointment that the men weren't with them. Every other Christmas, for as long as Janke could remember, her family had visited her grandparents for the noon meal. In the afternoon they'd walk to church together to listen to the Christmas service. It was the one time when Janke's family attended church. When she was in elementary school, Janke had enjoyed Sunday school. Alie's mother had been her Sunday school teacher. They often had made crafts, and she'd learned many songs, but the best part had been acting in the Christmas pageant.

"Look at you, staring out the window." Grandmother Janke, stocky and just reaching Janke's shoulders, embraced her in a tight hug. "The men are alright," she whispered. She looked over to Mother.

Janke followed her grandmother's gaze. She nodded and hoped they would be alright.

"I'll help you in the kitchen, Grandmother."

"Yes, you can bring in the coffee and the tray with cookies." The bright kitchen had two windows above the counter. Small terra-cotta pots with red geraniums filled the windowsill.

"How is your mother?" Grandmother kept her voice low. "She has lost weight." Grandmother poured coffee into the cups with the farmer pattern. "Her dress is way too loose, unlike yours." She eyed Janke's brown dress.

Janke's face colored. "Unlike mine. I'm bursting out of the seams and my fashion style is 'go short for the winter'."

Grandmother smiled. "You look good, Janke. You've grown into a beautiful young woman."

"Too bad nobody notices during a war."

"Oh, don't you worry." Grandmother pinched her cheek. "I'll see if I can't find you some better dresses. I have contacts." Her smile lit up her whole face.

"Mother has good days and bad days." Janke looked straight at her grandmother.

"And lately more bad than good days." Grandmother handed Janke the tray.

As Janke walked from the kitchen to the front room, where Grandfather was busy feeding the woodstove, she wondered how her grandparents, who were both so strong, could have produced a daughter who was not at all like them.

The coffee and homemade Christmas cookies tasted wonderful. Janke hadn't tasted real coffee for more than a year. With the coffee coupons they could only get chicory, a plant substitute for coffee beans, but Janke didn't like the taste. Her grandparents took turns talking about the weather, their rheumatism and the silly girls next door.

"I hope you didn't risk anything to get all these things." Mother's lip quivered. "You two should be extremely careful, with those Nazi sympathizers next door. I don't like the girls. They're always gawking through the window at anybody who walks down the street."

That was true, Janke thought. The lace curtains had moved when she and her mother had arrived. The neighbors were now probably wondering where the rest of their family was.

"Don't worry about us, Els. We have our ways to deceive them." Grandfather sipped his coffee.

"Both girls have German boyfriends." Grandmother looked at Janke.

"How old are those girls?" Mother picked up a cookie in the shape of a small wreath.

"Tine is only a few months older than Janke, and Jeltsje is ten months younger than her sister." Grandmother smiled at Janke. She really didn't care what the Tolsma girls did. She'd never liked them. They were snotty and thought every boy in town looked at them. She just didn't like the idea that they lived so close to her grandparents. Nazi collaborators were often dangerous informers.

The noon meal tasted delicious. Janke hadn't eaten succulent rabbit meat and pheasant since last Christmas. She suspected that her grandparents, "contacts" had helped them with the ingredients for this festive meal. No food coupons existed for rabbit meat or poultry. The potatoes fried in butter to a golden brown, the homemade applesauce and steamed cabbage all tasted like long-ago times. Janke treasured every moment, even though her thoughts were often with her father and brother. When the image of Helmut's face came to mind, she quickly erased that picture. A creamy custard pudding completed the meal.

"I'll do the dishes." Janke placed her napkin on the table and rose from the chair.

"I'll help." Grandfather stood up too. "The girls can stay in the front room and talk."

Janke and Grandfather carried the dirty dishes into the kitchen, where the kettle softly whistled. Janke washed and Grandfather dried.

"I'll come and get your mother sometime," he said in a hoarse voice.

It wasn't easy for Grandfather to admit that his daughter had problems, Janke thought.

"I know it's difficult for you and Jan and your father when your mother is upset."

Janke nodded. She couldn't look at her grandfather. Her throat felt thick. She scrubbed the cast-iron frying pan till it shone like the black belly of Marie's coal stove.

"She goes to bed when we're all out." Janke finally found her voice. "She is so afraid of the Germans next door."

Grandfather dried and dried the frying pan. "Maybe she would stay here for a while." He spoke to himself.

At three-thirty they all got dressed to go to church. They were not the only ones walking down the street. Because the Germans had forbidden groups of citizens to gather in the streets, many people met at church. Several German soldiers stood on either side of the large doors, their eyes roaming the crowd.

Organ music streamed out as people moved inside. The church filled up quickly and Janke recognized many of her former schoolmates. Alie waved at her from the front. She always helped her mother with the Christmas pageant. Marie waved and motioned there was enough room for the four of them in her pew. Mother moved in first to sit beside Marie, followed by Grandmother, and Janke sat beside Grandfather next to the aisle. Unfortunately they sat in the third row from the exit, and it would be hard to see the pageant at the front.

In the center stood the large Christmas tree. The scent of

pine filled the church. A candle had been placed at the end of each branch, and a man with a burning taper on a long stick lit the wicks one at a time. Candles burned in every little alcove between the Gothic windows on each side of the church. The fading afternoon light accentuated the colors in the stained glass windows. The lamps were turned off as the last flame flickered to life. Janke felt the magic of the wavering lights take over. The organ played "Oh come all ye faithful" and the congregation began to sing.

In his sermon, Reverend Bergman focussed on the tolerance the parishioners should have for each other, regardless of color, culture or religion. He mentioned the people who had endured terrible hardships in this past year and hoped that the new year would bring peace.

The Sunday school students performed their play, and when the little girl who played the innkeeper's wife stumbled on her line, Janke remembered that she had played the same role when she was seven. In front of a church full of people her nerves had won and she had been unable to say the words, "We have no room for you."

Alie's father prayed for peace for all people who were persecuted, imprisoned, working in Germany and in hiding. Peace for the Allies who risked their lives to help fight for liberation. Peace for the resistance workers and the people who opened their hearts and their homes to shelter those who had nowhere else to go. The congregation fell quiet when he prayed that they would celebrate next Christmas in freedom.

As the people left the church, they walked into the dark city. Anyone who stayed to chat with friends and family was quickly dispersed by the Germans, who were still there, shining flashlights into faces. Janke linked arms with her mother on one side, and Marie took her mother's other arm. Again they had to pass close by a group of soldiers. She noticed Helmut among them, searching the crowd. She didn't think he would spot her because there were too many people, but before they were on the road, she felt someone walking right beside her. Her heart jumped at the same time she felt his hand touch hers. A paper was thrust into her hand.

"Please take my letter," Helmut whispered close to her ear and disappeared among the people.

Janke quickly stuck the letter in her coat pocket. Her hand burned from his touch. For once she was grateful for the dark. She looked behind her and hoped nobody had noticed.

After big hugs from her grandparents, Janke, her mother and Marie went on their way home. The moon lit the way on this Christmas night. As they neared Marie's home, a shadow hurried toward them. A girl about twelve, whom Janke remembered from elementary school, stopped in front of them.

"What's wrong Aukje?" Marie unhooked her arm from Janke's mother's. "Tell me, did something happen?"

"No." The girl shook her head. "You have to take a message to Doctor de Wit." She looked from Janke to Janke's mother.

"It's alright, Aukje. You can say it." Marie placed her hand on the girl's arm.

"The wood will be delivered tomorrow morning at eleven. I have to go back now." Aukje turned and ran down School Street in the direction of Cornflower.

"Why don't you deliver the message to Doctor de Wit?" Marie said. "Els and I will have some tea until you come back."

Janke nodded. She looked at her mother. In her eyes she read fear and frustration.

The house was dark when she pulled the bell at 111 Marigold. The door opened and from the darkened foyer a woman's voice invited Janke in. As soon as the door closed, the light was switched on and Janke stood face-to-face with a young woman not much older than herself. Her hair was fastened in a thick roll, while auburn ringlets framed a perfectly made-up face.

This must be her, Janke thought. This must be the new assistant Alie had described. The perfect girl who had no flaws and had brought two Jewish children on the train from Amsterdam to Friesland.

"Why did you need to speak Doctor de Wit?"

"I have a message." Janke looked at the tall girl and realized Alie had not exaggerated.

"Doctor and Mrs. de Wit are out, but you can leave the message with me and I will pass it on."

"It is important." Janke hesitated.

"I know." The girl nodded.

"Tell the doctor that the wood will be delivered tomorrow morning at eleven."

"I will wait for them and tell him as soon as they come home tonight." Her voice was calm and pleasant. She stuck out her hand. "I'm Dinie," she said. "I hope we'll meet again."

"I'm Janke." She took Dinie's hand.

When she left, Janke remembered the letter in her pocket, but she didn't dare bring it out. She hurried to Marie's home. The two women were sitting at the kitchen table. The wood-stove snored contentedly, just like the lazy tabby in the basket beside it.

"We were just looking at the clock and thinking it was time for you to be back." Marie got up and poured Janke a cup of tea. "I told your mother that the men will come home early in the morning, before curfew ends. It's easier for them to see the night patrollers with their flashlights before they can be seen."

"Yes, if they don't get caught during whatever they were doing." Mother's eyes filled.

"They'll be careful, Mother. I know they will be." Janke got up and took her mother's coat and hat from the hanger.

"Thanks for the tea, Marie." Janke handed her mother the coat.

"Let's go home now," her mother said. "I want to lie down. I have a headache."

Marie looked at Janke. She read the concern in her eyes.

"I hope you feel better tomorrow, Els. I'll come and see you in the afternoon."

They left the house out the back. Tonight, Janke didn't feel like walking down School Street. She felt she had plenty to hide.

The secrets she carried about her father and Jan were serious enough, but she feared the letter in her coat pocket more.

After helping her mother get to bed with a hot water bottle for her feet and a cold compress for her forehead, Janke retrieved the letter and disappeared into her room. The headmaster's house was quiet. She heard the sounds of Christmas music coming from the school next door. They must be having a party, she thought. After lowering the blackout curtains, she snuggled into bed with her clothes on and turned on the bedside light. With trembling hands she looked at the handwriting on the envelope. "To Janke," it read. Carefully she ripped open the envelope and pulled out a single sheet of paper.

Dear Janke,

For the last two Sundays I have waited for you at the harbor, but you did not come. I have to think that you do not want to meet me. I am very sorry, because I would really like to see you again. I wanted to ask a favor. I would like to read some Dutch books that are not too hard for me. I am trying to improve my Dutch.

I wonder if you have some for me to read.

I hope I am not asking too much of you. I will wait for you this Sunday and the Sunday after that and every Sunday from now on.

I often think about you. I enjoyed talking to you when I met you at the harbor.

Thank you.

Helmut

Janke smoothed the paper. She had to smile when she reread the last lines. She knew he would be at the harbor every Sunday from now on. Her mind spun. But would she be there to meet him? She knew she shouldn't. She imagined his sad eyes when she didn't show up, but she also saw his face light up when he smiled, like today when he'd noticed her in the street. But she couldn't meet him on Sundays.

Janke checked on her mother, who was asleep. She went downstairs and locked the doors, but not before she left a key in a flowerpot on a shelf beside the shed.

Though it was still early, Janke decided to go to bed. But the events of the day had her mind in turmoil and sleep did not come quickly. She worried about her mother and the safety of her father and Jan. She wondered if they would see peace in the new year. And she couldn't help thinking more about the meeting with Dinie and the message she had delivered. But her last thoughts before falling asleep were concerned with figuring a way to get books to a German soldier who wanted to improve his Dutch. They had many books in boxes in the attic that were probably suitable for someone who knew little of the language, but was she going to take them to him? Before she had made a decision, sleep finally claimed her.

In the early morning hours, Janke woke to the sound of soft footsteps on the stairs. She left the warmth of her bed and opened the door. Her father, followed by Jan, met her at the landing.

"Everything alright here?" her father whispered.

"Yes," Janke said. "How about you?"

"Everything went according to plan. Did you get the message?"

"Yes."

"Go back to bed. Jan and I want some rest too."

Jan patted her shoulder. "Goodnight, Sis." He disappeared into his room.

6.

"Janke, open the door! Your grandparents are here!" Mother dried her hands on her apron and filled the teapot with hot water from the kettle.

Janke hurried to welcome her grandparents. As she opened the door for the elderly couple, a fierce January wind tried to force itself inside.

"Oh, that darn wind," Grandmother complained. She held out a box to Janke. "Here, take that to the kitchen. You might want to cut that. It's for Jan's birthday."

Janke rushed off to the kitchen, while her grandparents hung up their coats, hats, scarves and mittens. Mother stood at the counter. From a small tin can she scooped two tablespoons of tea leaves into the pot. Janke placed the chairs in a circle.

"Where is everybody?" Grandmother walked in, followed by her husband.

"Have a seat," Mother said. "The tea's almost ready. Janke, get your father and Jan. They've been upstairs all afternoon. They're not much help around here."

Janke sighed. She took the stairs two at a time. The door to the attic stood open, the ladder pulled down. Of course, Janke thought, where else would she find them but in the attic with their noses in the books. The attic had become the storage space for all the school supplies after the Germans had requisitioned the school building. Father, Janke and Jan had packed all the books from the library in trunks and moved them upstairs before the soldiers moved in.

At the beginning of the war, Janke and her brother had been able to go to high school, but a year and a half later the school had closed and the building was used by the Germans for storage. Since the closure, their father had taught them lessons in the evenings. Once a week they went to see Mr. Verbeek, a former high school, teacher to study English, German and French. Last fall their teacher had disappeared, and no one really knew where he went. His neighbor told Jan and Janke that Mr. Verbeek had gone to live in Limburg with his sister, his only family.

Lately, the work in the underground movement took up too much time and Father seemed less concerned about their education.

She should have a look in one of the trunks to find the books that she had read when she was in grades five and six. Now why would you do that? an inner voice warned. Janke's face colored. In the last few weeks she had often thought of Helmut and she felt guilty that she hadn't been to the harbor to bring him books. And why should she? she reprimanded herself. She shouldn't have anything to do with a German soldier.

She stepped into the attic. Two skylights in the sloping roof on either side of the house let in light. Underneath the windows, on the west side of the house, a small table and two chairs filled the space. Father and Jan occupied the chairs.

"The party has begun," Janke announced. She smiled at the sight of the two men dressed in their winter coats and wearing toques, sitting in front of the two small skylights, each reading a book. How alike they were, she thought. Both were tall, with curly blond hair, straight strong noses, square chins and their thin lips in a straight line except for the left side which was tilted up.

Her father looked up. "Come on, Jan. We can't be party poopers, and the light is fading anyway."

"Which trunk holds the books from grades five and six?" Janke trailed her finger along the top of a wooden trunk.

"The one you're touching," Father said. "Did you want to reread some of your old favorites?"

Janke nodded.

Father opened the trunk. "Here."

Janke looked through the stacks of books, at the titles. Most of them were familiar. She picked three and closed the lid.

With a big sigh, Jan closed the book he was reading and handed it to his father. "Keep this safe," he said in a heavy voice. Janke looked from one to the other. What was going on? A somber feeling settled into her chest. Was Jan saying . . . goodbye? Janke would be glad if he went into hiding. He would be safer then.

Father patted his shoulder. "You'll be alright, son. The war has to end soon."

Janke's mouth felt dry as she climbed down, ahead of the men. She took the books into her bedroom. On the second landing she waited for them. "Jan, are you leaving?" she whispered.

"Ssh, Sis. I haven't told Mother yet." He placed his hands on her shoulders. Janke looked up at her brother.

"The Germans will soon discover that I have turned eighteen, but I will be gone before they come and get me."

Janke blinked.

"You'll be alright, Janke." His hand ruffled her curls. "Promise to be careful and don't let Harm talk you into any dangerous stunts."

Jan left Janke as he bounded down the stairs. Father put his arm around her shoulder. "I need your help tonight, Janke."

"You can count on me," she whispered.

"Now we'd better put on our party faces." He pinched her cheek, lifted her onto the railing and gently pushed her. Janke slid down and jumped off in the hallway below.

After greetings and hugs from the grandparents, they all sat down. Janke watched her brother. A darkness shone from his eyes. The kitchen fell quiet. Mother poured tea for everyone.

"This cold weather we've had since Christmas is hard on people." Grandfather took his pipe out of his vest pocket. "There is such a shortage of wood, and people keep on cutting down trees. Soon we won't have anything left to heat with." His pipe pushed out blue ringlets of homegrown tobacco. Janke turned up her nose. She missed the smell of real tobacco.

"Did you hear that by now the Nazis have stolen the cast-iron bells from all the towers in Friesland?"

"It's a crime," Grandmother added, "but you know what Aaltje, the wife of the editor of the former newspaper, told me? In most towns and villages the people have found ways to chime the bells with iron pipes and pieces of railroad track."

Janke knew the bells at both churches in Bishopville sounded hollow. They used iron bars, too, but at least they chimed.

Father sat down. He pulled his tobacco pouch from his pocket and rolled two cigarettes between his fingers. He licked the ends and pinched them closed. One for himself and one for Jan. The cast-iron stove filled with logs and branches kept out the cold northwest wind, but somehow Janke couldn't feel the warmth.

"Did you look in the box yet?" Grandmother nudged Janke in her ribs. "It's for Jan's birthday."

Janke stood up. She opened the cardboard box. "A cake . . . a real birthday cake!" Blobs of whipping cream adorned the four corners. An oval of smaller blobs decorated the center of the cake. She turned around. "How did you do that, Grandmother?"

Janke placed the box in the middle of the table.

"Whipping cream!" Father roared. "Mmm, we haven't had that in ages."

Mother went to the front room, her face in a pout. Janke followed.

"Come on, Mother, don't spoil it."

"I was just getting the cake plates and I was only worried what your grandparents had risked this time to get special food," her mother snapped. "Here, you can cut the cake."

Janke returned to the kitchen, her face flushed.

"Do you need some help, Janke?" Father winked. "Just remember, the men get bigger pieces than the women. Our stomachs are bigger."

When everyone had received their cake and tea, Grandmother cleared her throat.

Janke smiled.

"And to get back to the birthday cake, I saved my ration coupons for flour and gave the baker two extra. I had traded some knitted socks for eggs. But that's not all. After the baker delivered the cake, it was your grandfather's idea to have whipping cream on top. He biked to Bosma's farm for fresh milk. We let it stand overnight in the cellar. In the morning a thick layer of cream had settled on top." Grandmother patted her stomach. "We took turns whipping it."

"Yes. We managed alright." Grandfather nodded and puffed his pipe. He looked pleased with himself. "We haven't had much practice decorating, as you can tell," he laughed.

"We don't care what it looks like." Father slapped Jan on the shoulder. "We know what it tastes like." He licked his lips.

The kitchen turned quiet while everyone sampled the cake. Janke held the whipping cream in her mouth for a little while before she swallowed it. Her tongue tried to take in as much of the flavor and the smooth, airy texture as possible. The sweetness made her close her eyes.

She looked across the table. Jan hadn't said a word. His deepset eyes looked somber. A sharp crease was drawn across his forehead. Mother's face shone pale in the glare of the lamp. Janke wondered if she knew about Jan's departure. They all knew that Jan had to work in Germany now that he had turned eighteen.

Father's jokes didn't have the usual effect, and Grandmother rambled on about her neighbors, the Tolsmas, and how their German boyfriends came to visit every night of the week.

"You should move," Mother said. "Now that those Germans visit the girls, I'm sure they watch what's going on at your house even more."

"They only seem interested in the girls." Grandfather shook his head.

The men smoked, and her mother stood ready to clear the dishes. Her father licked the last speck of whipping cream off his plate.

"I have something to say." Jan straightened.

Janke felt her body stiffen. She clasped her hands together in her lap and looked at her brother.

Mother sat down and Father took one of her hands in his. Grandmother looked at her daughter, concern in her eyes. Grandfather Pieter took the pipe from his lips.

"I have to go into hiding before I receive my orders to work in Germany."

Janke swallowed. She didn't want Jan to work for the Germans. She clenched her teeth together. How she hated, no, despised Hitler and his rotten war.

The grandfather clock in the front room struck five.

Mother pulled her hand away and pointed at Jan. "Why don't you just follow the order?" she burst out. "If they find you while in hiding, you have no chance. You might survive if you work in Germany till the end of the war." Her words came out rapidly.

Father placed his cigarette in the ashtray. He stared at his wife. Mother stood up, then sat down again. "The war can't last that long anymore. I thought the Allies would all come and liberate us." Her hands twisted the corners of her apron. "Where are they?" A long cry broke from her throat. "And the soldiers next door are getting on my nerves, too. I have the feeling they're constantly watching us. I can't take this any longer." She sagged down on her chair, hands covering her face. Her body heaved.

Janke looked from her father to Jan to her grandparents. She felt like a spectator in a play. She wanted to go on stage, but she couldn't. She was stuck. Stuck in the audience. Stuck on her chair.

Slowly her father rose. He placed his hand on his wife's shoulder. "You're right, Els. The Allies should've been here by now. But they aren't." His hand moved in circles around her shoulder blades. "The soldiers next door have never bothered us. I'm not so worried about them. The SS, housed in the buildings on Main Street, are the ones we don't want knocking on our door."

The choking sobs weakened. "Maybe we should move." Mother looked up.

"Maybe we should," Father sighed. "But we can't send Jan to Germany, Els. The circumstances under which the men have to work are inhumane. Besides, Jan will not contribute to Hitler's war machine by manufacturing the weapons that destroy our people. I will not let him!" His voice grew firmer.

Janke's mother pushed his hands away. She forced her chair back and stood up. Pointing her finger at them, she said, "I can't live like this. Now, Jan is leaving. Who knows when we'll see him again. Alive!" She shuddered. "You," she jabbed her finger at her husband, "are also very involved in illegal activities, even though you never tell me anything." She inhaled and let out the air violently. Her body turned and she pointed at Janke. "And you, young lady, don't even know what you're getting yourself into." Her balance wavered. "You all think you are so clever, you think you can outsmart the Nazis, but you can't."

Jan stood up. His eyes met Janke's. "I'll never go to Germany, Mother. I'd rather die."

His words were somber, but convincing, Janke thought. She watched him as he stood there. A feeling of sadness and pride came over her.

"I'm a member of the underground movement. I'll fight Hitler wherever and whenever I can." His eyes held Janke's. "As soon as I've found a safe address, I'll find out what action I can take from there."

Mother turned away from the table. She walked over to the sink, took the kettle with hot water from the stove and poured it in the dishpan. Like a windup doll, she began to wash the dishes. Janke grabbed a tea towel. With his eyes, Father told Janke to leave her mother alone. The kitchen fell silent, except for the rattling of dishes and the occasional bang of a piece of wood in the stove.

Grandmother cleared her throat. "It's time to go." She stood up and pulled her husband's sleeve. "We want to be home before curfew. I'm sure they have much to organize, now that Jan is leaving."

"I have to finish my packing." Jan hugged his grandmother. "I will be picked up tonight at ten."

"After curfew?" Grandmother buttoned up the cardigan she wore over her winter dress.

"That's better," Jan said. "We know all the little alleys. We're more protected by the dark. There won't be a moon tonight."

Janke's grandparents struggled into their overcoats. Mother kept busy with the cleanup. Father disappeared into the shed behind the kitchen, and Jan, after a quick goodbye to his grandparents, went upstairs. After she'd helped her grandparents onto their bicycles, Janke stood forlorn in the doorway. She stared into the dark. The night air chilled her. She shivered. How lonely she would be without Jan. She sighed and closed the door.

7.

Janke went upstairs. She paused in front of Jan's door. She heard him moving things around. Janke opened the door. On the bed sat Jan's old kit bag. From the closet he threw socks, underwear and sweaters on the bed.

"I'm almost ready." Jan stuck his head around the closet door.

Janke walked in and closed the door behind her. She could hear her mother downstairs in the kitchen, busy handwashing clothes.

"Do you know where you're going?"

"No." Jan looked at her. "And I won't send you a postcard."

Janke smiled.

"I'll be going from one safe home to another and I won't stay long at the same address. But don't worry, Janke. I'll be alright."

Janke nodded. Her throat felt swollen. "I need to help Father," she said thickly. She opened the door and went downstairs.

"Father is in the shed." Mother pinned towels, facecloths and underwear on a clothesline above the stove. It was a nightly ritual. Every night they had to find their way through the laundry. The air in the kitchen hung heavy and damp, but by morning most items would be dry.

Janke opened the door to the shed.

On his knees, his head inside an old chest, her father rummaged through the contents.

"I knew I had an old tin in here." He looked up as Janke walked in. "I just can't find it."

"You mean the green one?" Janke knelt beside him on the

cold, concrete floor.

"Oh, here it is. It used to be green." Her father pulled a large, square tin with a lid from underneath some rope.

"What did you want me to help you with?" Janke stared at the tin. She got to her feet and found a rag on the workbench. A cloud of dust flew in their faces as she wiped the tin.

"I want you to take all the family pictures. Put them in this tin and find a hiding place." Father opened the lid. Janke's eyes questioned him.

"When, or if, the Gestapo ever search this house, they'll find no pictures of the family. It will just be easier."

Janke nodded. It made sense. She'd heard of other people getting rid of their photos as well. Marie had told her that they had buried theirs in the garden, but she was worried that they might get wet.

"What will happen to Mother when the Gestapo comes knocking on the door?" Janke looked up at her father.

His face tight, he stared beyond her. "That will be a disaster, Janke. I hope it never happens because she won't be able to handle it."

"Would she tell them that we are . . . ."

In one brisk move Father put the tin on the floor and stood beside her, his arm around her shoulder. "We can't think of that happening, Janke." His voice quivered slightly. "All I can hope for is that I'm home when it happens, but I don't want you to worry about your mother. I will look after her." He squeezed her shoulder.

"Maybe Mother could stay with Grandmother and Grandfather for the next few days." Janke looked at her father's tight face.

"Yes, you're right. Can you take her tomorrow morning or do you have a job?"

"No, not until after the midday meal." Janke's brain organized her day. "If I take Mother in the morning I'll be back to make the meal."

"I'll be home at noon and we can eat together before you leave. That's settled." Father got up. He handed Janke the tin. "I want you to get rid of the pictures tonight."

Janke nodded. Tomorrow the Germans might come for Jan.

"Take them to Alie's and ask her father for a good hiding place."

Janke looked at the tin. "When do you want me to leave?"

"As soon as we've finished this evening's meal."

Janke took the tin into the front room where they kept all the family pictures in the oak armoire. She dumped everything in the tin and closed the lid. In Mother's sewing basket she found a piece of elastic which she pulled around the tin twice.

After their meal of sliced, dry bread, Jan followed Janke into the shed. "So, Sis, what are you up to?"

Janke tucked the tin under her arm. "I'm hiding the family photos."

"That's important," Jan said. "One less thing Mother has to deal with if the Gestapo search the house."

"I just wish Mother wouldn't be so afraid. She won't be able to be brave when the soldiers come knocking on our door." Janke's eyes filled.

"I know." He stared at the wall. "I'm worried about her, too, Janke." He put his hands on her shoulders. "Look at me. You're strong, Janke. We can't stop what we're doing because of Mother." Janke swallowed. She bit her lip. She placed the tin on the workbench and threw her arms around her brother. "Please, be careful."

"I will. You too. I'll miss teasing you while I'm away." Jan ruffled her short curls. "I'll make it up to you when I come back. I promise. After we've won the war." He passed the tin to her, opened the door and pushed her into the darkness of the evening. The door closed behind her.

For a moment, Janke stood still. The wind had died down. Her lungs filled with cold air and her breath came out in little, white puffs. She followed the path behind the houses until it crossed School Street. She wondered who would come to pick up Jan and how they would find their way to his hiding place.

The barking of a dog startled Janke and she crouched down behind a garden shed. All senses on high alert, she sprinted across the road to the next alley. Perspiration trickled down her spine. Her arm grew sore from pressing the large tin against her body. The sharp corners cut through her coat and sweater into her flesh. After taking a deep breath, Janke walked briskly down the alley. It used to be fun when Alie and Janke snuck behind the houses and secretly visited each other, but that was before there were blackouts, curfew, and German and civilian guards patrolling the streets at night.

She leaned against the last house, just before crossing Market Street. The sound of an engine stopped Janke in her tracks. She ducked. With her head down, she pressed herself against the wall as the headlights of a military truck came from the right. With screeching tires, the vehicle came to a halt. On her knees, the tin tightly clutched under her arm, she watched.

Soldiers jumped out of the back of the truck. Their flashlights pointed streams of light ahead of them. She could see two Germans running to the front door of one of the houses, halfway up the street. Two more followed. Their rifles ready. Her heart pounded. Oh, no, thought Janke. A roundup. Either Jews or divers. Her mind raced to figure out whose house it was.

"Open up! Quick!" With the butt of their rifles, they banged on the door. One of the Nazis took two steps back. He jumped and kicked the door open with his boot. The street trembled as more soldiers pounded the pavement and followed the first two into the house. Their screams and commands bounced off the walls and cut Janke's heart.

Arms up in the air, an elderly couple came out the door. Oh, no! Mr. and Mrs. Bijkerk. What in the world could they have done? They were such kind people. Mr. Bijkerk used to clean the school and played tricks on the children. Janke could hear the man's pleas being overpowered by harsh German commands. A soldier pushed him into the back of the truck. Mrs. Bijkerk struggled with another soldier who had taken hold of her arm. Janke heard the soldier swear as he forced her into the truck. Her heart froze when she saw another man and a woman, and then a young man about her age and a little girl being dragged from the house by soldiers. The boy stopped to grab the little girl's hand.

"Quick! We don't have time for slackers!" The German shoved the young man ahead. He struggled, bent down to pick up the little girl. Janke saw a teddy bear clutched in her arms. Another push. The boy tripped, then regained his balance. Something sailed through the air. For a moment, he looked Janke's way. The flashlight beam showed his face. Oh, no! No! She recognized Jacob. His four-year-old sister Rachel. His parents. The Schumacher family. Jacob had sat two desks ahead of her in high school. He'd been the smartest guy in the whole school. Her body shot up. She felt an urge to run out to the military truck. To scream, "You bastards! You can't do this!" She wished she had a gun. She would shoot them. All of them. All of those rotten, evil, ruthless savages. A monster invaded her brain, took control and ignited a fire. The fire to kill. "You can't take these people!" But not a sound left her mouth. Doors slammed. The engine revved. The truck backed up, turned and drove back in the direction it had come from.

Janke sat against the house. The street turned black again. The sound of the engine faded. Fumes of gasoline still hung in the chilly night air. Cold sweat trickled down her neck and back. Her hands felt moist. As if in slow motion, her body began to move. It seemed as if what she'd just witnessed was nothing more than a movie. It couldn't have been real. Numb and chilled, she lumbered ahead into the street. "Jacob," she whispered. Her foot squished something lumpy and soft. Janke stopped. She bent and picked it up. The teddy bear. She gasped. Rachel's teddy bear. In a flash she saw Rachel's chubby face framed with a wreath of auburn curls. A cry raw with disbelief escaped her throat.

She clutched the teddy bear against her chest. Tears wet her face. Soft moaning sounds wrung from the depth of her heart. She forgot to be attentive and watch for the guards who patrolled the streets after curfew.

Later, she couldn't remember how she'd reached the parsonage. Mrs. Bergman found her knocking at the back door. Her eyes wild and swollen, one arm clutched a bulge in her coat while the other held a teddy bear.

"Janke!" She pulled her inside. "What happened?" Gently, she pushed her into the warm kitchen.

Alie, her father and an older couple sat around the table, drinking tea, their faces aglow from the soft light of the electric lamp.

"Jacob's family and Mr. and Mrs. Bijkerk were all rounded up," Janke said in a choking voice. She let her coat and hat be removed by Alie's mother, who took the tin and placed it on the counter.

"Little Rachel . . . " She placed the teddy bear on the table. "She needs her bear."

Alie came over and placed her arms around Janke. Mrs. Bergman set a cup of steaming tea in front of her. They all looked at her with concern in their eyes.

"Drink first. Then you can tell us." Mrs. Bergman held out a chair. Janke sat down. She looked at the teddy bear and stroked its brown curly fur. Two black button eyes gazed at her.

"There was a roundup on Market Street," Janke began. "Jacob, his parents and little sister, and Mr. and Mrs. Bijkerk were taken away."

A cry escaped from the woman across the table. Her husband took her hand and patted it. He held it. Janke looked at the couple. She read the fear in their faces. Jacob's face came back to her. "He sat two desks ahead of me in class."

Reverend Bergman stood up. His hands balled into fists. "Someone must have informed the Nazis." He paced the kitchen. "They were only to stay at the Bijkerks' for two nights." His breathing was uneven now. "Their previous hiding place had become too dangerous. That's why I had them sent to Market Street. I organized a place for them in the eastern part of the country, but they couldn't go there until tomorrow."

Mrs. Bergman walked to her husband. She placed her hand on his arm. Janke looked at his pain-twisted face.

"Can you talk to the Germans tomorrow and find out where they went?" Janke looked at the bear. "We need to send the bear."

"They most likely went to Westerbork, a concentration camp near the German border, where they collect all the Dutch Jews. From there, a train leaves every Tuesday for Auschwitz, a concentration camp in Poland."

"Can we send the teddy bear to Auschwitz?" Alie took the bear from Janke.

"Auschwitz is a death camp," Mr. Bergman said softly. He stood behind the two elderly people. Tears ran down the woman's face.

Death camp. The words cut in Janke's head. Death camp. She saw Jacob picking up little Rachel. Her throat tightened. An uncontrollable shaking gripped her. Long sobs raked her whole being, and Janke collapsed onto the table.

Alie's hands touched her shoulders.

"This is awful," Mrs. Bergman said, when Janke finally raised her head.

"I'm sorry." Her voice was still thick from the tears. "I thought these people were sent to work camps."

"Some work," Alie's father said. "I know from reliable sources that Jews are forced into slave labor. The weak, the old and the little ones are . . . killed in gas chambers." His voice shook. "And you know the sentence for people who hide divers."

Janke knew. She covered her face.

Reverend Bergman blew his nose. "Mr. Bijkerk always told me jokes. Every Sunday he would say, 'Good morning, Reverend. This is another extraordinary Sunday. Do you know the one about . . .' "

The kitchen went silent. They all had too much to cope with and words were unnecessary.

"What's in the tin?" Alie broke the silence. She wiped her eyes with the back of her hand and walked over to the counter.

"I came to ask . . . if you would know a hiding place for our family photos?" Janke looked at Reverend Bergman.

"Alie knows a good spot." He winked at his daughter.

"And you should go soon," Alie's mother added. "Janke needs to get home."

Janke shivered. The thought of going back through dark alleys and crawling behind houses no longer appealed to her. She looked at the Jewish couple. Holding hands, the woman's face pale and wet, the man's lips drawn into a straight line, they weakly smiled at her.

The teddy bear on the table caught her eyes. "Can you talk to the Germans, Reverend Bergman?"

"I've tried that before, Janke. They just laugh at me. I'll look suspicious."

"But you're a minister," she cried.

"Even ministers are supposed to hate Jews." His eyes travelled to the people at the table. "The Schumachers and Minne and Baukje Bijkerk are gone, Janke. All we can do is pray that they don't suffer much. We will continue to fight in our own quiet way and try to save as many people as we can."

Janke took the teddy bear. She hugged it and stuffed it in her coat pocket. She stood up and wiped her face with her sleeve. "Alie, can you show me the hiding place?"

Alie took her coat and the two girls silently left the parsonage. "Where are we going?"

"To the church."

Janke followed Alie through an opening in a thick beech hedge. In front of them loomed the shadowy steeple of the church. In the dark, they maneuvered around headstones and large, concrete tablets.

"Ouch!" Janke hit her knee on the corner of one headstone.

"Ssh." Alie grabbed her arm. "I can hear the night guards talking in front of the church." She pulled Janke down. From behind the grave, they saw two tiny moving stars.

"Cigarettes," Janke whispered.

"We can't go to the side door until they leave." Alie's hand rested on her arm.

Again, the tin cut into Janke's arm. It felt heavy, as if lead had replaced the family pictures. She trembled.

Alie pinched her arm. "They're gone. Let's move."

Crouching low, the two girls moved around the headstones to the side door of the church. The door creaked its protest when Alie pushed it open. They paused and listened. The only sounds came from their breathing. Darkness swallowed them completely as the door closed.

"We have to find the stairs," Alie whispered.

Feeling along the walls with her hands, Alie guided Janke to the stairs. One tread at a time, they climbed. The stairs narrowed and curved. Some light shone through the openings of the stee-ple. A wooden ladder brought them to the top. Janke felt the night breeze cool her face. Their labored breathing echoed off the stone walls.

"Hang in. We're almost there," Alie panted.

A rustling startled both girls. They stopped.

"Bats. Or owls." Alie touched Janke's arm. "Ready for the last trek?"

"Yes" was all Janke seemed to have in her vocabulary. What she wanted most right now was to be home in the kitchen, with everybody around the table.

At last they reached the top of the bell tower. Even though the bell had been stolen by the Germans, every half-hour the caretaker and another volunteer took turns climbing the tower and hitting a piece of metal pipe on a chunk of iron railroad track to chime the time.

"Between these floor joists we've stored all our antiques," Alie whispered. "Give me the tin."

Alie took the tin from Janke's arms. She lifted one of the floorboards and placed the tin in the space underneath. Without a sound, she closed the space.

The night air came in through the openings in the tower. Janke welcomed the slight breeze caressing her face. Alie took her arm and pulled her over to the arched openings.

"Look up," she whispered. "The sky's calm tonight. No airplanes. No dogfights between German Messerschmidts and Spitfires. There's no war up there tonight."

"Yeah." Janke shivered. "Down below there is. Look down at our town, Alie. People are loaded onto trucks like cattle. Transported to the death camps." Her cheeks dampened.

Alie placed her arm around Janke's shoulder.

"And Jan went into hiding tonight," she added.

"Today is the eighteenth. His birthday. I hoped he would leave and not wait for the Germans," Alie sighed.

"Any news from Freerk?"

"We got a letter just after Christmas, but it didn't say anything. Their letters are censored. Father thinks that the food is bad and that they don't have heating because he wrote that many of the men had gotten ill and were in the 'sick ward', whatever that stands for. We know they're housed in wooden barracks."

For a moment the girls stood in silence, cloaked by darkness, thinking of their brothers.

"We'd better go," Alie whispered. "I'll walk you to the end of the cemetery."

"Thanks," Janke said.

"Will you be alright?"

"Yes. I just want to get home. Don't worry about me."

The friends climbed back down and out of the church.

Alie hugged her best friend before she let her go into the dark streets of the city.

Once in bed, Janke felt numb, and not just from the cold January night.

Her thoughts went back to the Schumacher family and the kind caretaker and his wife. Janke placed the teddy bear on the pillow beside her. "I'll save you," she whispered. If the Schumachers ever came back, she would return the teddy bear. Janke never prayed. Tonight she folded her hands. She squeezed her eyes shut. In the darkness of her room, she whispered, "God, if you are there, if you are watching all the horrific things the Germans do, please, do something about it. Make them stop. Let all the people who are in death camps come home . . . Amen."

Janke struggled with her blankets. She saw Jacob bending over to pick up his little sister. She tried to imagine what the death camps must be like. She visualized barracks, barbed wire and soldiers with machine guns pushing people. A face with sad eyes clouded the image, but Janke pushed it away. He was a German soldier. They were all the same. They were the enemy. Why had she even bothered looking for books for him?

No, she would fight the Germans. Nobody could stop her, not even her mother. It took a long time before the images faded and sleep secured her in its folds.

8.

"Grandmother has some wool for you to knit socks for Father." Janke helped clear the breakfast table. Father had just left for work. They'd had a hard time getting her mother up that morning. And now Janke wanted her mother out of the house because she feared the German police might come for Jan. Father had instructed her what to tell them.

"Your father has enough socks and I don't need to knit for Jan anymore." She wiped her eyes. A slice of bread lay untouched on her plate. Slowly she drank her tea. "I don't feel like going. My headache is bad today. I'm going back to bed."

"But they are expecting you." Janke took the tablecloth and shook it out in the sink. She folded it and placed it on a shelf in the pantry. "You must go, Mother. Here is your coat. The wind is cold. You need your hat." Janke placed the garments over the back of the chair and went back to the hallway to get dressed. What do I do if I can't get her out? she wondered. Janke's chest felt tight. When she walked into the kitchen, her mother glared at her.

"Is this some kind of plot?" Her eyes shot fire. "Do I need to be protected because the Nazis will be looking for Jan?" She stood up from the chair. Janke faced her.

"Did you and your father cook this up together? Did the two of you decide that I couldn't handle those Germans? Well, I'll tell you something." She strode to the counter and opened the top drawer. She pulled out a long, sharp, cutting knife.

Janke froze.

"I'll cut their throats before they enter this house and then they can shoot me." The knife clattered on the wooden floor. Mother sagged down on the chair.

Janke held her stomach. She felt sick.

"Put your coat on, Mother," she said as firmly as she could possibly manage.

Her mother looked at her. The fire had left her eyes. She stood up, took her coat and dressed mechanically. She walked into the hallway and opened the front door. With a heavy heart, Janke followed her mother into the cold January morning. They walked in silence: Janke still stunned over her mother's outburst; her mother fuming about the fact that her daughter and husband didn't think she could handle the Germans.

"Leave her with us until the Germans have visited you." Grandfather followed her to the door. "Even if she stays for a few days, we'll look after her." He patted Janke's shoulder.

"Thanks." Janke closed the door behind her and walked briskly out of Java Street.

Back home, she nursed the fire and made herself a hot tea. She picked the sharp knife off the floor and placed it back in the drawer. She folded the laundry and listened. She listened for a car to stop in front of the house. But her thoughts returned to her mother and how she appeared to be getting worse. Jan's leaving had affected her deeply.

She made the beds and decided to dust the front room. Not that there was any dust in the house — since Mother cleaned everything that was clean already — but just to keep an eye on the road. She waited for Father to come home. At least after the noon meal she would have to go to butcher Dijkstra to pick up instructions.

The grandfather clock chimed eleven and Janke didn't know what to dust anymore.

A feeling of uneasiness brought her upstairs to her room. The three books for Helmut sat on her night table. One was about a dog named Bijke, whose adventures on a farm had made

Janke laugh. The second one she'd picked was about a boy who was all alone in the world. The story reminded her of Helmut. The last one, her favorite, was called *Afke's Ten* and was about a poor family with ten children. She must have reread that last book half a dozen times. And now she was going to give these books to a soldier? "Janke, you are crazy," she said out loud. She opened her closet and shoved the books on the top shelf.

In her anger, she ran downstairs. She set the table for two and peeled three potatoes. There was some leftover cabbage from yesterday and Janke put the pot on the woodstove. She boiled the potatoes on a small oil burner. They were out of milk. Now that Jan didn't work at Harm's farm anymore, Janke would have to go there more often to buy milk and sometimes cheese and eggs. She should be happy. She would see Harm more often and who knows . . .

The back door slammed. Startled, Janke dropped the plate with cold meat. When Father walked into the kitchen, she was on her knees on the floor, picking up the meat with her hands.

"It would be a shame if you wasted it, Janke." Father laughed. "Come on. Put it back on the plate. You know the saying, 'a dirty pig is a healthy pig'."

Janke stood up. "I didn't hear you and when you slammed the door, I dropped it."

"Are you nervous?" Father's face had lost its laughter.

"Yes." Janke poured the tea.

"Did you have any problems getting your mother out?" Father checked the woodstove and sat down at the table.

"No," Janke said. It was no use telling father about the incident with the knife, she thought. He had enough to worry about.

"I'm trying to find another house." Father cut the meat in small squares. "I've asked around at the office, but there's no vacancy in town."

Janke sighed with relief. She didn't like living beside the Germans either, but in the almost four years that they'd been neighbors, the Nazis had never bothered them. She loved this house. It was the last one on School Street and had more property than the other homes. She loved the gardens in the summer and the big chestnut tree with its large canopy, shading the rooms from the summer sun.

Screeching car tires stopped her thoughts. Panic gripped her when the doorbell rang.

Calm, her father stood up. "Just keep on eating. I'll deal with it." He walked into the hallway and opened the front door. She could hear voices. German voices. The words "sohn" and "Jan" were easy to understand. Her heart pounded wildly when the kitchen door opened and a tall German officer walked inside, followed by her father.

"Good day, fraulein," he greeted her.

"Good day," Janke said shyly.

"And where is your son?" He looked at Father.

"Last week we had a message from my brother who lives on a farm in North Brabant." Father's voice sounded convincing and he spoke German fluently. "My brother had fallen ill and Jan has been asked to help out. It will only be for a couple of months." He looked directly at the officer.

The officer turned to Janke. "Have you been at this farm?"

"Yes, many times." Janke was surprised how clear her voice was. "But that was before the war," she added.

"We are trying to get his papers ready to have him exempted from working in Germany," Father caught the attention of the officer, "but as soon as my son returns home he will report to the workfare office."

The officer looked around the kitchen. Father opened the door to the hallway. The officer touched his cap, turned and followed her father out the door. She heard them exchange goodbyes and the front door closed.

The door opened and Father smiled. "So will you describe your uncle for me, *fraulein*."

Janke laughed even though her hands were still shaking. "You were very convincing," she said.

"My philosophy is to not show you're afraid. But I'm very glad your mother wasn't home."

"So am I," Janke agreed. "It wouldn't have been this easy."

"I'll pick her up tonight." Father buttoned his overcoat. "Be careful."

"You too." Janke closed the door behind him and finished the dishes.

At the butcher's on Market Street, Janke waited in line. When her turn came, Mr. Dijkstra merely nodded his head towards the back of the shop. Janke followed him into the small barn between the store and the kitchen.

"Can you pedal with another bike?" He took the handlebars of a bike with black saddlebags that was parked against the wall. He checked both tires.

Janke nodded. She didn't want to say that she hated it because it made her right arm hurt after a while. "How far is it?" she said instead.

"Small Port. Fifteen Harbor Path. About ten kilometers."

Janke knew the town and the street. The ferry to the island of Ameland sailed from there. She took the bike from him and went out the barn door. Her own bike leaned against the side of the store.

Mr. Dijkstra helped her on her way. Janke wobbled a little as she turned onto Market Street, but soon she found her rhythm. She turned right on Cornflower and followed the canal. At the Main and Cornflower intersection, she waited for a column of nine military trucks to pass, heading west. Janke followed as soon as they cleared the intersection.

She passed the checkpoint just beyond the bridge over the North Deep and pushed hard against the wind. Several times the handlebars of the second bike almost tangled with her own. She focussed on her task and didn't dare look around. She found it hard to bike through the small villages, because they were all built on manmade hills, called terpen, to protect them from the sea in the days before dikes. Once she had reached the church she could ease off since the road went downhill.

As she turned north, Janke saw the tall steeple in the center of Small Port. Beyond the town was the harbor and the dike. The wind blew her sideways. Janke had a hard time keeping both bikes on the road.

The town, with its quaint gabled houses, was popular with tourists in the season. Janke had loved walking along the harbor in the summertime, watching the ferry leave, seeing the many fishing boats lined along the quay, their nets pulled up high, hearing the seagulls fighting for leftover pieces of fish.

The streets bustled with people walking, cycling and pushing wooden carts. Janke needed to use her bell often to make her way through the traffic. She was relieved to finally reach Harbor Path, a narrow dirt road. The houses along this road were smaller. Square front yards were cluttered with children's toys, barrels and firewood. Clotheslines were strung from yard to yard with colorful items blowing in the wind.

Janke dismounted and walked. Ruts and holes made the path uneven. She read the house numbers until she reached number fifteen near the end of the street. Behind the house stood a large wooden shed, bigger than the house and leaning to one side.

Janke had just walked to the shed when a door at the back of the house opened and a boy of about eight or nine came outside.

"Go into the barn," he said. "My father will meet you there."

Before Janke could respond he'd disappeared in the house. Janke parked both bikes against the side of the barn and opened the door. Inside, two broken windows at the back provided the only light.

"Hello," Janke called. There was no answer.

"Better take these inside."

A deep voice made Janke turn. A man older than her father stood in the doorway. He held onto both bikes.

"Which one is yours?"

"The green one." Janke took one step toward the man. His

coveralls were stained with grease and his hair was curly and in need of a cut. Her eyes adjusted and she now noticed several parts of boats, engines, anchors and other ships' gear. He must run a repair shop, Janke thought.

"Did you bring the stuff?" he asked, unbuckling the saddle-bags from the second bike.

"No." Janke's eyes almost popped out when she saw the man take out a small, leather case from each saddlebag.

She'd never checked the saddlebags. She'd assumed they were empty.

The man walked over to a long worktable and opened one of the cases.

Janke's heartbeat accelerated. She knew before he opened the case what was in it. A revolver. She'd been biking with two revolvers in the saddlebags. If she'd been stopped and they had been found, she would have been shot, the sentence for posses-sion of weapons.

"You didn't know?" His smile moved up only one side of his face. "That's good," he said. " You would've been nervous all the way."

Janke managed a weak smile. "You're right. I better go home now," she said.

"You need the money." He walked over to a small unpainted cupboard and pulled a metal box off the shelf. He opened the lid and took out a wad of bills, held together with a rubber band. "For Dijkstra." He handed her the package.

Janke had never seen so much money. She wondered where she would keep it. It was too big to stick in her coat pocket and she didn't dare put it in the saddlebags.

"Hide it in your clothes." He tapped his head in salute and left the barn.

Janke opened her coat and stuffed the money inside her cami-sole. She didn't like the feel of the paper against her skin.

The ride home was much easier. The muscles of her right arm were sore from the strain of holding the second bike. She held her arm against her chest as if she needed to hold onto the money she was carrying.

Just before Bishopville, she turned south and found her way to Harm's farm. She hoped she would see him. The long lane to the farm was straight, with linden trees on both sides. She placed her bike against the side of the barn, took the small milk can she'd brought from her saddlebags and walked around to the stables. The warmth and the scent of cows and manure welcomed her. Her cheeks burned from the wind. She closed the door behind her. Two rows of cows lined the stable, with a path in the middle.

Mrs. Bosma, dressed in blue coveralls and a red handkerchief tied around her hair, came to empty her pail of milk into one of the large metal cans.

"Hello, Janke. How much milk do you want?"

"Hello, Mrs. Bosma. Not quite to the top." Janke held the lid while Harm's mother poured the milk.

"Thank you." Janke pulled her wallet out of her pocket.

"Don't pay me. We still owe Jan money for all the hard work he did. Did he get away alright?" Her dark eyes looked at Janke.

"We haven't heard anything. That must be a good sign." Janke wished they had heard from Jan, but it was too soon.

"We're so lucky that Harm has been exempted because of the farm. Oh, how I wish this war was over." She wiped her forehead with the sleeve of her coveralls.

"Yes," Janke nodded. "Then we could go back to a normal life."

Janke said goodbye and left the stable. She looked around the yard before she mounted her bike, but there was no sign of Harm. Perhaps next time, she thought.

Just before town, a black car slowed and stopped in front of her. Janke's breath caught. If she was searched now and they found the money . . .

"Janke." The driver opened the door and got out of the car.

"Helmut." Surprised, Janke dismounted. "Do you always drive a fancy car?" She couldn't believe how easy it was to talk to him.

He came over and smiled. He held onto her handlebars.

Janke's heart skipped.

"Yes, I am the private chauffeur of the commandant, who is also my Uncle Heinrich on my mother's side."

"Oh," was all Janke could say.

"But he has told me if I wanted I could use the car to drive a very special girl around."

Janke watched the shiny, black Mercedes. Never would she sit in the car of a Nazi.

Helmut's eyes followed her gaze. "You do not have to," he said.

Janke looked up at him. His eyes shone as he returned the gaze.

"Did you read my letter?"

Janke's face burned. "I have books for you, but I . . . " She couldn't think of any excuse why she hadn't met him at the harbor.

"Thank you. When will I get to read them?"

Janke smiled a small smile. "I will meet you on Sunday at four-thirty."

"Thank you." His hand shook when he reached out and touched her cheek.

Janke felt the imprint of his finger on her skin. "I have to go."

"I will see you on Sunday." Helmut turned and walked back to the car.

Janke waited till he started the engine and slowly drove past. He waved and she waved back.

Father sat at the kitchen table, smoking and reading a paper, when Janke walked in. She placed the milk can on the counter.

"Did you get Mother?" Janke noticed the deep lines in his face.

"Yes. She went straight to bed." He sighed and read on.

"I have to take something to the Dijkstras'. I'll be back shortly." Janke felt the bulge beneath her sweater.

Father didn't answer.

9.

Janke's days settled into a new routine now that Jan had left and her mother spent many hours in bed. In the mornings she did the housework, the shopping and cooked the noon meal if she wasn't away on a special assignment. On the days Janke was away, her grandmother came.

In the afternoons Janke went to the parsonage and helped Mrs. Bergman. Since the war had begun, Alie's mother's community work had doubled. She organized the distribution of clothes, footwear, blankets and household items to people who needed help. Janke and Alie often delivered items to poor families.

On Sunday afternoons Janke continued to visit Alie. After listening to the news they often practiced dancing in Alie's room.

This Sunday Janke had carefully packed the books for Helmut in the saddlebags of her bicycle.

After listening to the news of the invasion of Italy by the Anglo-American armies at Anzio, the girls became restless.

"The last invasion didn't succeed." Alie threw her hair back. "And Italy is so far away. Those Americans aren't helping us soon enough."

"We can't give up hope, girls." Reverend Bergman's face looked grim.

"Let's go to my room." Alie opened the door to the hallway and Janke followed her friend upstairs.

Soon the girls were dancing to the tunes of a Dutch orchestra.

"You're not with it," Alie complained when Janke lost count and tripped over Alie's feet.

"I get mixed up with my left and right foot," Janke apologized. Oh, how she wished she could just tell Alie about her secret meeting with Helmut. Alie had been her best friend since kindergarten, and in the past they had held no secrets from each other, but Janke felt intuitively that she couldn't share this with her.

Besides, what would she tell Alie? That this German soldier often occupied her thoughts? That she was drawn to his pale face with the sad eyes? That she found it easy to talk to him and that she didn't feel fear when she was with him? Well, she should fear him, Janke scolded herself.

The last notes of the orchestra faded away. Alie let go of her. "We need some serious practice." Her eyes gleamed. "I'll tell you, Janke Visser, when this war is over, we have to be ready. We will have to make up for all the lost time. In May it will be four years. Four valuable years. We don't want to look all rusty and stiff because we weren't allowed to dance." She grabbed Janke's upper arms and looked her straight in the face. "We will dance so smoothly and with such polish that every boy who comes out of hiding will want to dance with us."

Janke grinned at Alie's determined expression. "We will be ready, don't worry. We still have time to practice. Everyone is talking about the Allies liberating us soon, but they've been saying that since last fall."

"I know." Alie sat down at the end of the bed. "If we give up hope, we'll lose the war." In a dramatic gesture she threw up her arms and then flopped down onto the bed. "They should be here by now, but they aren't. We'd better not wait for them. We must continue to fight the enemy ourselves."

Janke nodded. But her thoughts were elsewhere. After leaving her best friend, she would bring the enemy some books to read so he could improve his Dutch.

"I have to get going." Janke stood up.

"I'll come with you," Alie announced. "At least halfway."

Janke nodded. Now she couldn't be at the harbor by four-thirty.

"I'm biking with Janke till Market Street." Alie patted her mother on the shoulder. Mrs. Bergman was sewing a button on one of her husband's shirts.

"Bye, Janke." Mrs. Bergman cut the thread with her teeth.

"Thanks for the tea." Janke waved as she followed Alie out of the kitchen.

Alie complained about the condition of her rubber tires as she noticed the rear tire of her bike becoming softer and flatter with every turn of the pedal.

"I'd better turn back, before I have to walk all the way home." She dismounted in the middle of North Street. "Come and see us soon." She waved as she motioned Janke to continue.

"I'll be there," Janke called back.

She turned her head once and continued down North Street. At the corner of North and Market Street, she waited. A police car roared down the street, its sirens blaring. Janke watched the people for a while. A man stood against the wall of the last house, reading a newspaper. Janke wondered if he was an informer. When she was sure Alie had had time to return home, she retraced her way back along North Street until she turned right towards the harbor.

She knew she was late when she arrived at the boat house where Helmut had found her the last time. As she approached, however, a figure appeared from the other side of the building. Helmut. She recognized him right away. He smiled when he walked toward her.

Janke dismounted and looked around.

"Do not worry; there is no one here." He took the bike from her. "Today it is too cold for people to walk along the harbor."

Janke smiled. It felt like he could read her thoughts.

"We can be out of the wind on this side of the building." He walked around to the front of the boat house. "Now we are really out of sight." Helmut placed her bike against the wall.

"I'm just here to give you the books." Janke hesitated when all of a sudden she found herself alone with Helmut.

"But you have time to talk for a few minutes?" His pleading eyes softened Janke's resolve.

She nodded. A silence grew between them while Helmut studied Janke's features. Heat crept up her face like a stream of lava coming down the mountainside. She noticed a tiny dimple in his chin and pale freckles covering his nose and cheekbones.

"You're not driving the Mercedes today." Janke's words broke the awkwardness.

"No, today is my day off." He looked at the harbor. "There is not much to do in your town."

Janke followed his gaze. "Did you have a choice where you were posted?"

"No." Helmut returned his gaze to Janke. "I was assigned to your town and to my uncle. I hate the war, Janke." His voice was harsh and Janke felt he meant it. "I hated your town, but now that I have met you, it is different."

Janke looked down. She didn't know how to respond to his last statement.

"I know how you feel about us and I am pleased you came today."

Janke thought of all the Sundays he had waited for her. "It isn't easy for me to come here," she said softly. "My mother isn't well." And that was not a lie, she thought.

"I am sorry." Helmut stepped closer.

Janke felt his warmth even though he wasn't touching her.

"Do you write home often?" Janke wanted to steer the conversation away from her mother and her family.

"No." Helmut looked at a seagull, which came screeching down and landed a few meters away from them. "I have nothing to write about to my mother." He kicked a small stone. The gull startled, scrambled away. Janke heard the anger in his voice.

"And your father?" Janke felt like an interrogator.

"My father is dead. He was killed in Africa during the battle of El Alamein over a year ago."

"I'm sorry." Janke read the loss in his eyes.

"I am very sorry he is dead." Helmut looked away; then he turned his head to face her. "My father and I had made plans, but . . . " He shrugged his shoulders. "I do not get along with my mother because of what she believes in." He looked intently at Janke. "And you? Do you get along with your mother?"

Janke shook her head. She couldn't tell him that her mother resented the fact that she and the rest of her family all belonged to the resistance. Again his eyes scanned her face. When she looked up, she felt caressed with a gentleness that warmed her insides. She felt a strong urge to talk to Helmut about the problems with Mother, to tell him that she missed her brother and worried about her father. Even though she found it easy to talk to him, there were too many topics they couldn't discuss. She had to go home or her mother would have another fit.

"What else do you do besides driving your uncle around?" she said instead.

Helmut smiled. He stepped closer.

She could feel his breath on her face when he spoke.

"I drive him to Leeuwarden many times because he is the commander of Bishopville, but he has no power of his own. He has to follow orders from the Ortskommandantur in Leeuwarden. He meets with him many times. He follows all the rules and lives for his Führer." The last statement came out mockingly.

"And you?" Janke asked.

"I follow the rules, Janke," he said softly. "I have no choice." His hand touched her cheek briefly, just like a feather of wind. "I also have to be in my uncle's office and do all the paperwork for him. He is too lazy, but he does not want to get into trouble, so I cannot make any mistakes."

"Do you go with him when there are roundups?" Was she hoping he would tell her that he saved people instead?

Helmut's face came close. "This is a test, yes?"

Janke moved away from him. She took a few steps towards the harbor, away from the shelter of the building. The wind whipped her face. She hugged herself and shivered with sadness, regret.

Two hands on her shoulders pulled her back behind the building. Janke didn't move. Helmut stood behind her.

"Yes, Janke. I am with my uncle when he orders a roundup." His voice spoke in her hair. "Often I am with him when people are chased out of their hiding places and loaded onto a truck. Sometimes I am with him when he interrogates a prisoner before he is sent to Leeuwarden to the House of Detention."

Tears ran softly down her cheeks. She didn't bother wiping her face. She just let them run like tiny rivers going nowhere. Why am I listening to him? she wondered.

He turned her around to face him.

"I have to go." Janke moved away. She grabbed her bike.

He stood beside her. His eyes, dark and sad, looked at her intently. "I hate war, Janke, and I hate violence."

Janke lifted her leg to mount her bike. "I have to go."

His hand touched her arm. He nodded.

Without looking back, she left the harbor and followed the North Deep. A cold wind blew from the northeast and daylight was fading fast. She didn't feel the cold from the outside. She only felt the coldness of her heart.

Out of breath, she opened the door to the shed. The books! She had never given him the books. They were still in her saddlebags.

The kitchen door opened.

"Janke, where were you?" Father's voice was heavy with concern. "Look at you. What happened?"

Janke's mind worked quickly. There was either something wrong with Jan or Mother. She wiped her face on the sleeve of her coat.

"I went to the parsonage, but you had left over an hour ago. What happened?"

"Nothing." Janke sought words for an explanation. "I went to the harbor. I sat there for a while. The time just went," she added softly. Her face burned and Father gave her a look of suspicion.

"The harbor is not a safe place for a girl alone." His voice was stern. "Harm was here."

"Harm," Janke repeated. Harm was here but she was spending time with the enemy.

"Harm has a job for you." Father paused. His eyes held hers. Janke felt sick. "Can, can I still do it? The job?"

"Tomorrow morning you bike to Drenthe."

"Drenthe?"

"Our Jan is hiding there. The people he's staying with can't get extra coupons or food. They are surrounded by Nazi collaborators."

Janke knew that in the province of Drenthe the Germans had more support than anywhere else in the country.

"You have to pick up food and coupons at the butcher tonight and take them to an address in the town of Roden. You will stay overnight."

"Will I see Jan?" She hesitated because she knew the answer.

Father shook his head. "It would put Jan and the people who are hiding him in danger."

"But why is Jan in such a dangerous place? Why did he not go south?"

"The night he left, they had trouble following their plan because there had been a betrayal. The chain of safe addresses had been broken. Jan had to make a detour, but he got stuck in Drenthe and has to sit still like a duck until it's safe enough to move on."

Janke nodded. She understood.

"You will deliver the food and the coupons to the local nurse. The couple Jan stays with is elderly and the man is not well. The nurse will deliver the items when she does her rounds."

Janke felt a rush of satisfaction that she would be able to help her brother and the people who were hiding him, but sad that she wouldn't be able to see Jan.

"Your mother doesn't know anything about this," Father whispered and nodded at the kitchen door. "You better go to Dijkstra's. It's getting dark."

Janke returned from the butcher's with saddlebags full of rutabagas, potatoes, cheese, a chunk of smoked meat and a wooden box filled with ration coupons. When she parked her bike in the shed, she took the books from the bottom of her saddlebags and hid them in a box on the shelf above her father's workbench.

In bed, her mind was restless. Her thoughts jumped from her time with Helmut to wondering why she thought so seldom of Harm lately. She'd had a crush on him since grade six. She had known him all her life. And what did she know about Helmut? He could have made up everything he'd told her just to get on her good side. He hated the war and he hated violence he had said, but was that true? Janke hadn't doubted his words at the time, but now she wondered. Maybe he was trying to get information from her. Maybe that was his job.

Alie had told her that German soldiers often used Dutch girls to get information on illegal activities. Well, Helmut could try all he wanted. She wouldn't tell him anything. She could keep a secret if she wanted to. She turned to face the wall. In the darkness she said softly, "There won't be anymore meetings with Helmut. He can find Dutch books somewhere else." She took a deep breath. Her decision made her yawn and curl up into a blanket cocoon.

10.

Father held the door open. "Are you dressed warm enough? The temperature is below freezing."

Janke nodded. She tied the hood of the blue, woollen coat snug around her face. New gloves, knitted from homespun wool by Grandmother Janke, warmed her hands.

"Can you handle this job?"

"Yes, Father." Janke smiled up at him. "I know I'm not supposed to carry this much food with me and it is forbidden to transport ration coupons."

Janke rolled her bicycle outside in the early morning darkness.

"I checked the tires for you. They should hold out." He pinched the rubber of the front tire. "You will travel east of Leeuwarden to avoid the checkpoints?"

"Yes." Janke remembered her instructions from Dijkstra. She mounted her bike and turned right. She heard the door of the shed close.

By the time she'd bicycled through the first village, she noticed a red glow in the eastern sky. Soon it would be light, with the promise of a clear sky and sunshine. The meadows were dressed in a cover of hoarfrost. Dark tree branches had been adorned with white lace. In the distance she saw the outlines of church steeples and factory chimneys of Leeuwarden. Few cyclists travelled the road but she met several military trucks.

Just before Leeuwarden, Janke turned into the lane of a big dairy farm. The frozen dirt road made for a bumpy journey. She followed a path through the meadows until she reached the canal that connected Leeuwarden with Bishopville.

A thin layer of ice had formed during the night, but it wasn't strong enough to support Janke or her bike. She walked until she reached the footbridge. Before she crossed the bridge she relieved herself in the reeds, startling two ducks. She knew she couldn't stop anywhere and use a bathroom. She couldn't leave her bike unattended.

Janke enjoyed her journey once she was biking on more even terrain. By noon she opened a package and ate a piece of bread. The road to the east was busy with traffic. Now she shared the road with more cyclists. The sun had melted the frost on the grass and the trees, and the wind picked up from the east. It blew right at Janke and slowed her progress.

At the edge of one town she had to show her identity card, but the soldiers didn't ask what was in the saddlebags. At all the other checkpoints the Germans just waved her through. Her thoughts often wandered to Jan. Just the thought that with every pedal of her bike she got closer to him made her forget how tired her legs were. How would he feel, being in hiding? He probably had to stay in a small cramped space all day. Janke shivered. She was glad she had decided to wear Klaske's warm coat today. She hoped the girl was alright in the camp in Vught.

Every time her mind wandered toward Helmut, she pushed harder on the pedals and forced herself to think of Harm. She should be glad that she would be seeing more of Harm. Harm would give her more jobs in the underground movement and she wouldn't have time to think of Helmut.

The sound of airplanes high overhead made Janke look up. Five stark white lines of condensation showed the aircraft heading east across the blue sky. Allied planes off to bomb the big cities in Germany, she thought. Allied planes no longer only flew night missions. This must be a good sign. "Good luck," she whispered and pushed on. Her legs ached when she finally saw the sign that said "Roden 10 km."

The town of Roden, a popular place in the summer, looked as if the war had missed it. She passed the church in the center and turned right. Following Aspen Road, Janke noticed large homes with manicured lawns on both sides of the street. Majestic chestnut trees flanked the road.

Stiff and tired, she turned into Heather Lane, where she stopped in front of number sixteen, a red brick house with a green door and thatched roof. Her legs trembled when she dismounted. She had to wait a minute to regain her balance. The green door opened and an older woman motioned her to come inside.

"Your bike, too." Her voice strained as she continued, "The neighbors just left and they are informers, so it's better that they don't see you."

Janke looked at the yellow brick house next door before she walked inside the hallway with her bike. The woman limped as she closed the door behind them.

"You must be tired. I'll make some tea."

Janke nodded. Her stomach gurgled and she realized that she had only eaten two pieces of bread during her journey. The black-bellied stove in the small kitchen glowed with warmth. A tableau of two peacocks in Delft blue tiles adorned the mantel. A round table with four chairs and a sideboard were the only furnishings. On the counter near the window stood an oil burner. Red-and-white-checkered curtains dressed the two windows.

"Give me your coat," the woman said. "You can call me Aaltje."

Janke sat down at the table while Aaltje bustled preparing the teapot and cups.

"Where shall I put the food I brought?" Janke asked.

"Just leave it in the saddlebags. It will be picked up tonight, after curfew."

Janke wanted to ask so many questions — about the people who were hiding Jan, and if Aaltje had seen Jan — but the stern face across the table kept her silent.

"I made your bed upstairs." Aaltje stood up to pull down the blackout curtains. She switched on the light above the table. "I caught one of the boys next door sneaking around my house last week, so now I close the curtains a little earlier."

Janke nodded. She felt uncomfortable. Aaltje's house felt more perilous than her own home beside the school. When she realized that Aaltje was an active member in the underground movement, even while she was being watched by neighbors, Janke's admiration for the woman grew.

In silence, they ate rye bread and cheese made from sheep milk. Then Aaltje rose and cleared away the plates and utensils.

"Come, I'll show you your room," she said. In the hallway she pointed up the stairs. "The little room on your right. You'll find everything you need. If not, let me know."

Janke climbed the stairs and opened the door to a small bedroom with a neatly made bed and a dresser against the wall. The blackout curtains had been pulled. On the bedspread lay a pair of rose-flowered pajamas and a towel and facecloth. Between the two windows hung a bookshelf. Janke read the spines. They were mostly children's books. One of the books was the legend of Ellert and Brammert, two giants who terrorized the fields of heather in Drenthe a long time ago. She pulled it off the shelf and took it downstairs with her.

"Thank you for everything, Aaltje." She sat down at the kitchen table. Aaltje had picked up her knitting.

"If you like the book, you may keep it," the older woman said. "You will have room in your saddlebags tomorrow."

"Thank you." Janke started reading the story that her father had often told to her and Jan when they were little. The print was large, the sentences short. It would be a good book for Helmut to practice . . . Oh, no, she interrupted her thoughts. There would be no more Helmut.

The small wooden clock on the mantel ticked away the time. Sounds from the woodstove and the clicking of needles filled the evening. Every now and then, Aaltje got up to add a log and nurse the fire. Every now and then, the sound of a car going down the street made both women pause and listen.

A noise at the back door made Janke look up across the table. Aaltje looked at her.

"Go upstairs," she said.

As Janke closed the door to the hallway, she heard Aaltje open the back door. On her tiptoes, she quickly ran upstairs, waiting at the landing for news. She heard muffled voices in the kitchen. There wasn't just one person coming for the food. She held her breath when the door to the hallway opened. Someone walked up the stairs. Janke froze.

"Janke," a familiar voice whispered.

"Jan," she gasped.

In a few strides, Jan had reached the top of the stairs. "In here." Janke grabbed his arm, pulled him into the bedroom and switched on the light.

For a moment they looked at each other; then Jan threw his arms around his little sister.

"What are you doing here? This is such a dangerous place." Janke's eyes filled with tears.

"I've been betrayed." Jan looked at Janke. "Tonight my contact came and said we had to get away as soon as possible. This place crawls with informers, Janke."

"But why did you come to Aaltje?"

"Because Aaltje has to leave too. They have been following her."

"The boy next door," Janke remembered.

"Quickly, get your stuff and come downstairs. We're leaving right now."

Janke didn't have anything except her coat.

Downstairs in the kitchen stood Aaltje, her hands resting on the shoulders of an old couple who were sitting at the table. They must be in their late seventies, Janke thought. A man with a dark mustache and a woollen cap pulled over his eyes stood at the door.

"Get your coat, Aaltje, and anything you need." His voice was curt.

Aaltje went into the hallway and dressed in a dark gray coat and hat. She grabbed her nurse's bag and pointed at Janke. "Take your bike through the kitchen."

"We can't take the bike," the man said. "We are climbing fences and it will be hard enough to carry Ben and Geesje."

"No, we need the bike." Aaltje spoke. "The saddlebags are filled with food and ration coupons. We can't afford to leave it here." She helped the elderly couple up from their chairs. Aaltje turned off the lights. The man with the mustache opened the door.

First the couple, then Aaltje, Janke with her bike, and last Jan stepped outside.

"Follow me," the man whispered. "Don't say a word and don't make any noise with that bike."

Janke and Jan followed behind the rest. They walked slowly. Once they passed the trees at the back of Aaltje's yard, it became harder to push the bike. There was no path, just tree roots, dead leaves and branches. Janke couldn't see much, only the dark outlines in front of her. Jan followed her and every now and then helped Janke lift the bike over obstacles. They stumbled along in the darkness, sometimes waiting for the old couple to catch their breath. No one spoke. The group halted when they came to a road. The man came back to Jan and Janke.

"We're crossing here, but not all at the same time. Aaltje and I will go first with Ben and Geesje. Wait five minutes, then make sure the road is clear before you cross. You'll see a white fence. Climb over it. Go straight through the gardens of the house on the other side. Stay away from the house as much as possible; the people are on the wrong side. We'll meet you past the second fence." He disappeared into the darkness.

"Come behind this tree," Jan whispered. "We can see the road."

They watched and saw Aaltje and Geesje cross the road. About five minutes later the leader followed with Ben.

As they waited, Janke realized how hard her heart was beating. She rested her head against the trunk of the tree until

Jan nudged her shoulder.

"Go," he whispered.

Janke pushed the bike out to the road. They looked both ways. The sound of an engine made her gasp.

"Back!" Jan pulled on the bike. Janke almost tripped as she tried to hold onto the handlebars.

"Down!" Jan threw the bike flat and pulled Janke behind the tree. With drumming heart, she watched a black car driving very slowly down the road. They stayed down and listened. As the sound of the engine faded, Jan got up.

"Stay here," he said. "I have a feeling it will come back."

Jan didn't even make it to the road before Janke heard the sound of the engine return. Had they been discovered? Were the others captured?

Jan dashed back beside her. "I don't like it." he said "They must be patrolling the area because of an incident. Maybe they raided Ben and Geesje's house and found everybody gone."

Cold sweat ran down Janke's spine as the car came to a halt a few meters away from them. They heard the doors open. In the next moment, light beams were crisscrossing through the trees beside them.

Jan's arm pushed her head down. Janke smelled and tasted the dirt of the forest floor. She tried to block out all feeling and waited for the Germans to pounce on them. Jan's uneven breathing beside her was all she heard. Finally they heard doors slam closed and the car drove slowly off.

"Let's go." Jan pulled her to her feet. He grabbed the bike. "Let's cross the street before they come back. I was worried about dogs."

Janke didn't answer. They made it across the road. Together they lifted the bike over the white fence. As quickly as they could, they made their way across the lawn to the second white fence. The small beam of a dynamo light waved back and forth from behind a tree.

Janke just hoped it would be their leader, the man with the mustache.

"Are they on our tail?" Jan asked as soon as they could identify the man.

"We must assume they are." He didn't wait, but walked away from them.

Jan took the bike from Janke. She lifted the carrier seat every time the bike got stuck. Twigs and branches scratched her face as she trudged along. It felt as if hours had passed, but she realized they had not covered a great distance. When they halted, the leader spoke to Jan.

"We'll soon come to a farm where we'll stay for a few hours. We can't trust the farmer, but we will leave before he gets up."

They stumbled on until they came to the end of the forest. A field lay ahead of them. Janke felt very exposed. Now they wouldn't be able to hide from any searchlights. In the distance she could just make out the outlines of several buildings. They hurried through a wooden gate.

"We'll go down to the left," he said. "We can hide for a few hours in the equipment shed."

What would happen after a few hours? Janke thought. How would she be able to find her way back if she wasn't discovered before? What would happen to Jan and the others? To her horror, Janke noticed they were not the only ones in the shed. Two other men had joined the group.

"Don't worry," the leader whispered. "They're members."

They found Aaltje and the couple huddled in the corner, sitting on a pile of burlap sacks.

"Listen, everybody," the leader spoke in a low voice. "Jan will go with these men. They have a place for him. Aaltje and I will take Ben and Geesje to a nearby address until we can place them somewhere else. At about five-thirty, the girl will take her bike and leave the shed."

Janke shivered. "But I don't know my way," she whispered.

"When you come out of the shed, keep to the left until you're on the road. Turn left and bike until you get to the intersection. There will be signs to guide you home. Here is a dynamo light, so you can check your watch."

They sat together in the dark. Janke felt sleep take her away for a few moments. Then Jan's voice woke her.

"You won't hear from me for a while, Janke." He spoke softly. "It might take a long time for me to get to the south. I might even try to go to England."

Janke nodded. She wouldn't tell him how afraid she was for his life.

"But I will be alright. Don't worry. Promise?"

"Promise," she said softly.

"There are rumors that the Allies are planning a big invasion along the coast and it won't be like Dieppe." His voice sounded passionate. "I'll try to join them and then I'll come to liberate you." He squeezed her arm tightly. Janke smiled despite the fact that she found it very unlikely that this would happen. Dieppe, the disastrous landing of Canadian troops on the coast of France in August of 1942, had been a failure and had cost many lives.

At about four o'clock the leader sprang into action. "Time for us to leave."

Jan and Janke hugged. They didn't speak. She touched his face and felt it was wet.

"Be careful," Jan said. "You'll be biking during curfew for the first half-hour.

"I know." Janke blew her nose.

Before they left, the leader divided the food. He gave everyone some ration coupons and returned the empty boxes to Janke's saddlebags.

After quick goodbyes, the others filed out of the shed. Now that she was alone, Janke became aware of every sound. A twig rustling. The little feet of mice or rats. The minutes crept by until at last she dared to check her watch. It was time to leave. Janke followed the instructions, keeping an eye on the other farm buildings. No sounds yet, but she imagined that any minute the farmer would start milking his cows.

She found the road. The darkness protected her. She kept

looking behind her, worrying about cars. The road signs at the intersection told her she was north of Roden. Now she wouldn't have any trouble finding her way. Tired, but relieved that curfew was over, Janke journeyed homeward. Was it only yesterday that she had cycled these roads?

11.

On a dreary Monday afternoon in March, Janke stood in line at the butcher shop on Market Street. Winds coming from the northeast made it feel like January. Women and children and a few old men, ration coupons in hand, waited to buy whatever the butcher had been able to get his hands on. Each family received only one meat coupon for the week, and some Mondays there were more customers than meat.

"This is the coldest day in March I can remember!" a woman ahead of her shouted. She held onto a little boy who was hopping up and down to keep warm.

Today, the lineup moved quickly.

"He got two yearlings last night," an old man named Klaas told Janke. A wad of brown tobacco landed beside her on the cobblestones. Janke jumped. The man bared his brown smile.

"Don't like that, eh? You should try it sometime. It's good." Klaas chewed on. "It's better than cigarettes. I'll do little jobs for them."

Janke looked confused.

"Our friends the Germans. They pay me in tobacco. Real tobacco." He laughed.

Bile rose into Janke's mouth and it wasn't just from the sight of brown juice dribbling down his chin. She turned away from Klaas. He probably wasn't a Nazi collaborator, she thought, but one of those people who didn't care whom they dealt with as long as they could make a profit. Father had warned her about people like Klaas. This old man, without loyalties except to money, could be more dangerous than any sympathizer.

People tried to push their way through the doorway to escape the cold, and Janke felt squished between several older women. Janke watched the butcher, who chatted to his customers about food and fuel shortages. On Mondays she usually received her assignments for the week, although at Harm's farm she often got additional or last-minute instructions. The underground movement was a tight network of people connected throughout the country.

What better place than a shop for exchanging information and goods, Janke thought. She hoped that this time the assignment would involve more real work, like rescuing people or hiding secret information.

"Did you hear the Germans have cut down most of our forests?" A young woman with two children made her way to the counter.

"As if we have much forest to begin with." Mr. Dijkstra took her coupon. "They rob us of everything, Martsje. If you need wood for the stove, you ask old Klaas." He laughed. "I'm sure he can get you some. He has connections."

Klaas mumbled and gave his coupon.

"The wife would like some help in the kitchen," Mr. Dijkstra said when it was Janke's turn. She had heard the butcher speak this line many times in the last six months. Janke walked around the counter. No one in the store would find it suspicious that a young girl would help out at such a busy place. She opened the door behind the butcher and walked into the warm kitchen.

Mrs. Dijkstra turned from the counter to face her. She wiped her hands on her apron. "Have a seat, Janke," she said, as she pulled out a chair for herself.

Janke sat down and folded her hands in her lap, waiting. She watched the plump face in front of her. Three chins rested on the large, heaving breasts. Perspiration trickled down Mrs. Dijkstra's forehead, and the red, curly hair lay damp and plastered against her skin.

"From now on you will have different jobs, Janke." The woman looked at her intently. "You will need to stay at a different address because your work will be more dangerous."

Janke nodded. Her tongue wet her lips. She felt Mrs. Dijkstra stare at her. Her face blushed. All her life she'd known the butcher and his wife, but it felt like Mrs. Dijkstra saw her for the first time.

"Do you know where Douwe and Afke Jansma live?" Mrs. Dijkstra smoothed the tablecloth with her hands.

Janke nodded. "Their farm is east of town and about one and a half kilometers off the main road. The farm buildings are hidden by tall linden trees. They have no children."

"From now on, that's where you'll be staying." With the tip of her apron, Mrs. Dijkstra wiped her forehead. "And here is your uniform." She reached for a green bag underneath the table and pulled out a navy blue dress and headdress, a white apron and a medical bag.

"You'll find everything a nurse needs in here." She handed it all to Janke. "Take it to the Jansmas'. They'll tell you when to wear it. For certain jobs it's better to wear the uniform. It will get you through checkpoints much faster."

"Can I visit home?"

"Only at night and make sure nobody sees you. We don't know how much the Germans next door are watching your family."

"I worry about my mother," Janke said softly.

"It must be hard on your mother," Mrs. Dijkstra sighed. "First your brother and now you. Did the Germans come looking for him?"

"Yes, but luckily Mother wasn't home. Father dealt with them."

"Your father has a way of dealing with that riffraff." Mrs. Dijkstra smoothed the fabric of her apron. Janke stayed silent, contemplating her new situation. The leaders of the resistance trusted her enough to give her more dangerous work, she thought. A surge of adrenaline rushed through her veins. It felt good to be needed. She was going to really fight those German bastards. Her hands clenched together.

"What's the job?"

Mrs. Dijkstra cleared her throat. The features in her face softened. "Tonight at eight, an Allied radio technician will be dropped near Bass Lake. Your job is to lead him to a small houseboat that's hidden on the northeast side of the lake. He'll stay there until his contact arrives tomorrow."

"How will I find him?" Janke asked.

"You'll meet my husband and some others at the old boat house on the lake. You know where this is, don't you?" Janke nodded, recalling swimming off the dock on summer outings in better times.

Mrs. Dijkstra continued, "The men will be with you until you make contact; then you'll be on your own. It might be a bit difficult to find the houseboat. It's not very big and is mostly hidden by bushes and undergrowth. So I'll draw you a sketch."

Mrs. Dijkstra took a piece of brown paper from the counter. With a stub of pencil, she drew a circle. "From the lake to the north is the River Pike that leads to the sea. Off the river is a narrow inlet." She drew a line on the right side of the river. "You simply follow the shoreline from the lake to the river. So long as you keep to the right, you can't miss the inlet."

Janke quickly memorized the drawing. Then Mrs. Dijkstra crumpled the paper, opened the door of the woodstove and threw it inside.

"When you get to the houseboat, tell the Englishman to stay out of sight. He can feed himself. There are canned goods in one of the cupboards. Someone will come for him. He's to stay hidden until he hears someone whistle the song 'It's a Long Way to Tipperary.' Once you have the solder settled, you go to the Jansma farm. Don't go home."

"What if I don't get to the Jansmas' until very late?"

"Just go into the barn and make yourself at home in the hay until morning." Her eyes never left Janke's face. "Understood?" Mrs. Dijkstra's voice was firm.

Janke nodded.

"You can go now." She rose from her chair. "Here's your mother's meat." She picked up a package from the counter. "I don't need the coupon."

Janke took the newspaper-wrapped package from Mrs. Dijkstra and walked to the door.

"Janke." Mrs. Dijkstra's voice called her back. "This is not child's play."

Janke looked at her. Their eyes locked.

"This is war."

"Mrs. Dijkstra?"

"Yes."

"Why me?"

"Your English is good."

Janke opened the door and walked out. With the bag slung over her shoulder, the package of meat in one hand, Janke biked home.

The lessons from Mr. Verbeek and the homework her father had forced her and Jan to do now paid off. She pondered her new assignment as she pedalled home.

When she entered the kitchen, her mother sat at the table, her head in her hands. Her eyes were red and swollen.

"What's wrong?" Janke looked at the thin face.

"I have a headache."

"Why don't you lie down?" Janke put away her coat.

"Where were you all afternoon?" The sharpness of her mother's voice made Janke cringe.

"I stood in line for a while to get meat," Janke answered in a neutral voice.

"You were out all afternoon. Your father's never home. I'm left to do everything. Everything." Her eyes welled up.

"But I had to get the meat from the butcher." Janke clenched her fists. A stream of angry words rushed, ready to escape. Words that would do no good. She unclenched her fists and walked over to her mother. She sat down beside her, placed a hand on her arm. How could she tell her that she wasn't coming home anymore? That her daughter had been drawn into the real dangerous work of the resistance. A soft cry escaped her lips instead. A sound that was between laughter and a sob. Janke took a deep breath.

"It's hard for everybody, Mother," she said as evenly as possible. "Father's risking his life to save others and to help get rid of the Nazis." She swallowed. "And I got you the meat and an extra coupon."

"I'm so tired of the war," Mother lamented. "Those stupid ration coupons. I'm tired of not being able to buy the things we need. Every day I have to figure out how and where we're going to get our next meal. How to get wood for the stove." She wiped her eyes with the back of her hand. "Look at your clothes, Janke. Everything is too short, worn and shabby. I'm too embarrassed to let you walk around like that."

Janke sighed. Her eyes travelled from her patched stockings to the gray, woollen skirt, its hem reaching just above the knee, which wasn't the style. She wore two sweaters and a cardigan that day, all of which had seen better times.

"I'm not concerned about fashion," she said flatly.

"I'm constantly living in fear, with those Germans next door." Mother took a deep breath and raised her head to look at Janke. "And if that's not enough, you and your father think that you can outsmart the Nazis. But you will pay for it." Her breath quickened. Her voice rose. "Why can't you live as quietly as possible, instead of getting involved? Every time the doorbell rings, I jump. Every time a car comes down our street, my heart stops. I can't take it anymore!" Her head sagged down on her arms and she sobbed. "And I don't even know where Jan is. He could be dead."

Janke placed her arm around her mother's shoulder. She felt a mixture of pity, anger and frustration rise toward her mother. "We can't do much to fight the Germans, but every little action helps. And we must fight them." Her voice rose. "If we all sit back, this war will never end. And Father is still looking for another home, away from the school."

"But I like this house!" Mother raised her head and looked at Janke. "I want those Germans to leave and I want you and your father to have a little more consideration for me." Her head fell down on her arms again.

The grandfather clock in the front room struck the half hour. "I'll cook dinner," Janke said. "Why don't you lie down and I'll call you when it's ready."

Without a word her mother went upstairs. Janke looked for butter, but the butter dish was empty. She filled a pot with water instead and put it on the stove. The unwrapped package contained four sausages and two large chunks of beef. Janke searched the cupboards for salt, but all she could find was a tin with pepper. She sprinkled a tiny bit on either side of the beef. She placed the beef in the boiling water. The sausages followed. Janke stirred the pot without looking. Where was the mother who sang songs with her? Who made her frilly dresses and danced with her through the front room? Who told stories about gnomes and fairies and made up riddles? The mother who loved to wear pretty dresses, makeup and high heels? Who loved to go for strolls on Sundays, her hair all put up, her face pretty and smiling?

A shadow crossed her mind. Janke paused. That same mother had another side, as if she were two different mothers. The light Mother and the dark Mother, Jan had jokingly said without smiling. Once when dinner had burned and Father had been late and Janke had ripped her new coat while climbing a tree, her lively Mother had screamed hysterically that they would drive her into a mental hospital. It wasn't the only incident she remembered. As the war went on, the light Mother was gradually taken over by the dark Mother, Janke thought.

A commotion at the back door shook Janke from her thoughts. She closed the lid on the meat.

"Mmm, smells good in here." Father's head peered around the door. "Where is your mother?"

Janke nodded her head in the direction of the stairs.

"I see," was all he said.

"She's upset." Janke looked at her father.

Father nodded.

"Can you get Mother? The meat is ready."

Janke heard her father taking the stairs two at a time. While she waited, she set the table for three. And after tonight, the table would be set for two people, she thought.

"She doesn't want anything." Father closed the door behind him and sat down.

"I'll make some tea for her later." Janke placed the meat and some bread on the table. She sat down across from her father.

"I won't be coming home tonight."

Father looked her over. "Are you old enough for that?"

"It's because I can speak English," Janke said, as if she wanted to blame her father for the hours of homework he'd put her through.

"I see."

"I haven't told Mother and I'm worried how she will react."

"I'll talk to her. Is it just for tonight?"

"No." Janke shook her head.

"Where can we reach you if we need you?"

"For now, I'll be staying at Douwe and Afke Jansma's."

"That's a good place. And you won't go hungry," he smiled. "You better get ready." He walked over to the windows and pulled down the blackout curtains.

Janke went upstairs. She took the few clothing items she owned from her closet and tucked them inside a pillowcase. She looked around her room. The bed was neatly made with the burgundy quilt and the crochet bedspread on top. The small teddy bear, that had belonged to the little Schumacher girl, sat on the bookshelf. Janke took the bear and looked at the black, beady eyes. "I'll keep you safe," she whispered. She stuffed the bear inside a shoe box and placed the box on the floor of her closet.

The door to her parents' bedroom stood ajar. Without making a sound, Janke tiptoed to her parents' bed. Her mother's eyes were closed. She bent and kissed the white skin of her cheek.

"Mother," she whispered, "would you like some tea?"

Her mother didn't move. Janke touched the curls on the pillow. Her chest felt tight when she left the room and went downstairs.

"I'll keep tabs on you." Father stood up from his chair. With one hand on her shoulder, he added, "Promise to be careful?"

"If you make the same promise to me." A lump closed her throat. She felt the pressure of his hand. "And watch Mother."

"I'll arrange for her to stay with your grandparents every now and then, until I've found another house."

12.

With her few belongings and the nurse's bag packed in her saddlebags, Janke found her way to the boat house. The last part of the road was difficult to bike. Deep ruts had made the path uneven. She moved as quietly as possible. Shadows stood against the outline of the building.

"Come over here." She recognized the butcher's voice.

"We'll put your bicycle inside." He walked nearer and took the bike from her. Janke followed him. Two other men grumbled their greetings. Janke didn't recognize either of them.

"A few more minutes." The butcher closed the door to the boat house.

"How does the pilot know where to drop this man?" Janke asked.

"Every area has been mapped out, and those maps with the exact spots have been sent to England. They are all labelled with silly sayings like 'Jan is a tall boy' or 'The worm has two ears.' When this saying is broadcast in the afternoon by BBC Radio and later on by Radio Orange, then we know where the air drops will take place that night."

Janke couldn't believe the preparation and organization that was involved in an operation like this. And this was not the only dropping tonight. All over the country, people, weapons and newspapers were dropped.

"Every dropping takes an army to organize," Mr. Dijkstra said. "Not only local people, but men and women in England help plan these operations as well."

Janke listened. She only heard the lake murmuring quietly.

"It's time." The butcher straightened his back. The two men followed him, with Janke closing the ranks. Her body tensed. She kept up with the men, walking through the reeds beside the lake. The dark sky didn't reveal any planes. Perhaps it was better for the plane to hide in the clouds.

Janke stumbled. One of her shoes stuck in the mud. When she freed her shoe, it was full of water. She emptied the shoe and pushed her foot in quickly. Janke tried to ignore the ice-cold dampness that penetrated her skin and crawled up the rest of her body. The men had walked ahead of her and she needed to catch up. She didn't want to lose them in the black night. Danger could be close. What if the Germans had picked up the saying on the radio this afternoon? What if they had broken the code?

The small group halted.

"This is our spot." Mr. Dijkstra addressed the other two men. "Take your positions. As soon as we hear the engine, we'll give the signal. You have the flashlights ready? Janke, you stay close to me." He held her elbow and guided her ahead.

"Down." The butcher's words forced her to the ground. She lay in the wet mud. Her heart pounded in her ears. She wouldn't be able to hear the engine of the plane if her heart didn't quiet down. The minutes stretched. The wind chilled her damp clothes as she listened intently.

A soft growling from the west alerted Janke. "I hear something," she said to the butcher.

"They'll hear it," Mr. Dijkstra said.

When the sound of the plane drew nearer, Janke held her breath. Three white lights formed a triangle in the field and flashed a signal to the plane. Again and again, they repeated the signals. Janke scanned the area around her.

"Look." Mr. Dijkstra touched her arm. "Look to the north. See that white shape?"

Janke squeezed her eyes until what looked like a white balloon came into focus.

"You take care of the man. We'll look after the parachute and the equipment. Go! Run!" He pulled her to her feet and pushed her in the direction of the parachute.

Janke stumbled across the meadow. Running was difficult on the uneven surface. She kept her eyes on the parachute. If it got out of sight, she would never be able to find it. Now she'd lost track of it. The parachute must have come down. Her eyes caught a billowing white shape close to the lake. What if the man had landed in the water? She ran faster. Her feet hurt in her thin-soled shoes. The soggy earth sucked at her strength with every step.

Out of breath, she stopped near the parachute. "Are you alright?" Janke tried her best English.

"Yes, I'm alright." A voice came from the reeds. "I'm a bit tangled up in the lines. Can you give me a hand?"

In the darkness, Janke found her way to the shadowy figure huddled among white cloth on the ground.

"Quick," Janke said. "We have no time to lose. You must leave the parachute here and follow me."

Pulling the man to his feet, she supported his full weight. He groaned. Janke removed the ropes and fabric.

"I'm Peter." He extended his hand. "I might have sprained my ankle."

Oh, no, Janke thought. That'll slow us down.

Mr. Dijkstra and the other men came running to them.

"Quick. Fold the parachute."

The men grabbed the silky material, which resisted when they tried to fold it up. The air kept bubbling up the fabric until one of them put his weight on it to get the material under control.

"The radio equipment?" the butcher asked.

"It fell over there." Peter pointed to the east.

"Hurry, Janke," Mr. Dijkstra urged. "You're taking too much time. Do you know where you are and how to get to the boat?"

"Yes."

Peter leaned on Janke as they stumbled off. In the distance, they heard the engine of a plane.

"It's coming back," Peter said, breathing hard.

Janke looked up. She hoped the plane would get away unnoticed.

Suddenly the sky lit up, and searchlights crisscrossed overhead in front of and behind them. As if on signal, the two of them dove into the reeds. The sharp edges of the tough leaves cut Janke's face. Mud caked her clothes.

The rat-tat-tat of the anti-aircraft guns shattered the stillness of the night. The two lay still. Beams of light flew overhead like attacking birds.

"We have to move on." Janke's voice was calm. "Can you crawl?"

"I'll try," Peter said.

Soon the night quieted again and the lights faded. The Allied plane must have made its escape. Far in the distance, Janke heard the barking of dogs. Were they German dogs? Or dogs from neighboring farms?

"It should be here." Janke stood up. She followed the small inlet to the right. Darkness, trees and shrubs made it impossible to see the houseboat.

"Wait here," she said to Peter. Janke felt her way through twigs and branches that swept in her face and scratched her hands and cheeks. She stumbled across roots and climbed over dead trunks lying scattered in the grass. She almost lost her balance when she fell against something hard. The houseboat.

"Here," she breathed. Janke retraced her footsteps as closely as she could, until she found Peter. Together they managed to get to the boat.

"Hold onto me," Janke said. Carefully trying to step between the roots this time, they reached the gangplank. Janke opened the hatch and helped him climb inside the cabin. She felt her way around inside, while Peter leaned against the wall. Solely by feel, she managed to find an oil lamp with a box of matches beside it.

She lit a match and quickly scanned the hold. Blackout curtains were drawn. She lit a second match and the lamp. The cabin was spartan. A small table was built into one wall, along with a wooden cupboard. A bunk lined the opposite wall.

Janke motioned towards a chair. "We better have a look at your ankle."

Peter stumbled toward her, his eyes smiling. Janke colored. Her clothes were caked with mud, her hair tangled with it, and her hands a muddy brown.

He reached for her hand.

"I'm . . . Janke." She quickly pulled her hand back.

"I'm from Canada," Peter said. In the light of the lamp, his skin looked dark, his eyes sparkled. "Thanks for helping," he smiled. "I never expected to be rescued by a young lady."

"Lady?" Janke looked down at her clothes. They both burst out laughing.

"Even your nose is black." Peter touched her nose with his finger.

Janke laughed.

"I'll see if there's something to wrap around your ankle. I have to go back tonight. You're to stay here until your contact arrives tomorrow. He will whistle 'It's a Long Way to Tipperary'."

Peter softly whistled the tune, but as he took off his boot and sock he groaned. The ankle was indeed red and swollen. On a shelf Janke found a small first-aid kit. She hadn't expected to practice her pretend nursing skills so soon. She bandaged the swollen ankle as best she could.

"Thanks," Peter said. "That feels much better."

"I have to leave now," she said. "There's food in the cupboard when you get hungry." She indicated the small one-burner stove on the counter. Janke walked over to the bunk and pulled a box out from underneath. She piled the blankets on the mattress and pushed the box back.

"Will I see you again?" Peter leaned on the table. His dark

hair fell across his forehead. His eyes were deep and charcoal, his smile pleasant.

"No," Janke said. "Other people will take care of you. My job is finished."

"Thanks again." Peter hobbled after her and escorted her out into the dark night. The stillness absorbed them and they stood quietly for a moment.

"Goodbye, Janke," he said before he secured the hatch behind him.

13.

Janke shivered. She looked in every direction, afraid of Germans combing the area. As fast as her feet would take her, she followed the lakeshore to the boat house. Her footsteps sounded on the wooden dock. Janke tried to tiptoe to quiet the noise, but her legs were too tired to obey.

She listened before she opened the door. Would her bike still be there? Her body slightly bent forward, she felt around the walls, and within steps she touched a bike which she assumed was hers. The saddlebags were there, and inside she felt the pillowcase with her clothes and the nurse's bag.

The road back proved difficult to bike on, but this time she didn't walk. She still had a long way to pedal to the Jansma farm. Drizzle fell softly as she neared the main road. Before the first houses of the town began, Janke turned left, to the east. She now felt the wind behind her, gently pushing her in the right direction. Janke kept her eyes down and ahead. It would be too easy to drive off the road and land in the water-filled ditch.

The light sprinkle turned into rain and seeped through her clothes. She wondered how Mr. Dijkstra and the other men had fared. As she neared the turnoff to the Jansma farm, Janke heard the sound of a truck coming from behind. She jumped off her bike. There was only one place to hide. The ditch. Janke quickly pushed her bike down the muddy slope. The truck drew nearer. Without thinking, she pushed the bike forward and jumped into the frigid water.

The ditch was deep enough that only her head was above the

water. She could feel her bicycle on the soft bottom. She moved as close to the bank as possible, hidden by the long reeds along the edge. Her teeth chattered. Janke closed her eyes and blanked out all feelings while the military truck rumbled by.

As soon as the truck's lights disappeared down the road, Janke tried to climb out of the ditch. Numb, her clothes heavy with water, her first attempt failed. Then she remembered her bicycle. She had to duck under the water to reach the handlebars. She pulled the bicycle up and propped it against the bank. Now she had no strength left. *I have to*, she thought. *I have to*. Only determination allowed her to pull herself up onto the steep bank. She flopped down on the damp grass; the water ran from her clothes and body.

Finally she stood, back on the road, still dripping water. She looked both ways. All was quiet again. The bike squeaked and groaned when she finally mounted it. She swayed and wasn't able to stay on the side of the road. The cold had numbed all feeling in her limbs. She'd lost control of her steering. Several times she dismounted, walked a few steps and tried to bike again.

Soon she was relieved to see the two stone pillars that marked the entrance of the Jansma farm. She forced her legs to move on, for now she knew she was safe.

Following Mrs. Dijkstra's instructions, Janke opened the side door of the barn. She pulled her bike inside. She half-expected to meet a barking dog since most farms had guard dogs, but all stayed silent and black. Forlorn, Janke stood against the wall. She had no idea where to go. Her clothes were drenched, her body completely numb. Her tears ran freely. She wished she was back in her mother's kitchen.

Her knees buckled. Janke sagged down against the wall. She closed her eyes.

Something warm tickled her nose. The beam from a flashlight blinded her.

"Max here heard someone come in." A woman's voice woke

Janke. Her face was licked by a warm tongue.

"But, child, you're soaking wet," the voice spoke again. "We have to get you out of these clothes or you'll catch pneumonia." The woman pulled her to her feet.

Janke recognized Afke's voice. Just then Janke noticed the large German shepherd. The dog sniffed her wet clothes, his tail wagging.

"Janke, this is Max." Afke guided her through the barn. "I kept him with me in the kitchen tonight. He goes half-mad with barking when someone enters the barn. I didn't want him to scare you."

All Janke could do was nod her head.

"Where did you get into the water? My golly, you look like a drowned cat."

The door to the kitchen opened. Afke pushed a chair in front of the woodstove. "Here. You sit down while I get a basin with warm water and dry clothes."

Janke almost hugged the stove.

"Take your clothes off." Afke bustled about at the sink. She filled a metal tub with water, added hot water from a kettle from the stove and carried it over.

"My clothes are in the saddlebags, but they're soaked, too." Her voice quivered. "I had to dive into the ditch, just before the turnoff to the farm." Afke's eyes grew large. "M . . . Military truck was right behind me. I didn't know what else to do."

Afke shook her head. "Oh, boy. Oh, boy. That was the only thing you could do to save your hide."

Janke had managed to take off her wet coat and three sweaters. Her shoes had been ruined and it was the only pair she owned.

"Don't worry about the clothes." Afke placed a facecloth and towel next to a glass of milk on the table. "Here are a pair of pajamas," she added. "I'll leave you, so you can get yourself washed up."

Janke washed the mud from her face and shivering body.

After she dumped the water in the kitchen sink, she placed her wet clothes over a wooden drying rack beside the stove.

"I'll show you your bed." Afke's head stuck around the door. "You have to share. We're a little crowded."

Janke looked at the woman walking ahead of her. Her gray, braided hair crowned her head in a wreath. Her body was stocky, a little bent, but not heavy. Her soothing voice had comforted Janke. She still felt shaky, but also safe and immensely tired. It didn't really matter if she had to share a bed, she thought. If only she could lie down and get warm.

They went up two steps and Afke opened the door. In the small room stood a double bed. A bulge on the far side showed it wasn't empty.

"Her name is Annie," Afke whispered. "She's six. She's my niece from Amsterdam." Afke lifted the blankets and helped Janke onto the bed. "There's a hot water bottle for your feet."

"Thanks," Janke murmured.

"Good night, Janke." Afke stroked her forehead.

The night disappeared into a black well.

She woke when the blankets pulled away from her warm body and a draft of cold air greeted her.

"Who are you?" Two dark eyes and a head full of black ringlets bent over Janke's face.

Janke smiled. "I'm Janke and you must be Annie."

"Yes." She sat up straight now, pulling the blankets with her.

The room was bathed in morning light. The sun peeked inside and threw pale yellow rays on the wallpaper.

"Aunt Afke opened the blackouts and she told me to be very quiet and lie very still and not to wake you. Did I?"

"Oh, no," Janke smiled. "You were very quiet. Let's get up. You have to show me the way."

On a chair beside the bed Janke found a pile of clothes. She dressed quickly in a navy blue skirt, a gray sweater and a burgundy cardigan. As she followed Annie, she combed her hair with her fingers.

Every chair at the large kitchen table was taken.

"Douwe, we need two more chairs." Afke had risen and busied herself with plates at the stove.

"Everybody, this is Janke."

They all nodded and murmured, "Good morning, Janke."

Douwe, a tall, skinny man with a balding head and a twinkle in his eyes, added two chairs. One for Janke and one for Annie.

"I'll introduce you to everybody." Douwe smiled. "To begin at that side of the table," he pointed to the two young men at the left, "are Bill and Jim, both pilots from America shot down by the Germans, but fortunately rescued by our people a week ago."

Janke nodded at both men, who looked to be in their early twenties.

"Beside me is Bert. He is our farmhand."

Janke looked at the boy. He must have been about fourteen. With his short, dark hair and brown eyes, Janke knew he was no farmhand, but a Jewish diver, and so was Annie.

Janke watched the little girl as she climbed onto Douwe's lap. A rag doll, dressed in red-and-blue gingham, dangled from Annie's arm. An image of the little Schumacher girl flashed through Janke's mind. She shivered. She hoped Douwe and Afke had made them a good hiding place.

"Here, sit down. I made you a plate of hot wheat porridge. You need a good base in your stomach."

Janke realized how hungry she was and, without speaking, she dug into the steaming breakfast.

"You have a big day today, Janke," Douwe began. "Our two pilots need to be taken to Den Bosch. They're going back to England."

Janke's eyes grew large. She looked the two men over. Her heart skipped. Janke had heard how Allied people were taken from safe address to safe address, travelling from the Netherlands to Belgium, through France, over the Pyrenees, through Spain and from there to Portugal. It took weeks before they reached Portugal. From Portugal, they went back to

England by boat or plane.

"They've practiced bicycling for almost a week," Douwe smiled. "They've made good progress. I think they're ready to bike to Leeuwarden and take the train to Den Bosch."

"That's twenty-five kilometers." Janke looked at the men.

"It's safer that the men take the train in Leeuwarden, rather than from town." Douwe nodded at the two, who couldn't understand the Dutch conversation.

"Where do I leave them in Den Bosch?" Janke took a large spoonful of the sweet wheat porridge.

"A girl, dressed in a long blue coat and blue hat, will be just outside the station. You walk up to her and say, 'It's a nice day for travelling'. Her answer has to be, 'Especially on a sunny day'. She'll find you a place for the night and take care of our boys."

After breakfast, Afke gave Janke a gray, woollen coat with matching hat, scarf and mittens. The coat was oversized, but a great improvement over her own shabby one. She was glad she hadn't worn Klaske's winter coat the night before. It would've been ruined, and she still hoped she could return it one day.

"You can use my bike." Afke busied herself with packages of food for Janke and the men. "You buy three return tickets at the station," she said. "The Germans are less suspicious if you buy return tickets. As you step into the train, you slip the tickets to one of the men. You sit in the same compartment, but not together. You are travelling by yourself, visiting an aunt in Den Bosch. The men are travelling together." She looked at Bill and Jim. They were now dressed in civilian clothes. Both wore trench coats. Jim's was brown, Bill's beige. They also wore hats, one just slightly darker than the other.

"And remember, boys." Afke jabbed her finger at them. "You both can't speak. Not to each other. Not to Janke. Not a word, understood?"

They both looked at Janke. She repeated the words in English. In unison, they nodded. Bill tapped Afke on the shoulder.

"We do exactly as our pretty guide here tells us." His wide

smile reached his ears, and Janke smiled back.

After hugs and thanks for Douwe, Afke, Bert and Annie, the three took their bicycles and set off.

They were lucky the wind wasn't too strong yet. The cycling trip took them through several villages. Janke stayed quite a distance behind the two men, to keep an eye on them. She watched how they talked and laughed, as if they were on a fun outing, she thought.

Several army trucks passed them, but the soldiers didn't pay any attention to the cyclists. The boys laughed so hard when they met the local taxi, a Model-T Ford pulled by a horse, that Jim steered straight for a fence. He teetered, and just when Janke was sure he would crash into the wooden railing, he veered away from it and regained his balance. Her insides hurt from laughing, but it also worried her, especially when they neared the big, concrete wall outside the town of Leeuwarden.

Quite a lineup of military trucks, German cars and bicycles had formed at the checkpoint. Janke's stomach knotted inside her. She looked at the boys, who had instructions to just show their identity cards and not speak a word. They dismounted from their bikes as the line moved slowly through the checkpoint.

Ahead of Janke, a woman, dressed in many layers of clothing, said, "They're looking for weapons."

Janke sighed. At this point she couldn't do anything for the pilots. She watched them as they held out their identity cards. The German waved them both through. The next two people were sent straight through as well, but the woman who'd told her about the weapon search was subjected to an extensive inspection. Two soldiers went through her saddlebags. All they found was turnips, packages of butter and buns. Janke saw the look of disappointment on the Nazi faces. With a growl, they waved her through, but not before they had taken all the food away from her and one of the soldiers had spit on her shoes.

Janke's throat closed. A wave of humiliation swept through her. She forgot all about the pilots. She wanted to help the woman, say something comforting to her, but one of the Nazis pushed her bike and barked at her that she had to get out of the way. They didn't even look at her identity card.

Shaking with anger, she mounted her bike. As Janke passed Jim and Bill, she noticed their pale faces. They had been thrown into this war like birds falling from the sky. A war they had heard about and of which they'd seen pictures. They'd flown over occupied territory and thrown bombs at an invisible enemy. Today they were confronted with the reality of war. They'd learned the brutality of the Nazis firsthand.

At the train station they parked their bicycles in the bike racks. After Janke had bought the tickets, she waited until an elderly couple got up to board the train. With the two tickets in her right hand, she made sure she waited for the pilots. The station crawled with soldiers. They all carried rifles and bags and were busy getting on as well. At every corner stood a Nazi with a machine gun.

Special coaches were reserved for the Germans. They travelled first class. The seats in their compartments were soft and comfortable. The civilians were packed into the smaller compartments like cattle and sat on wooden benches. In these cars, the heating had been turned off and the windows were closed.

People behind Bill and Jim were starting to push. Janke took her time and waited for the elderly couple to climb inside. Bill stood beside her. Janke pressed the tickets in his hand.

She found a place across from the couple, but was able to keep an eye on the pilots, who sat two seats ahead, facing her. Soon the compartment filled with old men, women and children. A heavyset woman lowered herself on the bench beside Janke and squished her against the wall.

"Nobody wants to sit in the first compartment because of attacks on the locomotive." Her breath gurgled and came out uneven.

Janke tensed. She hadn't thought of air attacks. She looked at the two pilots. They each held a Dutch paper, pretending to read. Slowly, the train set off. Through the small window, Janke saw the buildings glide by. Just outside the city boundaries, the ticket collector, accompanied by a soldier with a machine gun, entered their compartment. The two of them took a long time, punching the tickets and checking identity cards. Janke held her breath when they neared Bill and Jim. The Nazi studied Jim for what seemed a century before he handed back his identity card. Janke's hands felt slick with sweat.

The train chugged along past meadows and villages.

Just before the town of Zwolle, the engine slowed. They were in the middle of the fields. Why would the train stop here? Janke looked around. The whistle blew continuously.

The ticket collector stuck his head through the door and yelled in Dutch, "Air attack! Get off the train!"

People scrambled to get to the door. Janke was pushed and shoved by other passengers. She jumped off the train and landed in a large puddle. Men and women and children fell all around her like a sudden rainstorm. An arm pulled her up. Janke scrambled to her feet. From other compartments, the German soldiers were running away from the train.

"Where to now?" Jim asked.

"As far away from the train as possible," Janke panted.

Jim ran beside her, while Bill followed. They jumped over narrow ditches and ran until they heard the grumbling engines of the RAF planes.

"Down," Janke screamed. She threw herself behind a ridge, feeling the cold and dampness of a swamp. Reeds scratched her legs.

"Oh, shit!" Jim lay close to her.

The pilots were now on the receiving end of the war. She looked up and saw three planes. The planes dove, their engines cried. The rat-tat-tat of machine guns shattered the air. People screamed. Bullets bit the ground around her. Janke covered her ears and closed her eyes. Would she die now? she thought. Die from a bullet of their allies? Die here in a wet field without family or friends? Jim placed his hand on her arm. In his eyes, Janke read the pure terror of war.

The attack had only lasted a few seconds, but when Janke and the pilots got up, the world had changed. The field before her lay scattered with bags, parcels, clothing and people. One by one, the terrified passengers scrambled to their feet and moved back to the train. The locomotive had been hit. Large bullet wounds gaped in the iron engine.

Two bodies stayed still beside the tracks. Janke shivered. A young man, lying face down, had been riddled by the bullets. His beige coat was spotted with holes like a leopard's skin. The ground underneath him had changed color as the puddle of his blood grew larger. A little further down, a woman lay on her back. A cry escaped Janke's throat when she noticed her face all bloodied and shattered.

Janke hesitated to go back on the train. She looked behind her at the sky. What if the planes came back? Bill and Jim didn't follow the other passengers onto the train either.

"I always thought we shot at trains full of Germans," Jim said in a soft voice.

"They're only in special designated coaches." Janke quickly pointed at one section of the train.

Jim winced. Janke touched his sleeve. In a whispering voice, she continued, "The more the Allies attack, the better, and the sooner this rotten war will end."

Jim didn't answer. They were the last ones to climb back into the compartment. Janke returned to her seat beside the large woman, who was crying softly.

Nobody spoke. The silence closed around them, until it was shattered by three whistles. Engines sputtered and slowly the damaged locomotive pulled its cargo of terrified passengers. Numb, Janke stared out the window. Her muddy clothes made her shiver. She looked at Jim and Bill. They better get back to England safely, she thought, as the train rattled into the station of Zwolle.

Still shaken, the passengers clambered off the train. Janke

looked for the sign to Den Bosch. Before she changed platforms, she checked to see if the Americans were following her.

For the next few hours, on the second train, they travelled through parts of the country Janke had never been in before. The scenery changed from farmland to more wooded terrain. Small villages popped up and passed by. Different people travelled with them. A woman carried a wicker basket with a live chicken. She was accompanied by five dirty-looking children, ranging in age from about five to twelve. The kids were noisy. Two boys, close in age, bickered constantly over a small metal car. A little girl sucked her thumb, her pale face streaked from a dirty nose and tears. The others stared with a blank gaze out the window.

Her two companions continued "reading" their newspapers until they reached Den Bosch.

This station was packed with soldiers and travelling people. Janke panicked. How would she recognize the woman in blue in these crowds? And where would she spend the night? The train emptied and Janke looked for the exit sign. She checked on the next day's train schedule back to Zwolle before she left the station. Soldiers watched from every corner. She slowed down until she was sure her companions followed her through the gate, past another checkpoint and onto the road.

Her eyes roamed the streets. She'd never been to Den Bosch before. The high buildings and rows of duplex houses surprised her. The streets were dirty and there were people everywhere. Across from the station stood the remains of what had once been a building. Among the rubble and debris, people scrounged for useful items.

An older woman, with a blue coat, walked ahead of her, but she wore a scarf around her head. Janke crossed the street and looked again for the woman in blue. She had no idea what to do if the woman didn't turn up. On a bench just past the main entrance sat a woman in a blue coat and hat, reading a book. Janke walked past her. She bent to tie her shoelaces.

"It's a nice day for travelling."

The woman continued reading. "Especially on a sunny day. Walk to the end of this street and wait for me."

Relieved, Janke walked on. The street wound around a large building. Three military trucks passed in front of her. Their brakes squealed and Janke gasped. They stopped at the train station. Soldiers jumped out of the back and ran into the building. An abandoned warehouse stood at the corner. At the top, the windows were boarded up with planks. Jim and Bill passed her, followed by the woman in blue.

"So long, Janke," Jim whispered.

Bill nodded and tipped his hat. They walked on around the corner, out of sight.

A few minutes later, the woman returned. "You can stay the night." She showed Janke upstairs to a room in the warehouse.

14.

Her train left the station at ten the next morning. Janke transferred in Zwolle again. The wind howled between the buildings and the blue sky had been replaced by dark, gray clouds.

A large poster on the wall of the main building caught her eyes. The Nazis always posted lists of those who had been shot, mostly out of revenge or retaliation for sabotage actions by the underground movement. Janke read the names of ten men, with their ages written beside their names. The youngest was eighteen, the oldest, sixty-seven. She thought of their families. Jan was eighteen.

Women with small children and old people filled the benches of the compartment, as did the smell of unwashed bodies and foul tobacco smoke. As the train neared Leeuwarden, the sky grew even darker. Rain pelted the windowpane. The compartment turned dark and lights were not allowed on until the blackouts had been pulled down.

The train station in Leeuwarden filled up with people as the train emptied its cars. A group of SS soldiers stood near the exit. Janke tried to breathe evenly. She had nothing to fear. Her identity card was correct and she didn't carry anything with her that would put her at risk. Just ahead of her walked a young woman in a tweed coat. She wore high heels and real nylons. Her auburn hair was put up in a fancy roll with long ringlets on either side. A golden fox stole hung around her shoulders.

Janke watched how she smiled through the row of soldiers. They all smiled back. As she turned her head, Janke recognized her. Dinie van Echten, the girl who worked for Doctor de Wit.

The girl who had taken Jewish children to Friesland.

Janke didn't want the Germans to smile at her, and she would never smile at them, but maybe that was Dinie's secret. Maybe her smile had got her past the Nazis with two small children.

Janke didn't look at the men when she held up her identity card and handed her train ticket to the first soldier.

"And what did you do in Den Bosch?" he asked in German.

"I visited my aunt." Janke replied in perfect German.

The Nazi looked at her identity card.

"Safe trip home," he said.

Janke hurried outside the train station. She made her way through the crowds. The heavy rain continued. Dinie stood on the sidewalk, covering her hair with her purse. Janke watched as a black Mercedes pulled up beside the stylish woman. A German officer got out. He walked around to the passenger side and pecked Dinie on the cheek. They smiled at each other; then the officer opened the door and she climbed in. The engine revved and the car sped away along Station Road.

Janke's mouth had dropped open. Now she was confused. Did Dinie work for the resistance? Or did she work for both sides? A chill crept up her spine.

As she turned and started for the spot where she had left her bike, another black German car came to a halt. The chauffeur got out, came around and opened the door for an officer. The man strode into the station. As he turned, the chauffeur looked at her. Janke recognized Helmut and quickly looked away. She followed the sidewalk to the bicycle racks. The hairs on the back of her neck stood on end. She didn't look back, but knew she was being followed.

Just get the bike, she thought. She placed her small purse in the saddlebags and pulled the bike out of the stand.

"Janke?"

Startled, Janke turned and bumped into the person behind her, her face in flames.

"Sorry. I did not want to frighten you." The words came out slowly.

Janke's breath caught in her throat. His eyes looked at her intently, searching.

"I have not seen you at the harbor?" He stepped closer.

"I've been busy every Sunday." Janke averted her eyes.

Helmut stayed silent, his eyes on her face. "I am driving back to Bishopville alone. I can give you a lift?"

"No." Janke shook her head. She shouldn't. If she accepted a lift from Helmut she was as bad as Dinie.

"The weather . . . " he hesitated. "It is bad. The wind." He pointed north. "It is strong."

It wasn't the first time Janke had biked twenty-five kilometers with the wind against her and the rain attacking her, and it wouldn't be the last.

"I can't accept," she said again.

"I can take the fahr . . . bicycle inside the car. Just before town I will let you out. Nobody will see that you rode with me."

Surprised, Janke looked at him. She almost smiled. The invitation was very appealing. She was starving and wasn't looking forward to the long bike ride.

"I understand," Helmut continued. His voice was pleasant. The accent charming. He tried hard to speak Dutch. She should feel scared. Her brain tried to think of an explanation, but it wouldn't obey. His uniform was immaculate, his hair combed neatly to one side. She wasn't afraid of this soldier. She remembered his eyes and his touch. Involuntarily, Janke's hand went up and touched her face.

Helmut watched her gesture. "I would like to talk to you," he said, "about the books I have not read."

Janke looked into his eyes. "I have them for you," she said softly. They were still in the shed on the shelf, if mother hadn't cleaned them away in one of her unnecessary cleaning moods. "I'll bring them on Sunday." Before she realized it, she had agreed to see him again.

"I will take your bicycle." He took the handlebars from her and walked her bike to the car.

Janke followed at a distance. She looked at the people rushing by. She didn't want to be recognized. By the time she reached the Mercedes, Helmut had packed her bike in the trunk and held the door open for her. Now if someone saw her getting into a German car, they would think she was a . . . She thought of Dinie.

"It is cold." Helmut touched her shoulder and Janke got into the passenger seat.

They didn't talk much while driving through Leeuwarden. Janke looked at the buildings, the houses and the people walking on the sidewalk. Traffic teemed with bicycles and motorbikes. A few buses and taxis were still running, but every bus was guarded by a German with a rifle. When they passed through the last checkpoint, Helmut sighed and glanced at Janke.

"I am happy you came with me," he said.

Janke looked at his serious face. "But I shouldn't have accepted," she said.

"No," he said with a straight face, " because I am a bad man."

Janke chuckled. "I'm sorry. I'm afraid to see you. I'm afraid someone will see me with you."

"But you are not afraid of me?"

She shook her head. "Should I be?"

"No, Janke. I do not want you to be afraid of me. I do not want you to think of me as a bad Nazi. I am not an active member of the Nazi Party and I never have been. And neither were my father and my uncle." He honked the horn at two cyclists who were using the entire width of the road.

Janke saw them shake their fists when they realized who was honking. She made herself as small as possible in her seat.

"Before the war started, we had a big fight at my house." Helmut glanced at her again. "My father and my uncle wanted to move to Canada. They did not like Hitler." He paused and swallowed. "My uncle went. He has sent me his address. I have memorized it. He lives in Ontario in a town called Waterloo. He owns a bakery. My mother would not hear of it. She supported Hitler. Then, you know what happened to my father. When I turned seventeen, I was recruited and sent to your town. I hate the war. I only wished to be with my uncle in Canada."

"Can't you ask your uncle the commandant to help you get away?"

"No." Helmut shook his head. "I told you before he has no power. He thinks the war is good for me." Helmut sighed. "My only chance would be to escape and hide and try to go to Canada on my own."

Janke laughed. "Escape? Do you know how hard it is to hide?" She blushed. What had she said?

"Do you know how difficult it is to hide?" His eyes didn't leave her face and he almost drove off the road. Now he knew, she thought. She had given herself away.

"I will not ask you to help me hide," he said in a soft voice.

"I cannot help you." Janke wasn't going to say anything else.

Helmut stared ahead at the road. Janke looked out the side window, where farms and pastures and houses passed, but she didn't notice the view.

The car slowed down. Janke looked at Helmut. She felt his regret and a sadness closed around her heart. She wanted to say something, touch him, but the words didn't come. Her hands stayed in her lap. Helmut stopped along a stretch of the road where there were no houses. He quickly stepped out and went around to the trunk to take out her bike. Janke climbed out of the passenger seat. She took the bike from Helmut. He placed his hand on hers.

"Will you bring the books on Sunday?"

"I . . . I don't know." She looked up at him.

"I will be there. I will wait for you." He let go of her hand and returned to the driver's seat.

Janke stood beside her bike and watched him drive away. As she slowly mounted, she just wished that Helmut was a Dutch boy. A boy she could meet openly. A boy she was allowed to like. But he wasn't, and if she continued to see him, then she had to be prepared to make sure they wouldn't be discovered. She would have to carry the secret with her for as long as this war lasted.

15.

"Can I get up now?" A mop of dark curls rolled out of bed. "Janke?" She stopped in the middle of her tumble. "Aunt Afke makes me stay in the room until she's finished milking the cows."

"Aunt Afke is smart." She lifted the little girl up into her arms. "Wow, you're getting heavy." She twirled Annie around and held her tight. Annie squealed in delight.

"Janke?"

"Yes."

"You know what Bert and I have been practicing?"

Janke looked at the little face. The dark eyes glittered excitedly from underneath the curls.

"We practiced going into our hiding place." She stood up straight. "I can crawl in really fast. Bert is too clumsy. His arms and legs are too long." She stretched her arms to show Janke. "It stinks in there." Annie pinched her nose. Janke couldn't resist a smile.

"That sounds like a good game you and Bert are playing." Janke bent down and stood her on the floor. Annie pulled back.

"It's not a game." Her face was very serious. "When the bad soldiers come to the farm, Bert and I have to go into our hiding place as quick as a bunny." She took a deep breath. "If they find us, the soldiers will kill us. And Douwe. And Aunt Afke. And you, if you are here. Aunt Afke said so."

Janke swallowed. She didn't know how to respond.

"Let's go for breakfast." Annie took her hand. " I'm starving."

"Me too." Janke and Annie bounced down the stairs.

Douwe and Bert trooped into the kitchen, where Afke placed steaming hot plates with wheat porridge on the table.

"Did you two have a good sleep?" Douwe looked at Janke and patted Annie's hair before he sat down.

"Oh, yes, we did." Annie climbed on her chair. "And I never wake Janke. But I told her what we've been practicing."

Janke watched as Douwe and Afke exchanged glances.

"Perhaps Janke can time you today." Douwe winked at Janke. "I have to fix the fence at the end of the three-hectare pasture. Tomorrow, we'll move the cows there."

"Will you time me and Bert, Janke?" Annie's eyes pleaded sweetly.

"Of course I will." Janke looked at Douwe.

"You should eat more, Janke." Douwe dug into his food. "You're too skinny."

Janke smiled at him. "It's not the food. It's all that biking that keeps me thin."

Especially when you sit comfortably in a black Mercedes, a voice in her head nagged. She felt her face burn and quickly looked at her plate. Annie climbed on the chair beside Janke. She chatted away about the calf that had been born yesterday.

"You know why Uncle Douwe named it Annie?" Her eyes smiled.

Janke shook her head.

"He says it looks like me. That is silly."

"I told you," Douwe chuckled between spoonfuls of porridge. "That calf has the same big, questioning eyes as Annie."

Even Bert laughed, a sound Janke hadn't heard before. Annie looked at Janke with her round, questioning eyes. "Are you going away again today?"

"No," Janke answered. "You and I are going to help Aunt Afke today. She needs a break."

"From us?"

"No, silly. From all the hard work she does every day."

"Yippee." Annie skipped around the table.

Later in the morning, Annie helped Janke hang sheets and pillowcases on the clothesline. A spring sky and April sun had opened the blooms of yellow daffodils along the brick wall of the farm kitchen. In the flower beds the young shoots of tulips and hyacinths were ready to burst into bloom. The pastures were dotted with dandelions and meadow daisies. A soft wind blew the sheets back and forth on the clothesline as Annie handed Janke the pieces of wet laundry and Janke fastened each item with wooden clothespins on the line. They were singing about little ducks swimming in the water when Bert came around the corner.

"Quick, Annie! Come with me! The bad soldiers . . . !"

Annie dropped a pillowcase on the grass. Bert grabbed her by the hand and together they ran into the stables.

The holding tank for the manure, Janke thought. She didn't know what to do. The sheet stuck to her hands. She heard the sound of trucks. Max's loud barking. The calming voice of Douwe, restraining the dog. Should she hide too? But where?

"Keep doing what you're doing." Afke's head poked around the corner and disappeared again.

Janke wished, with all her might, that the ground would open up and swallow her. She felt in her skirt pocket. Her identity card was tucked inside. Afke had told her right from the beginning that she was to say she was their maid. Afke had problems with rheumatism and needed help with the chores.

Annie's clothes? Janke wanted to run inside and hide the little girl's things. She heard the slamming of doors, orders being shouted in German on the other side of the building. Her feet wouldn't obey. Janke stood rooted in the grass, the sheet clutched to her chest, when three soldiers came running around the corner. They stopped in front of her. The Nazi with a high cap checked her identity card.

"Janke Visser?"

Janke nodded.

"What are you doing at a farm?" He looked at her intently over his glasses.

"I help Mrs. Jansma. She has rheumatism," Janke answered in perfect German.

He nodded and looked at her picture again. "We have heard that they are hiding Jews here."

Janke looked straight at the officer. She shook her head.

"No. There are no Jewish people here."

"You have to come with us." His voice became louder.

Janke, followed by the soldiers, walked to the front of the house. Douwe and Afke stood in the front yard. Max had been tied to a fence post. The dog bared his teeth and growled. A soldier stood to one side, his rifle pointed at them. The sounds of slamming doors, furniture being moved, heavy boots and loud voices from the invaders came from inside the farmhouse.

One of the soldiers pushed Janke forward to stand beside Afke. She looked at the faces of her hosts. Douwe's showed anger and contempt; Afke held her head high. Her mouth formed a thin, straight line. Their expressions made Janke calm. Even though her chest hurt, her head was clear. No one spoke. The three of them waited. There must have been at least twenty men, searching the house, the stables and the barn.

The voices became angrier. Janke hoped it was because they didn't find what they had expected.

Finally, the commanding officer whistled. They all came running. One of the men screamed like a happy child. He waved a rag doll in the air. Annie's doll. Janke held her breath. He gave it to his superior. The man studied the doll, walked over to Afke and thundered, "Whose doll is this?"

"Mine, when I was a little girl." Afke pointed at herself.

The officer smiled. He looked at the doll once more. "Liar!" He spit on it, threw it on the ground and stomped on it with his gleaming boots. Janke watched as the crushing weight of the Nazi pulverized the glass eyes. Then he ordered his men to get back into the trucks, frustration dripping off his face.

The three of them stood like statues until the last of the trucks had left the long lane and turned onto the road, heading into town. Afke moved first. She picked up the doll and looked into its empty, squished face. Tears ran down her cheeks. "This could have been Annie," she said, her words barely audible.

Without a word, they walked inside where chaos greeted them. The contents of every drawer and cupboard had been dumped on the floor. Pieces of broken plates and cups lay everywhere. Afke sat down. Douwe stood behind her, his hands resting on her shoulders.

"I'll get the children." With angry strides, he left the kitchen. Like a machine, Janke started clearing the mess. First the debris from broken china; then the pots and pans and other kitchenware.

The high-pitched voice of Annie brought Janke back to the world. Tears of relief flooded her face when Annie and Bert walked into the kitchen. Bert's face white as a ghost. Annie's cheeks red from excitement.

"I was real quiet, Aunt Afke." She ran into the older woman's arms. Afke held her tightly, without words.

Douwe placed his arm around the boy, who surveyed the kitchen-turned-war-zone with trembling lips.

"You had . . . to go through this . . . for us," he stammered.

"We don't care about the mess, Bert." Afke wiped her eyes on the bottom of her apron. "We're so grateful they didn't find you."

"But they could never find us, Aunt Afke. Bert and I were really, really quiet."

"Yes. You and Bert were so good, they could never find you." Afke kissed the girl on both cheeks. She stood up and put Annie on the floor. "We better clean up and make some food. I bet you everyone is hungry after such a fright, and it is time for our noon meal."

Janke didn't think she could ever eat again. Her throat felt thick and closed. She watched the two hardworking people who would give their lives for the children they were hiding.

"It's time this goddamn war ended." Douwe threw the cutlery back into the drawer.

"Douwe!" Afke turned away from the hot stove and placed her hand on his arm. "The children," she said in a calm voice.

Douwe bent his head. He grabbed a broom and dustpan from the bottom of the pantry and started to clear away the broken china.

Afke put a pot with peeled potatoes, carrots and onions on the stove. The five of them cleaned until the food was ready, and Afke set the table with china that had survived the raid. They ate their meal in silence. Douwe's outburst had shaken everybody. They'd never heard him being angry. Janke had only known him as a kind, quiet man who liked to make jokes.

"The strain of this war is getting to everybody." Afke stroked Annie's curls.

"When are the good soldiers coming?" Annie looked up at Afke.

"They're on their way, dear. They're on their way."

16.

Alie arrived one afternoon at the beginning of May. She found the family in the kitchen, cleaning up after the noon meal. Annie chattered away while standing on a chair in front of the sink, washing the dishes.

"I heard about the raid last week, but I couldn't come. I was away."

"It was really bad, Alie." Annie waved the dishtowel. "The soldiers threw everything out of the cupboards. They were so mean. But today Aunt Afke will make me a new rag doll."

Alie looked at Janke.

"It's true," Janke nodded at Annie. "But Annie and Bert have a really good hiding place."

Afke poured a tea brew she had made from dried herb leaves in her garden.

"Thank goodness we didn't wash clothes that day, just bedding and towels." Afke sighed. "We are more careful. Every night we put everything that doesn't belong to the three of us in a hiding place before we go to bed. Next time, we might not be so lucky."

After they drank their tea, Afke sent the two girls outside.

"The sun is out there, waiting for the two of you to catch up on your news." Afke took Annie by the hand. "We are going to look in my basket of remnants so we can make you a new rag doll."

Janke smiled when she heard Annie giving Afke advice about how big the new doll should be and what kind of hair and what color eyes it should have.

"She's a sweetheart." Alie took Janke's arm as they set out

toward the fields where singing birds and a yellow carpet of dandelions greeted them. "You're quiet." Alie inhaled the fragrance of the meadows.

"Yes." Janke looked at her friend. "For some reason I believed Douwe and Afke's farm was a safe place."

"There are no safe places," Alie responded. "But don't let this get you down. There are rumors that it's happening very soon."

"What?"

"The liberation by the Allies, of course. And I have some news about Freerk."

"What news?" Janke stopped in front of her friend. "Why didn't you say so right away?"

"Because I'm scared." Alie's face turned serious. Little lines etched her forehead. "He's going to escape from Germany. He can't take it any longer. He's been sick and . . . "

"How do you know all this? From his letters?" Janke wanted to pull the words from her friend's mouth. "Tell me, I'm bursting."

"If you let me." Alie smiled weakly. "A friend of my father knows someone who gets information from the Germans about the workers in the factories." Alie took a deep breath. "This man also has connections with the resistance. The next time someone in Freerk's barrack dies, they're going to change his identity."

"How?" Janke could hardly contain herself.

"They will give the body Freerk's identity and ship it to us."

"What?" Janke clasped her hands together.

"We will have a funeral, with just the family and Freerk will escape and go into hiding."

"But what about the real family of this dead person?" Janke couldn't believe this would work.

"We will notify the family, and after the war we will rebury the person in his own hometown."

"Oh, Alie." Janke placed her arm around her friend's shoulders. "No wonder you're scared and worried."

"I'm so afraid Freerk won't succeed." Her eyes filled and Janke hugged her tight.

"He will, Alie. You have to be positive. He has to escape."

"I know." Alie wiped her face on the sleeve of her beige cardigan. "If he doesn't get out of that place he will die. This person my father knows said that nobody can survive the harsh conditions any longer than a year. And Freerk has been there almost that long."

Janke opened the gate to the pasture where the cows grazed. Some looked up, but most kept on grazing when the girls walked by.

"You can't talk to anybody about Freerk." Alie looked at Janke.

"Don't worry." Janke looked away, her face turning red. "I'm very good at keeping secrets."

"Mm," Alie eyed her friend with suspicion. "I assume you are carrying some deep secrets."

Janke nodded.

In the distance two black horses, Abe and Sijke, pulled a mower under the guidance of Douwe. The girls climbed the gate to the next pasture.

"And that brings me to our next assignment." Alie held out her hand to help Janke jump down.

"Both of us?" Janke asked.

"Tomorrow morning we are to bike to Leeuwarden. We have to go to a house on the Wilhelmina Quay and ask where the shipment of tea has arrived and when we can pick it up."

"Oh, I'm glad we can do this one together," Janke smiled. "What do you think the shipment of tea is?"

"It could be people, food or weapons." Alie shrugged her shoulders. "Nothing surprises me anymore. I have carried it all."

They followed an old path that lead to the end of Douwe's fields. Here the fresh, young tips of wheat and oats were sprouting up from the warm soil. The ground was soft under their shoes as they followed the ruts in the path. Crested plovers dove at the girls, defending their nests, until their attention was caught by two black crows.

"Look at us, Alie." Janke's voice sounded flat. "What has become of us? We're as bad as the boys. All we can think of is the next assignment. I was home today, helping Afke, but I'm already restless."

"I feel the same," Alie said. "I'm so full of hate. I'm even willing to kill them and I think I could, too."

"After what happened last week, I feel capable of killing, too. I just hope I never have to make that choice." Janke shivered in the warm May sun.

"You're right." Alie hooked her arm through Janke's. "But whenever I feel so full of hate, I push it away and force myself to dream of boys and dances." Alie let go of Janke and pretended she was holding a boy in her arms. She sang about a blue river and waltzed around the pasture. Janke stood and watched, her eyes smiling.

"Come on, Janke," Alie sang. "Dance with me. I don't see any handsome boys out here. Do you?"

Janke laughed. "You're obsessed with dancing." She took Alie's hand and placed her other hand on her friend's shoulder. Alie lead the two in a roundabout waltz, until they tripped over each other's feet and landed in the grass. They quickly stood up and brushed off their clothes. Their laughter startled a pair of sparrows.

Their stroll took them to a field with soft clover. Alie pulled Janke down on the bank of the water-filled ditch. "Look at that sky." She pointed at the soft clouds overhead. They lay on their backs and stared at the sky. In between the clouds, white lines of condensation streaked the blue. White lines from Allied bombers on their way to Germany.

Janke closed her eyes briefly. Oh, when was this war ever going to end? She felt so tired, so tired. Once more she opened her eyes and followed the white clouds. One cloud looked like a sailboat. If she could just climb aboard and sail away. Her eyes closed. The sailboat moved, gliding along an ocean of blue sky. At the helm sat a young man. He steered their boat to safe havens. His face looked familiar. His eyes were kind, but sad. Those eyes smiled at her with tenderness and she smiled back.

With a shock, Janke sat up. Heat flushed her face. She wiped the grass from her dress and stood up. She couldn't think of him now. Not with Alie right beside her. Not when they had just talked about killing Germans.

"What's wrong?" Alie's puzzled look made Janke look away.

"I don't know. I feel strange."

Alie pulled herself up. "We need the danger."

"Do you ever wonder what we'll do when this war is over?" Janke looked at her friend's face.

"We can't just go back to school. We can't pick up where we've left off." Alie looked at her. "Maybe I'll travel to America to escape for a while."

Or Canada, Janke thought, but she shook her head instead. In silence, the girls walked back to the farm.

17.

In the weeks that followed, Janke biked across the countryside finding safe addresses for divers as the stream of people from other parts of the country increased. More and more people believed they would be safe in Friesland. Janke now felt very much at home at the Jansma farm. Sunday nights she visited her parents, and most Sunday afternoons were spent at the parsonage.

On a Sunday in early June they listened to Radio Orange and heard about the invasion of the Allied troops in Normandy.

"Finally," Mrs. Bergman said. "We've waited for this for so long."

"With the Russian armies moving west and now the Allied troops moving north, it can't be long." Reverend Bergman wiped his eyes.

The bell rang and Alie's father went to answer it.

"Let's practice, Janke." Alie pulled her friend upstairs to her room. "We have to be ready for the liberation. I want to party for weeks when this country is free."

Janke laughed. She should feel happy, but a small voice tugged at her heart asking what would become of Helmut. They practiced dancing to the music of pre-war records in Alie's room.

Before visiting her parents, Janke met Helmut behind the boat house at the harbor. There were more people walking on this sunny afternoon. Janke still tried to make sure no one saw her. She wouldn't stay long, as Father had grown somewhat suspicious since the Sunday when Harm had come with a message and Janke hadn't been at Alie's.

Janke now brought Helmut a new book every week and they often talked about his dream of going to Canada.

"Canada is an enormous country," Helmut said. "When my uncle arrived, he sent me pictures. I even got a calendar with photographs of the Rocky Mountains, the prairies and a huge natural area in Ontario called Algonquin Park." His eyes travelled far away.

Janke watched how his face became light with excitement and longing for this great country on the other side of the Atlantic Ocean.

"Aren't you worried about the Allied troops and what will happen to you when this country is liberated?" Janke taunted.

"Yes, I am. But I am very glad the Allied armies are coming. It means this terrible war is coming to an end." Helmut turned to face her and grabbed her hands. "Come with me, Janke." His eyes pleaded. "We could build a life together far away from this war."

Janke smiled. "You are a dreamer, Helmut. We are still in the middle of this war. We are still enemies, you and I. How can you even think that we can go to Canada together?"

"Are we enemies?" He threw the words right back at her.

Janke blushed.

"You come to see me every Sunday because I am your enemy, yes?" His voice tightened, his face shadowed by tension.

"I have to leave." She pulled her hands free of his. Defeated, Helmut turned away. He walked towards the water's edge and stared. Janke's hands trembled. She took her bike and waited.

She wished. She wanted . . .

Helmut didn't turn.

Janke mounted her bike and pedalled home, her face wet, her fists clenched.

"Janke." Father opened the door. "What's wrong? You look upset."

Taken off guard, Janke pushed her bike inside. She needed a moment to think.

"I'm so tired of the war." She walked past her father into the kitchen. She felt his eyes on her back.

"I guess we all are." She turned to face her father. She thought how hard it must be for him to deal with Mother's mood swings, Jan in hiding, his own illegal activities and her absences from home. Father patted her shoulder. "We all are," he said, "but I do have some good news."

Janke looked at his smiling face. Mother wasn't the only one who had grown old quickly, she thought. The war had eaten her father's years away as well.

"I've rented a houseboat for two weeks in July."

"A houseboat?" Janke sat down. "How did you manage that?"

"I've been looking for another place to live and I'm always asking people. Yesterday, I got the news."

"Who and where?" Janke turned her head as the door to the hallway opened. Mother, dressed in a blue-and-burgundy-flow-ered dress, walked into the kitchen. Her eyes smiled. She'd washed and put up her hair, Janke noticed.

"Well, hello, stranger." She walked over to Janke. "What do you think? We'll get a two-week break from our neighbors." She nodded her head in the direction of the school.

"I think it's fantastic." Janke felt warm inside when she saw her mother smile at Father. "I still don't know where this house-boat is."

"Not far from here. On Bass Lake." Father placed his arm around Mother's shoulders.

That would be close to the small houseboat where the under-ground movement was hiding people, Janke thought.

"I'll love it." Janke stood up and hung up her coat.

"Marie made us bread." Mother sliced a loaf of grey-looking bread.

"And I brought some cheese from Afke." Janke went back to the shed to retrieve the treat from her saddlebags.

"I have one condition." Mother placed the bread on the table, while her father cut the cheese. "No illegal activities while we're vacationing."

Janke looked at her father. The war wouldn't stop for two weeks while they were in the houseboat.

"It all depends, Els," Father said.

"That's not good enough." Mother's voice rose. "I'm not going to be on a houseboat for two weeks all by myself in the middle of nowhere!"

"It's a big boat with two bedrooms." Father looked at his bread.

"That was not what I asked." Mother stood at the table.

Janke sat down. She agreed with her mother.

"You're right, Els." Father, too, sat down and arranged slices of cheese on his bread. "Janke and I have to make an effort to stay home as much as possible for those two weeks."

"An effort? I want a guarantee," Mother nagged.

"Oh, Els. I said we'll do our best, but people depend on us."

"I also depend on you, but that doesn't count." Mother threw her knife on the table.

Janke held her breath.

"Els, that is not fair and you know it. If every family provided two or three people for the underground movement, the war would end sooner, but if everyone acted like you . . . "

"You always have your answer ready." Mother jumped up from the table. "You're so clever. The headmaster knows everything."

"Oh, Mother." The words were unfair, but Janke swallowed her remarks. They wouldn't do any good. All of a sudden she felt itchy. The small kitchen, the air thick with tension, confined her. Her mother's remarks irritated her. She sprang to her feet.

"You're leaving already?" Mother's shrill voice startled Janke. "You just got here. Can't you even make time to visit us?"

Janke plopped down on her chair. She looked at her father. He nodded.

"Could you stop now, Janke?" He checked his vest pockets for tobacco.

"No." Janke shook her head. Some days she hated taking risks to save strangers. But the more she got involved, the more she needed it. What else would she be doing all day?

"People depend on me, too," she said softly.

"Don't forget, Els, that the Allies are in France." Father placed his arm around her shoulder. "That news gives us hope that changes are coming."

18.

"You don't need to bring much." Janke stood at the kitchen door of the parsonage.

"I'm so glad you invited me." Alie stuffed her clothes in a large canvas bag. "I have two bathing suits."

"I just hope the weather will stay warm while we're at the houseboat." Janke took the bag from her friend and carried it outside, where two bikes leaned against the wall.

Mrs. Bergman followed the girls outside. "I won't take any messages. You two should rest for a week." She wrapped two loaves of bread in a tea towel and packed them in Alie's saddlebags. The large bag would be tied onto Alie's carrier seat. Janke had already tied two sleeping bags on her carrier with twine.

"What about our special assignment?" Alie looked at her mother.

"I don't expect you're needed until the end of the week." Mrs. Bergman smiled. "Your father and I will come down to the houseboat and let you know as soon as possible." She kissed both girls on the cheek.

It was about Freerk, Janke figured, but she didn't ask. Alie would tell her. Her heart skipped. All she hoped for was that Freerk would be safe.

Dressed in shorts and capped-sleeve blouses, the two friends set off. It was a sunny Saturday in July. The breeze played with their hair. They took the main road to Bass Lake — not the path that Janke had biked to the houseboat which the resistance used. This was a dirt road that followed the west side of the lake to the mouth of the River Pike. Meadow birds followed the two on their journey, their songs adding to the vacation mood. The pastures celebrated with an array of yellow buttercups, red and white clover and tall red sorrel.

"I can tell you about Freerk." Alie pushed the pedals of her bike, her face bright with excitement.

Janke's eyes followed two small sailboats on Bass Lake. She quickly turned her gaze to Alie. "Where is he?"

"He's left Germany. He's somewhere between here and the German border. That's all I know. I'm scared and excited and worried."

"Oh, Alie. I hope he'll make it."

"Me too." Alie nodded. They passed two older cyclists and their conversation halted until they were out of hearing distance.

"We need to practice our sailing skills." Alie turned to Janke. "You and I will have to take him by sailboat to East Port. From there he'll try to reach Sweden by fishing boat."

"That will be difficult," Janke said. "I've heard the Germans search every boat that leaves the harbor. They have caught on that many people escape that way to Sweden."

"I know." Alie nodded again. "I still don't understand how Sweden has managed to stay neutral all this time, but at least it's one of the two countries in all of Europe people can try to escape to. And Freerk has no other option. Sweden is his only chance."

Soon the girls reached a wooden gate closed for grazing sheep and cattle. Janke opened the gate, and both girls took their bikes into the pasture. They were met by curious sheep, whose woollen coats had been sheared. Four yearlings ignored the girls as they wobbled along the sun-baked ruts of the path. Two more gates had to be opened and closed before they finally reached the houseboat, which lay peacefully moored at the bank of the river.

Janke's father waved his fishing pole when he saw the girls approaching. Her mother got up from a canvas chair at the edge of the river and walked towards them. Janke heaved a sigh of relief when she saw her mother in a pale blue sundress, her hair tied in a ponytail and a smile on her face.

"Ready for a swim, girls?"

"I think we'd like to explore our vacation home first," Janke said as she untied the sleeping bags from her bike.

"It's no palace, but it will do if the weather stays dry." Father had joined them. The houseboat was a rectangular box about ten meters long; its paint-peeled wooden sides had once been green. "Are you any good at catching fish, Alie?"

"Oh, yes, Mr. Visser. But I always seem to catch the small ones that taste like mud."

"Well, if we don't catch anything else, we'll feast on those."

The girls walked to the front of the boat and opened a door that had once been painted brown.

"I wish we could get some paint," Janke said. "I would love to brighten this boat up."

"It's hard enough to get food these days," Mother followed the girls inside, "let alone paint and other luxuries."

They entered a small kitchen-sitting area with benches on either side of the room. In the corner was a sink and a two-door cupboard for dishes and food. A pair of tiny bedrooms, one behind the other, occupied the rest of the boathouse.

"At least there is an escape window big enough for us to crawl through." Alie pointed at a large window at the end of the second bedroom. "In case of an emergency, we don't need to go through your parents' room."

"And it's faster to the outhouse," Janke laughed.

It didn't take long before first a blue and then a burgundy bathing suit dipped in the clear water of the River Pike. The water felt cool at first, but after a few minutes a wonderful feeling of freedom overcame Janke as she swam.

"Oh, this feels like living!" Alie shouted. She splashed wildly till Janke dove under to dodge the sprays of water.

"You girls are disturbing the fish." Janke's father reeled in his line and moved further down the bank.

"We'll send them your way," Janke laughed.

The girls swam until their skin was wrinkled and goosebumps covered their arms. Finally they dried themselves and stretched out on their towels to warm up in the sun. Janke looked at her mother, who was sprawled comfortably in her chair. Her face was relaxed at last. Janke wished life could stay like this. The clear blue sky, the warmth of the sun caressing her skin, and the freedom she'd felt in the water took away some of the worries of the war.

The peacefulness surrounding the vacationers and the murmur of the water in the reeds allowed Janke to doze off. Then Alie's voice startled her awake. "Now, you are a lot of fun!"

"I can't believe I fell asleep!"

"Yes, you were snoring lightly." Alie stood up beside her. "You were probably dreaming of that special someone you won't tell me about."

"Who? Why?" Janke's face burned.

"Hey, I'm just kidding." Alie hit her on the shoulder. "You never talk about Harm anymore. It's no fun."

"I told you, Harm is too busy with the resistance." Janke walked towards the houseboat. "I'll make some tea," she called over her shoulder.

"You're too late." Mother came outside. "I made a large pot. You can help me bring the tray outside and call your father."

The four of them sat around an old wooden crate that Janke turned upside down to use as a table.

"After tea we can row over to Keestra's." Father pointed to the west. "The farm is just past the bend. He owns this houseboat and said we could borrow his sailboat as well."

"Oh, wonderful!" Alie cried and spilled tea all over her bathing suit. "I . . . we . . . uh, like sailing, right, Janke?"

"Yes, we better brush up on our sailing skills." Janke winked at her friend.

"You will like Keestra and his wife, Els." Father rolled one of his skinny cigarettes. "They are really nice. They told us we can get eggs, milk and butter any day. And they have a large vegetable garden."

"It will be so nice not to worry about ration coupons and food." Mother stretched her arms and laughed at Father.

"I think we should brush up on our sailing skills, too, Els. That is, when the girls will give us some time." His eyes sparkled and Janke felt warm all over.

At night they pointed out the Big and Little Dipper and listened for the planes going east.

The days of the week swam together as one sunny day followed another. They enjoyed the water, caught fish, rowed to Bass Lake and sailed down the River Pike close to the Wadden Sea. They visited the Keestra farm to buy food almost every day. Slowly the tensions of war left their bodies as they enjoyed the feeling of freedom.

Janke was grateful that Alie had been allowed to stay with them for the week. They had a chance to catch up on many aspects of their lives. All except one. Even though Alie now spoke openly about her feelings for Jan, Janke tried to avoid the topic of boys and often found herself steering the conversation in other directions. Still she worried about where Jan was and if Freerk was safe.

Janke hadn't met Helmut since that Sunday when they had quarrelled, but her thoughts were with him all the time. Though she told herself that they could never be together, she also felt that her feelings for him would never change. She knew she cared deeply about the kind boy trapped in his Nazi uniform. But she vowed this would be a secret she would carry for the rest of her life.

As the week progressed, Alie tensed. They expected word from Alie's parents about Freerk's whereabouts. Now that she felt rested, Janke admitted that she was ready to tackle new resistance jobs. Friday afternoon, two cyclists climbed the gate. Alie jumped up from her towel when she recognized her parents. The Bergmans brought food and good news about Freerk. They stayed for tea.

"Freerk didn't wait for someone to die. He escaped on a day

pass on his Sunday off." Reverend Bergman's voice quivered. "He stole a woman's clothing from a clothesline and walked all day. At night he followed the railroad tracks until he reached the border. He crossed in a forested area and made his way to a farm."

Janke watched Alie's mother hold her hands clasped together. Her face showed she was reliving her son's dangerous journey.

"How did he know he could trust the people on the farm?" Alie's cheeks were bright red.

"He didn't, but he was lucky. The people were involved in the resistance. They contacted our members."

"Where is he now?" Alie sat at the edge of her chair.

"Let me finish," her father smiled. "Freerk became seriously ill and had to stay on the farm." He cleared his throat. "We have been so lucky. The people did everything they could to save him. The resistance stole penicillin from the Germans. Without the medication, Freerk wouldn't have made it."

Janke couldn't believe it. Again, she was amazed how people took enormous risks to save strangers.

"And now? Where is he?" Alie jumped up from her chair. "Tell me!" She pounded her father's shoulder.

"He's very close. I have an assignment for both girls, if it's alright with Janke's parents."

"She's never asked permission before," Janke's mother said. With that she hurried into the houseboat. Janke's chest tightened. All of a sudden the tension returned.

"It's alright." Janke's father stood up. "I know Janke will want to help."

"Should I talk to her?" Alie's mother asked. "If it's better that Janke isn't involved . . ."

"No, Mrs. Bergman. It wouldn't really help and I want to go with Alie." Janke touched Alie's mother's arm.

Mrs. Bergman went inside the boat to talk to Janke's mother, while the girls received their instructions about how and where to pick up Freerk the next day.

"And today we heard on the radio that the Allied forces have finally broken out of their encirclement in Normandy." Reverend Bergman walked towards the river. "If they move up north fast, we could be free before the winter."

"I hope you're right." Janke's father had come to stand beside him. "We can't take another winter," he said. Both men stared out over the river and the land beyond.

Janke thought about the Allied troops chasing the Germans back. A new fear entered her chest, a fear for Helmut's safety.

19.

The next afternoon, Alie and Janke went sailing on Bass Lake. A light breeze filled the sails and the boat glided across the lake in the direction of the canal.

"The resistance houseboat is hidden just off the lake." Alie's long hair was tied back in a ponytail.

Janke nodded and watched her friend, who seemed nervous and excited at the same time. She knew exactly where the small houseboat was hidden.

The warm afternoon brought some pleasure boats and a family with rowdy children in a rowboat onto the lake. Janke tried to enjoy the wind in her hair as she secured the large sail, but Alie's tension rubbed off on her, and by the time they reached the inlet, her chest felt tight.

What if Freerk wasn't in the boat? What if something had happened last night?

The wind slapped the sail. Janke quickly secured the rope.

"I'm so glad you came with me." Alie blinked back the tears. The girls didn't talk until they gently maneuvered the boat into the narrows. Janke jumped ashore and tied the boat to the branch of a willow tree. Alie whistled "It's a Long Way to Tipperary."

The girls waited, crouching down in the reeds. A warbler sang in a clear voice and interrupted the silence. They listened. The water rippled onto the shore. The sun beat down and added heat to their already warm bodies.

A door closed. A whistled tune answered. Alie dashed ahead, tripping over reed clumps. Janke followed quietly and at a distance.

"Janke!" Alie's voice sang with relief. "Come! She looks wonderful."

Janke laughed when she saw Freerk dressed in a yellow dress covered with daisies. He wore a wig of brown, curly hair and had a bonnet tied under his chin. His feet were clad in white socks and matching sandals. He looked thin, his cheekbones stuck out. His skin had a pale color.

"Janke, let me hug you. How good it is to see you." He smiled and placed an arm around each girl. "I can't believe how grown-up the two of you look."

If they could just go home now, Janke thought. "We better go," Alie took control of the situation. "You'd better take this." She handed him his new identity card.

"Looks good." Freerk showed them his picture. The card said he was Baukje de Groot, housewife, thirty years old, born in Leeuwarden.

"We have to leave," Alie repeated.

They untied the sailboat and sailed back to the lake, then onto the canal.

If only this could have been a normal summer, Janke thought with regret. They'd had such a great week, filled with laughter and outdoor activities, but today, once more, the threat of being caught sailed with them.

A majestic yacht, flying the swastika, cruised the canal as well. On board they saw a group of high-ranking German officers accompanied by several young girls. Janke squinted her eyes. On the top deck was a slim, young girl. Beside her, with his arm draped around her shoulders, stood an officer. Janke didn't know if it was the same Nazi who had been at the station, but she was very certain about the girl. They waved at the sailors and Alie and Freerk returned the greetings.

"Did you recognize the girl on the top deck?" Janke asked as soon as their boat stopped bouncing on the waves from the wake of the yacht.

"No," Alie said.

"She looked like Dinie."

"I don't think so." Alie shook her head in disbelief. "The boat was too far away to recognize the people. And why would she be with them?" She pointed at the yacht and turned up her nose. "She works with us."

Janke turned away. She didn't want to tell Alie and Freerk what she had witnessed at the train station. What was she going to tell them? That Dinie works for the resistance, just like I do, but she is seeing a German officer, just like I see Helmut? It was better to let them believe that Janke was mistaken.

For the last part of the trip, they had the wind against them. They tacked the boat back and forth the width of the canal, Janke and Freerk ducking their heads every time the jib swung across to take the large sail to the other side.

The waterway became busier as they neared the harbor of East Port. Small and large fishing boats lined the quay. Their eyes searched for the name *Anna Maria*, the fishing boat that was to take Freerk to Sweden.

"There," Freerk pointed to a brown boat with a large trawl net at the back. The skipper stood on deck, peering down the canal with binoculars. They saw him look at his watch. They found a spot nearby and moored the sailboat. Janke spotted a group of soldiers just to the left. Two German shepherd dogs accompanied them.

"It's best to pretend we're tourists," Freerk suggested. "We'll wait in the boat."

Seagulls screeched and dove at the boats, hoping to pick up scraps of fish. Fishermen gathered their nets, which had been spread out on the quay, and carried them back aboard their boats.

"The Nazis are searching every boat for divers," Freerk explained. "Several boats have a hiding place built in underneath the hold, but the dogs can sniff out stowaways easily."

An older man, smoking a pipe, approached them. Janke watched. His sleeves were rolled up and his arms were covered with blue tattoos. He wore a black, leather cap. Slowly, he walked past the boat. They barely heard his words. "As soon's those rats are out of sight, Baukje can come to the boat. The sailboat should leave immediately."

They sat some more. All three kept an eye on the Nazis and their dogs. They acted as if they had all the time in the world, but Alie and Janke had to be back by curfew.

A yelp from across the harbor made the Germans jump into action. Their boots thundered on the cobblestones. Quickly, Freerk hugged both girls and climbed ashore. "Be careful," he said in a thick voice. He threw them the rope. Alie's face was wet, but she reached for the helm. Janke took her spot to guide the sails. They saw Freerk climb aboard and then he disappeared.

With the wind in the sails, they left East Port and Freerk.

20.

Janke's parents stayed another week at the houseboat, but Janke returned to the Jansma farm and Alie went home. The warm weather stayed. Janke enjoyed being outside, and it made her biking trips easier.

The resistance had been hit hard during the month of July. Two important leaders had been murdered by the Gestapo, and there were rumors that the movement had been infiltrated by spies. Members were warned to act more carefully and to report anyone who seemed suspicious.

"Paris has been liberated, Janke." Douwe had just placed the radio in its hiding place under the stairs when she walked in the door.

"That's good news." Janke washed her hands at the sink.

"You must be hungry." Afke put a pot on the stove and stirred.

"Let's get the map." Douwe opened a drawer in the sideboard. He unfolded a map of Europe and smoothed the creases as he spread it out on the kitchen table. Afke, Bert and Janke bent over when Douwe put his finger on the capital of France.

"That's still a long way from Friesland." Afke shook her head and returned to the stove.

"But if they keep this up, they should be here before the year is over."

Soon Janke's vacation was forgotten as her daily jobs took up all her time. Her parents were back home and slowly Mother slipped back into her dark moods. Janke visited them every

Sunday in August that she could.

The fourth of September brought chaos as the Allied troops liberated Brussels and the Germans panicked. Many collaborators fled east. Rumors that Allied troops had entered the southern parts of the Netherlands made the Germans increasingly nervous. Curfew was now from eight at night until six in the morning. Men between seventeen and fifty-five were ordered to dig trenches in the province of Drenthe. Buses and trains were taken over by the Nazis, but the employees went on strike, which meant they had to go into hiding. Unfortunately the rumors proved to be false. The Allied troops were only at the Dutch border. They had liberated Belgium, though.

Life became more miserable as the Nazis intensified their hunt for divers and members of the resistance. As a result of the liberation, many Belgian SS commandos were dispersed in Friesland, where they took high-ranking positions. Many political prisoners soon experienced their brutal torture tactics.

One night in mid-September, Douwe woke everybody, even Annie, to see the spectacle above. They all watched as the sky above Leeuwarden looked like it was on fire.

"It must be the air base," Douwe said as he pointed at the planes crisscrossing north of the city.

Janke watched fireworks explode in the night sky. They heard the wailing of the sirens and the droning of planes. They heard the German fighters as they tried to attack the Allied planes.

"I don't think Annie needs to see this," Afke picked up the crying little girl and carried her inside.

"Well, I think they hit them hard," Douwe said.

Bert's face beamed as he watched the fighting planes.

When the quiet finally returned, they went back to bed, but the sky over Leeuwarden was still ablaze. Full of hope, Janke pulled the blankets around her, but fear for Helmut kept sleep away.

The next morning, Janke went to check on her mother. As she biked into town, she could feel the excitement of the people, even though gatherings of more than two persons in the street were still forbidden.

Father met her at the door.

"Did you hear? The whole air base has been destroyed!" His eyes sparkled.

"Good," Janke said. "Where is Mother?"

"She's in the kitchen. I'll see you." He tweaked her nose and was gone.

Janke entered the kitchen where her mother sat at the table, holding a cup of tea.

"Mother, it's good news, isn't it?"

"Your father didn't tell you that some of the bombs missed and that seven people got killed."

"Oh, that is terrible." And again Janke realized that the price for freedom was high.

"Could you go to Harm's and get some milk for us?"

"Yes, and I brought you some beans and butter from Afke."

Janke drank tea with her mother before she left to get the milk.

She took an enamel can with a lid and handle and placed it inside her saddlebags. A light rain turned the landscape into a gray world as she left the streets of Bishopville behind. The road ahead wove straight through fields of cut wheat and harvested potatoes. Farmers were busy digging up sugar beets. Clouds of seagulls followed the men, women and the machines.

Two white, stone pillars marked the entrance to the long lane to Bosma farm. As soon as Janke neared the farm buildings, she saw a figure waving at her. It was Harm. She met him behind the stables.

"Janke, it's lucky you came today," he said. "I was going to come for you. I have an assignment for you."

Janke nodded. She looked at the young man in front of her, his face serious. Janke realized suddenly that all she had felt for Harm was friendship. Her heart no longer beat faster when she stood close to him. This realization caught her off guard, but she wasn't surprised.

"We have a job for you . . . a dangerous job." His eyes watched her face. The tension in his voice shook Janke. Meeting his gaze, Janke nodded.

"You are to pick up a young Jewish girl in Amsterdam," Harm said, his voice now softer.

"A Jewish girl," Janke repeated, startled by what this might mean.

"Yes." Harm stepped closer. He grabbed the handlebars of her bike. She smelled cows and hay on his coveralls. She looked up at his face, but his eyes were distant.

"Tomorrow morning, you must bike to Leeuwarden. From there you take the train to Utrecht." Harm was all business, as if speaking to an acquaintance.

"But are the trains still running after the strike?" she asked.

"Yes, but they're being run by Nazi collaborators. They are not always running on schedule."

Janke nodded. "I guess I will find out when I get there."

"Yes," Harm agreed. "When you get to Utrecht, you transfer to the train to Amsterdam. Before you leave the train, put this on."

Harm pulled a red scarf from his pocket and handed it to Janke.

"At Central Station in Amsterdam you will see a woman in a gray raincoat, wearing a green hat with a feather. Don't approach her, but follow her at a distance. Got that so far?"

Janke moved her head slightly. She felt she was dreaming. Slowly the impact of his words sank in. She'd never been to Amsterdam. And now she was trusted to do something really dangerous. Just like Dinie, who worked for Doctor de Wit.

"The woman in the green hat will take you to 18 Emperor Street. Keep that address in your head, in case you lose each other. Once at the address, she will give you instructions about how to get the girl and bring her here."

"Here!" Janke couldn't believe it. "You mean I take her to the farm?"

"You bring her to the barn. Make sure nobody sees you or the little girl coming to the farm. You hide inside and wait for me."

Janke looked at Harm. His orders were short. His face stern. Janke felt instinctively that Harm's feelings for her had changed as well.

"It's a dangerous assignment, Janke." His voice was much softer now. "You're sure you can handle this?"

"How old is the girl?"

"I don't know. Little."

"A baby? A toddler?"

"I don't know, Janke." He looked at her closely. "I get orders and only know so much." He sighed. For a moment Janke saw the weariness in his face.

"All I know is that if we don't get this little girl, her life and the lives of the people hiding her are in danger." He let go of the handlebars. "Listen, Janke. If you don't want to do it, let me know now. We have to find someone else."

Again, Janke thought about Dinie, who had travelled with two Jewish children on the train. Maybe Harm was thinking of her as well.

"I'll do it." Janke stuck out her chin. She was more determined than ever to fight the Germans.

"Good." He touched her face. "Remember the instructions?" She nodded.

Harm made her repeat the assignment. "You'll have to stay overnight in Amsterdam. You can't travel past curfew."

He didn't have to tell her that. Her head spun. Amsterdam, she thought. She'd always wanted to travel to Amsterdam.

"I need milk," she said quickly.

"My mother will meet you in the stable." He turned and left before Janke could catch her breath. Even though her feelings for him had changed, she wouldn't let Harm or the resistance down, she thought.

When Janke delivered the milk, she stayed to help her mother and kept her company until after the evening meal. Just before curfew, she rode back to the Jansma farm.

21.

Early next morning, Janke arrived at the train station in Leeuwarden. She was lucky; a train stood ready for departure to Utrecht. This time she made sure she sat in one of the compartments far away from the locomotive. The memory of the attack on the train during her last trip still gave her shivers.

A man in his late sixties, smoking a big cigar, sat down beside her. Janke was overwhelmed by the stench of the smoke. The man sagged against her and closed his eyes as soon as the train set off. Janke kept an eye on the cigar, now dangling from his mouth.

The trip took forever. Her body ached from the man's weight. At noon the train stopped in Utrecht. The platform there was crowded, and everyone seemed determined to get on the train before the arriving passengers had a chance to get off. Janke hurriedly found the train to Amsterdam. She had only minutes to spare. When the station guard blew his whistle, Janke had no choice but to board the first compartment behind the locomotive. At least this time she had a bench to herself. She just hoped there wouldn't be any air attacks.

At two, the train arrived at Central Station in Amsterdam. Janke looked outside, anxious to see the gabled houses, the canals, the dam and the Royal Palace. What if she couldn't find the girl? Janke remembered the red scarf in the pocket of her light jacket and tied it around her neck.

Her eyes scanned the people as she walked toward the exit. A young woman stared at her with hollow, hungry eyes. German soldiers barked orders at the passengers. They were herded toward the exit, where everyone was checked thoroughly.

Outside Central Station, Janke took a deep breath. Her eyes scanned in all directions. A soft nudge on her arm made her look up. Her eyes met those of a young woman wearing a green hat with a feather. After a moment she followed the woman down the street. The gabled houses Janke had wanted to see so much stood gray against a cloudy sky. Her hands felt cold. This big city, her assignment tomorrow, the little Jewish girl, all the details made her nervous. It had been so easy to play the heroine in front of Harm, but now that she was in Amsterdam, Janke felt very small. She'd never seen so many soldiers with machine guns. They were everywhere, on every street corner, in front of every store.

The woman in the green hat walked at a fast pace and Janke had trouble keeping up with her. A few times she almost lost sight of her on the crowded streets. They travelled for about an hour until they finally arrived at the address on Emperor Street. Without a word, the woman opened the door and Janke followed her inside.

"I'm Thea." Her eyes scanned Janke's face.

"I'm Janke."

She led Janke up the stairs and stopped in front of another door. Thea took off her hat and Janke noticed how young she looked. Her brown hair had been bleached, as well as her eyebrows. Her eyes were blue with shadows underneath. She looked thin.

Three times the young woman knocked. The door was opened by a girl about Janke's age.

"This is Celia." Thea and Janke followed Celia inside. Two men in their early twenties were sitting at a square wooden table. Their heads were bent over maps.

"Hey," Celia said. "This is Janke. She's come all the way from Friesland."

"Did you bring us some food?" One of the men, with dark

hair, peered over wire-rimmed glasses to get a better look at Janke. He smiled.

"Wouldn't she have looked suspicious carrying food around in a city that is starving?" Celia shook her head.

The man sighed and returned his gaze to the map. The other man never even glanced at Janke.

"Keep your jacket on. It's chilly in here." Celia walked over to a small table against the wall. She stirred a pot on a propane stove. A faint smell of soup filled the room and suddenly Janke remembered how hungry she was.

The three girls ate their soup sitting on the floor. Thea didn't speak. She looked like a frightened bird, Janke thought.

"Piet, not his real name, is the head of the organization." Celia pointed at the dark man. "He's also being sought by the Gestapo. That means we have to change locations every five or six days."

Janke's stomach tightened. The watery soup didn't taste good anymore. She felt an urge to run outside and fill her lungs with air, but where would she go in Amsterdam?

"There's a bathroom down the hall and a small bedroom." Celia took the bowl from her. "The three of us have to share the blankets tonight."

Thea got up from the floor. "I still have a job to do." She looked at the two men sitting at the table. "Don't worry if I'm not back. I have a safe address."

Piet turned and looked at Thea. "You know your code?"

Thea nodded. Piet took a revolver from his coat pocket and handed it to Thea. She placed the revolver inside her clothes. Janke's chest tightened. What was Thea's job? Janke's eyes followed the young girl as she walked to the door.

"Try not to use it," Piet warned her. "You know the consequences. Ten of us for one of them."

"I'll do what I have to do." Thea closed the door behind her.

Panic struck Janke. Was Thea going to kill someone?

After the blackout curtains had been pulled, the men read by the light of a candle. Celia motioned Janke to come with her. The girls went down the hall to a small room. On the floor lay a mattress with a thin blanket.

"We're sending more and more divers to Friesland," Celia said as she unfolded the blanket. "The Gestapo has been crazy. They've held more raids in the last few months than in the previous years. Every day, parts of the city are closed off by the Germans. They search every house, warehouse and store. It's harder and harder to keep people safe."

And Janke had thought that it would be easier to disappear in a big city than out in the country.

"Aren't you scared?" she asked.

"Everybody is." Celia sat on the mattress. "After the Jews were forced to live in the ghetto, they have been loaded on trains and sent to the death camps in Germany and Poland. The few we save have to go into hiding."

Death camps. The words gave Janke an ice-cold feeling. Her thoughts went to the Schumacher family. "That's why I'm taking a little girl to Friesland tomorrow?"

"The people who are hiding this Jewish family are getting scared. There have been too many roundups in their neighborhood."

"Why only the girl?" Janke asked.

"It's too risky to move the parents to the same place." Celia lay down and pulled the blanket on top of her.

"You're keeping your shoes on?" Janke sat down as well.

"Just in case we have to leave in a hurry."

Janke pulled the blanket over her fully-clothed body. She thought she'd be listening for boots on the stairs all night instead of sleeping, but sleep must have claimed her tired body. The next thing she heard was someone calling her name. It took her a few seconds before she remembered where she was and why she was here.

"Time to go." Celia stood ready at the door. Janke looked at the bed. Thea had not slept beside her.

"No." Celia shook her head. "We don't know where she is, but we're moving again and I'll take you to your address. Sorry, but we've run out of food."

Celia pulled a black felt hat with a narrow brim over her head.

"You think Thea is alright?" Janke tried to keep up with her as they walked down the street beside one of the canals.

"I can't think about what might have happened to Thea. It will drive me crazy." Celia looked at her briefly. "Do what you have to do. Don't think. It only gets you into trouble." Celia's face looked blank, as if she had blocked out all her emotions.

"Why do you do it?" Janke couldn't resist the question.

"It happened gradually. Somebody asked me to give some-one a message and, before I knew it, I was deeply involved." She shrugged her shoulders. "At first it was like a game. I liked it when we outsmarted those stinking Nazis. Now it's much more dangerous. A few times I've been lucky. But what else can I do? I'm used to it now. I need to feel the danger. It's like a drug. When the adrenaline rushes through my veins, I feel high. I'm addicted to danger." Celia laughed, but it didn't sound like laughter.

Janke recognized those same feelings.

"For Thea, it's different." Celia's voice was serious. "Her parents were murdered by the SS because they were hiding Jewish children. Two weeks ago they shot her boyfriend."

Janke swallowed hard. So much hate. What did Thea have left to lose?

"We're almost there. You'll get further instructions at the house." Celia kept her voice down.

"Here it is." Celia stopped in front of a green door, which had the number sixty-one on a white oval plate. She rapped the knocker three times. They waited. Footsteps sounded, coming down. Janke looked at Celia.

"Good luck." Celia tapped her on the cheek.

Before Janke could respond, Celia had disappeared around

the corner.

The door opened. Janke wrung her hands. In front of her stood a lady with a pale, gentle face. Her silver-colored hair was held back with a blue ribbon.

"Good morning. Ah . . . " For a moment she'd forgotten her code. "I, ah, came to pick up a kitten."

"Yes. Come in." The door closed behind her and Janke followed the lady into a vestibule.

"The family is in the living room," the woman whispered. "As you can imagine, the parents are very distressed to let their little girl go. We will miss the little one and her parents , but it's too dangerous. There have been so many raids and . . . "

"Yes, I know," Janke said softly.

Janke's hands felt moist as they walked into the living room. A little girl, Janke guessed she was about four, with long, brown braids, played on the floor. She was struggling to put a stuffed cat into a knitted blue coat. She didn't look up when the two women entered. On the sofa sat a young couple, their eyes glued to the child.

"Sarah, Zacharie, this is . . . "

"Janke."

They stiffly rose from the sofa and shook hands with her.

"And dressing her kitten to go on a train trip is Irene."

Now, the little girl looked up, her dark eyes full of excitement. "Choo, choo. Kitten on the train! Kitten on the train!" She made the furry, stuffed animal hop on the carpet.

"She's still getting used to her new name," Sarah spoke to Janke. "We've been calling her Irene, after the princess, but she doesn't always respond."

Janke nodded.

Sarah whispered, "It's best that you leave quickly. We don't want to drag this out. We've told her she's going on a trip to a farm. We've tried to teach her all the names of the animals. We . . . " Sarah swallowed hard. "We've told her we would see her soon."

Janke's throat closed and her chest tightened. The husband

hadn't said a word. Janke saw him wringing his hands.

"Here is a small bag with some clothes."

Suddenly, the little girl was dressed in a red cotton jacket with a matching bonnet. Her mother tucked her braids inside and tied the ribbon. Her hands touched the little girl with so much tenderness that Janke had to turn away.

In the vestibule, the woman who'd let her in gave Janke instructions.

"You can't go back the way you came. There have been problems on the train to Utrecht. From here you take the trolley bus to Central Station. Buy two return tickets to Enkhuizen. I don't know when the train leaves. The schedules are all off since the strike."

Janke nodded. It meant they would take the ferry to Friesland, she thought.

"After the train to Enkhuizen, you take the ferry. A man carrying a basket with eggs will meet you when you get off." She handed Janke the money.

"Do I need a password?"

"If you do, I don't know it." The woman shook her head.

Tears flowed during the quick goodbye. For a moment, Irene couldn't let go of her father, but when her kitten fell, she was eager to rescue her pet off the floor. Janke used that moment to take Irene's hand and gently lead her out of the house. Janke didn't look back. She just walked, remembering the words Celia had said earlier that morning. Don't think. It will only get you into trouble.

22.

The trolley bus, packed with people, jolted and jerked its way to Central Station, stopping and going, letting passengers on and off.

Irene sat quietly on Janke's lap. She held her kitten, sucked her thumb and watched the outside world. Who knows how long she'd been cooped up in the house? Janke thought. She probably hadn't had any contact with other children. She'd heard of divers who didn't feel fresh air for months while they hid behind walls and in small cramped spaces.

"We're here." Janke lifted the girl off her lap, and the two of them headed for the ticket master at Central Station. After she'd bought the tickets, she smiled at Irene and pointed at the trains. The smell of coal smoke and the noise of engines scared the little girl. She clung to Janke.

"You have to help me find Platform 2 North, Irene." Janke bent down to look at Irene's face. With eyes as big as plates filled with fear, Irene waited for what would happen next.

"Over there." Janke pointed to a large number sign. They found a bench in a half-empty compartment. Janke slid Irene over to the window.

Just before the train was to depart, after the whistle had already sounded, the door opened. A German officer with a red face walked in.

"Identity cards, please!" he hollered in German.

Janke held out her card. The officer looked at her. Irene stared out the window.

"And where are you travelling to?" The voice wasn't unfriendly.

"We are visiting our aunt in Enkhuizen," Janke answered in German.

"When will you return?" His eyes never left her face.

"Tomorrow," she said in a calm voice.

The German nodded, glanced at Irene, who still stared out the window, and returned Janke's papers. When he finally left the compartment, Janke felt the tension leave her body. She hugged the little girl beside her.

"I want Mama and Papa." Irene's lip trembled.

"I know," Janke stroked the child's face. "Soon," she whispered and she hoped with all her heart that it wasn't a lie.

Finally, the train moved out of the station. Janke pointed to everything that passed their window to keep the little girl occupied. After an hour, the train suddenly stopped in the middle of nowhere. Janke looked out the windows to see what was the problem. Another Allied air attack? Panic flooded her mind, but then she remembered how the train's whistle had blown uninterrupted that other time.

She heard the shouting of soldiers outside. The door to their compartment opened and a Nazi ordered everyone to leave the train.

"The bridge has been damaged by air raids!" he yelled. "All passengers walk across to the other side! Another train is waiting for you!"

Carefully, one behind the other, the people walked across the damaged bridge. Janke had a hard time keeping Irene from falling between the tracks. The soldiers screamed behind her, hurried them across like cattle. When Janke bent to pick up Irene, a German grabbed the little girl from her. Janke froze. She watched as he carried Irene in his arms to the other side.

"And what about you, young lady?" he yelled, waiting for Janke to follow. "Do you want me to carry you, too?"

Janke swallowed a gulp of air, unfroze and hurried to the soldier holding Irene.

"She looks like my daughter," he smiled at Janke as he handed her Irene. "Here, back to your mommy. Quickly board the train."

Janke's whole body shook. She found it hard to breathe. Irene started to cry.

The train had fewer compartments than the one they'd left, so the passengers were crammed together on the hard benches. Janke held Irene on her lap, and she felt comforted by the little body next to her. A great sense of responsibility flooded her. In her mind, she saw the two parents who had entrusted her with the care and safety of their only child.

When they left the train station in the town of Enkhuizen, they were relieved to feel fresh air. The wind blew hard in the small harbor town where the ferry waited. Janke secured Irene's bonnet before she bought their tickets and carried Irene up the gangplank. The men on the quay were already untying the ropes. The ship's horn blew and the engine idled. Irene looked with bewilderment at the people who'd crowded onto the ferry. Many farmers had traded eggs and butter for live chickens, ducks and fresh produce at the open-air market in Enkhuizen. Now these people and their noisy cargo travelled back to Friesland.

Janke and Irene settled inside. A man carrying a basket full of eggs winked at her. Janke thought she was to meet a man after the ferry ride, but she decided to keep an eye on him.

The wind blew from the west and bounced the ferry on the waves. Irene fell asleep against Janke. As the child slept, Janke relaxed a little. She watched the German soldiers drink coffee. They didn't seem to take much notice of the people aboard the ferry.

After the two-hour trip, they moored in Wharfside, a small harbor town on the southwest coast of Friesland. As Janke got up, she lifted the still-sleeping Irene in her arms. The man with the basket looked at her. Janke let him pass ahead of her in the line of women, children and older men, all anxious to get off the ferry.

Irene woke up while Janke carried her down the gangplank.

"Which way you goin'?" The man waited for her to catch up.

"I have to go up north," Janke looked at him.

The farmer looked her over. "That's what I thought." He nodded. "Come with me."

Janke hesitated. She looked around. There was nobody else who seemed to be looking for a young woman and a little girl. The man must be her contact. Having no choice, she nodded at the man and followed him.

Down the street stood a horse and wagon. A woman sat on the wooden seat. She looked up as the threesome approached.

"You can hitch a ride." The man pointed to the wagon.

Janke hoisted Irene onto the back of the wagon and jumped up beside her.

"I see you picked up more than eggs," the woman greeted them.

The man chuckled.

"Giddy up, Watse." He took the reins and sat down beside the woman, whom Janke assumed was his wife.

Irene came to life at the back of the farm wagon. She talked about the horse. She pointed at people riding their bikes. She laughed when two ducks flew low over them. Janke smiled, relieved they had made it this far. She stared at the scenery passing by and listened to Irene's babbling.

The wagon finally stopped close to the barn and stables of a large farm. Janke took Irene in her arms.

"Come inside for a cool glass of milk." The woman walked toward the living quarters while Janke followed. The farmer took the horse to the pasture beside the barn.

"You look like you had quite the trip bringing this little girl to safety."

Shocked, Janke stared at the woman. Her mouth fell open.

"Is it that obvious?" she asked. She didn't even know if she could trust these people.

"To me it is," the woman smiled. "Most people assumed you were a young mother travelling with her child. But we knew that a courier with a child would be on the ferry either today or tomorrow."

"I didn't have a password." Janke looked into smiling, warm eyes.

"Sometimes we get the message too late, but we're always on the lookout."

"Is this the farm?" Irene wriggled out of Janke's arms and skipped ahead. "Can I see the animals? Mama said there would be lots of big and little animals on the farm."

"Not this farm." Janke saw the disappointment rush across the little girl's face as they sat down at the large table in the farm kitchen. The woman placed two glasses of milk on the table. Then she pulled a loaf of bread out of the cupboard. Janke's mouth watered as she spread a thick layer of butter on two pieces of bread.

Irene had spotted a cat in a basket beside the stove, and as soon as she'd finished her food she slid off the chair and knelt down beside the cat.

"She likes her belly stroked," the woman encouraged Irene. "You have far to go?"

Janke nodded. She looked at the woman sitting across from her. Her face was round with plump red cheeks.

"I'll give you my bicycle."

"No." Janke shook her head. "You can't give up your bike. How will you get your things from town? I mean . . . ?"

"Don't worry. I have Watse and the wagon. At least then I don't have to pedal."

"Thank you." Janke rose from the table.

The woman stood up. "You better get going if you want to make it before curfew."

Irene held onto the black tabby with white socks. He had nestled himself snugly in the little girl's arms. His purring accompanied Irene's babbling, high voice. Janke looked at the woman.

"This is her second goodbye today."

The woman shook her head. "You can't stay. Our farm is

being watched and often searched because we're so close to the ferry. The Nazis suspect this place is a haven for fugitives."

Janke understood. She picked up Irene, despite her protests. Encouraged by the woman's kindness, she mounted the bicycle. Irene sat behind her with her legs in the saddlebags. Janke didn't think the little girl had ever had the chance to ride a bicycle with her parents. Soon after her birth, she'd been forced to go into hiding.

The wind blew from behind and the first part of the journey went quickly. Every now and then, Janke reached back to check that her little passenger was still sitting on the carrier. She travelled on the back roads, avoiding towns and villages, but that route took longer. She couldn't handle anymore checkpoints.

She had to stop once when she felt Irene release her grip on her coat. The little girl had fallen asleep. She hung heavily on one side. Janke tried to keep her straight by holding Irene's arm. It was awkward to bike like that, and Janke had to stop a few times to rest her arm. She was now fighting against both time and the wind.

With only an hour before curfew, Janke knew she might not make it to Bosmas' farm. Her speed had slowed. Her arm was numb from holding onto her precious cargo. As her feet turned the pedal, she thought, *I must deliver her safely. I have to deliver her safely.*

A sigh escaped her when she finally turned into the lane to the farm. She headed straight for the barn behind the stables. She leaned the bike against the side of the barn and carefully lifted the little girl off the carrier. Irene slept on and seemed to weigh a ton.

Janke opened the door. The barn was quiet. For a moment she leaned against the wall, checking the contents. Her eyes adjusted to the fading light that came in through the high windows. On one side stood the farm equipment. On the other side, wooden crates were piled high.

A soft coughing sound startled Janke. She turned. Her mouth flew open and she almost dropped Irene. Not Harm, but Dinie, carrying a flashlight, stepped from behind an old threshing machine.

"Hi. I hope I didn't startle you."

Janke wondered why Dinie hadn't been chosen to bring Irene here.

"Hi," Janke found her voice. "I didn't expect to find you waiting for us." She clutched Irene tightly, which woke the little girl up. Irene stared at Dinie.

"I'll take her to her hiding place. You must be tired."

For an instant, she doubted Dinie. Was she an informer? A spy, who worked for both sides? She had seen Dinie with that officer on the boat. What about you? a voice in her head nagged.

Irene rubbed her eyes. She looked from Dinie to Janke. Her arms went around Janke's neck. She pressed close. Janke held her in her tired arms.

"Where's Harm?" she asked.

"He isn't here. He had a job to do."

"Where are you taking Irene?"

"It's not far. Just on the other side of town. Please," she added in a gentler voice. "It's late. I'd like to get going and you must go home, too."

"Irene," Janke said softly, as she pried loose the little girl's arms. She gently set her on the ground. "This is Dinie. She is going to take you to the farm where all the animals are."

Irene hesitated.

"It isn't far." Janke tried to reassure her.

"Will Mama and Papa come soon?"

"Yes." Janke avoided Irene's eyes.

"Will you come and see the animals?"

Janke looked at the little girl who had trusted her even though she'd only known her one day.

"I'll try," she said. "Say hi to all the animals from me. Especially the horses. I like horses."

Dinie took Irene's hand. Janke opened the door. Dusk had created a world of shadows. Dinie lifted the little girl onto her own bike.

"I won't take the main road." Dinie put her hand on Irene's shoulder and looked at Janke. "There is a path through the meadows that I can follow. It's just hard to see. But I'll make sure she's safe." Dinie and Irene disappeared behind the evening shadows of the barns and stables.

Janke returned to the barn. She made up her mind to wait for Harm. She just wanted to make sure that she was to deliver Irene to Dinie. If not, then she would have to tell Harm about the officer. She sat down on the floor and rested her head against one of the crates.

The sound of footsteps woke her. Dazed, she scrambled to her feet. The barn was pitch-black. Time had slipped by. She listened. The footsteps came nearer. The door opened. Janke held her breath.

"Dinie?" Harm's voice broke the tension.

"No, it's me," Janke said as calmly as possible.

"Janke?"

"Yes."

"I don't understand. What are you doing here? You should have been back at the Jansma farm."

"You should have told me who was going to take the little girl to the next safe place."

"I didn't even know at the time." He looked at her.

"Where is she taking the little girl?" Janke walked toward Harm.

"It's better that you don't know, Janke. Your job is done and you did very well."

"Was this a test?"

"If you want to call it that." He chuckled.

"But Dinie has done this work before."

"We can't rely just on Dinie. There are so many children who need to be saved."

"I see." Janke walked to the door.

"You better get going. It's after twelve. You can't go through town."

Harm followed her outside. The night air made her shiver. He brought her bike from the side of the barn. He held onto the handlebars as Janke mounted.

"Go now," he said in a much gentler voice. "And Janke?"

"Yes?"

"Dinie is a very important courier. She works for the leader of the movement in Friesland." Harm paused. "I know that she gets her instructions directly from our head man." She heard the admiration in his voice.

As Janke prepared to ride off, Harm still held on. He looked at her. Janke met his eyes. She could see that the beautiful Dinie had captured Harm as well. With a push in the small of her back, he sent her into the night.

2 3 .

On the first of October, Janke celebrated her seventeenth birth-day by bicycling across the province. Her saddlebags were filled with false identity papers, ration coupons, food and clothing. Her clothes hid a secret message, a map and even a microfilm. The underground movement buzzed with illegal activities and more and more people joined.

Janke stayed with Aunt Anna several times. Her aunt had moved to another house to join a group of four women living in a large mansion outside of Gateway. Ten hectares of land, with orchards and large vegetable gardens, gave the women enough work to con-ceal their real activities. Several times Janke collected pilots from the mansion who'd been shot down and were saved by the resist-ance. By bike, she took them to safe addresses.

A Canadian had set up a radio transmitter in the attic. From his hiding place, he had a great view of the road leading to the house. As well as receiving messages from England, he also guarded the fortress, as Aunt Anna called it. In the cellar, the printing of one of the illegal newspapers took place. One of the women owned a small press. A third woman was in charge of distribution.

Janke felt swept up by the activities during her stay at the mansion. The women supported each other, and the hard work in the resistance gave them strength to cope with the loss of loved ones. After Mad Tuesday in September, with more people in hiding, the couriers were busier than ever.

Once the Nazi collaborators realized that the Allied troops were not yet liberating the country, they slowly returned with their families from the east. But the air base near Leeuwarden had been completely destroyed during the night of the sixteenth of September, and the Germans didn't rebuild. The fighter planes that hadn't been destroyed moved back to a base in Germany.

Outside the town, on the stretch of road near the Jansma farm, a little boy and a man were shot in the neck at close range. Janke didn't know the man or the boy, but the fact that this murder was uncalled-for added to her bitterness against the enemy.

The Dutch Interior Armed Forces were formed, called the NBS. Prince Bernhard led as chief commander. Many young men in hiding signed on with the new army. They would help the Allied troops liberate the Netherlands. Instructions for the underground movement now came from the government in exile in London. All activities had to be typed out in triplicate. Before, there had been no paperwork involved. And even though names and places were written down in code, it would be easy for the German intelligence department to decipher the codes.

"In London, they don't know what it's like," Mr. Dijkstra growled.

Janke sat at the kitchen table in the butcher's house. It was early afternoon. The butcher shop was closed due to the lack of meat.

"It's easy for them to dream up rules and regulations, but we have to do the dirty work." He hit the table with his fist. Cups rattled in their saucers.

"The reason you're here, Janke, is because we need you to attend the ball next week."

"What ball?" Janke grabbed the edge of the table.

"The Nazis are celebrating some kind of harvesting feast at Hotel Canal View. They harvested our goods and have organized an enormous ball. They've invited an orchestra from Austria and they're in the process of stealing cattle and other food. Wine is coming in by the truckload. Meanwhile, our people are starving." He took a gulp from the teacup. "As always, they've invited local girls. This time, we want you and a friend to go."

"I'm not going." Janke pushed back her chair. "I've vowed never to set foot in that ballroom until this bloody war is over." She marched to the door. "If that's what you needed me for, you've wasted your time."

"Janke! Sit down!" Mr. Dijkstra's voice ordered her back. "I know you're angry. I'm not asking you to dance with that riffraff. But we need you to be there and do a job for us."

"What's the job?" Resigned to follow orders, Janke perched on the edge of the chair. She could just imagine those arrogant bastards prancing the floor, eating their food, drinking expensive wine and flirting with all the girls, but if she needed to do something for the resistance, she would.

"Is it alright if I ask Alie?" The butcher had mentioned a friend.

"Yes," the butcher stood up, "but you can't tell her what the job is."

Janke nodded.

"I'll let you know on Saturday."

Janke wondered what she could possibly do at the dance that would help the resistance. By the time she reached the parsonage, she figured it must be a spying job.

Alie laughed her worries away. "Who cares, Janke? For once we can look at their fake world. We can giggle and laugh and forget about the whole war. And I want to dance. We're wasting our best years." Her eyes sparkled.

Janke smiled. "How can you forget the war in a room full of uniforms? I won't let any of those bastards touch me."

Except for one soldier, a nagging voice reminded her. Janke shook her head to shake out that last thought. "You won't see me dancing. I'll dance when the war is over."

"We need dresses. My mother has a chest upstairs with clothes from when she was our age."

Mrs. Bergman came upstairs with the girls. She spread out her ball gowns on the bed in what used to be the spare bedroom.

"Janke, this one would look gorgeous on you." The fabric was a mauve satin. Tiny roses in a slightly darker shade were embroidered along the neckline. Janke slipped the dress over her head. The full skirt reached her ankles. Cap sleeves covered the top of her arms. Her hands smoothed the softness of the satin.

"Oh, Janke. Turn around. You look like a princess."

Stunned, Janke admired herself in the large mirror of the armoire. She didn't recognize the girl who looked back at her. In the last couple of years she had worn drab-colored hand-me-downs that were either too small or too big.

Mrs. Bergman stroked her hair. "I know your dilemma, Janke. I'm sure there's a good reason they want you at the ball."

Janke looked at Alie, who'd just wormed herself into a long, slender dress made of ice-blue taffeta. The style made her look taller and slimmer than she already was.

"I'll put my hair up." With both hands Alie pulled her hair into a ponytail and then coiled it on top of her head. "Maybe you'll have to assassinate a higher ranking Nazi while you're dancing with him. Maybe you'll get one of those little snap-out knives to keep in your purse."

"Alie!" Mrs. Bergman chided. "I didn't know my daughter had such a murderous mind."

By the time they had shoes, purses and dresses all coordinated, Janke had caught some of Alie's dancing fever. The shoes were a little on the large size, but Mrs. Bergman filled the toes with pieces of balled cotton, and if she didn't do any acrobatics, Janke would be fine. Alie's mother even taught them the steps to the polka, a dance the Germans liked.

It was soon time for Janke to leave. As she biked down the road towards the Jansma farm, a black car approached from the other direction. Janke looked up. Hadn't she watched every black German car in the last few months? Her heartbeat danced as the car slowed down. She jumped off the bike as she recognized the chauffeur. He was alone. She pretended she was checking her saddlebags. The car stopped. The driver got out.

"Janke." In a few strides he stood beside her. Janke looked up. His face looked thin.

"I missed you." His hands caressed her arms. His face was close. His eyes studied her face.

"Janke, I was a fool. I said very dumb things to you."

"It doesn't matter." Janke's hand touched his face.

Helmut took her hand and kissed her fingers one by one. The feel of his lips on her skin made her stomach flutter. His hand traced her jaw line. Janke stood still.

"You look tired." Helmut bent his head. His mouth brushed her lips.

Janke forgot the world around her. She forgot that anybody on the road could see her.

"Are you going to the dance on Saturday?" she whispered.

Helmut pulled back to look at her. "The harvest ball?"

Janke nodded. Fool, she scolded herself. Why had she asked?

"I was not going, but why do you ask me?" An urgency shone from his eyes.

"Because I want to dance with you."

"Janke!" His arms flew around her and he pressed her tight. Janke almost lost her balance and her bike.

"I have to go." She panicked when she heard the rumbling of a military truck in the distance.

"I will be there," he whispered. Helmut returned to the car. The door closed. The engine revved. The car disappeared in the direction of town.

And still Janke stood beside her bike. Her fingers touched her lips. She trembled. Her heart wanted to sing, but she didn't allow it to find the tune.

24.

On Saturday afternoon, hours before the ball, Janke received her instructions. She was to spy on Dinie van Echten. She had to find out if the girl danced with the same Nazi all night, and if she did, she was to find out his name.

"Let me take your picture." Alie's father walked over to the antique cabinet in their living room. Both girls were dressed and about to leave. Alie's mother had brought out a lipstick and powder box that she kept in her bedroom drawer for special occasions.

"Ready? Smile." The click of the camera shutter made the girls burst into giggles.

"I can't believe how lovely the two of you look." Mrs. Bergman wiped a tear from her cheek with the back of her hand. "I'm afraid you'll make many wrong heads turn."

Janke wished her mother could see her now. "Let's go." Alie was already at the door.

Janke pushed thoughts of her mother away. "Thanks," she hugged her friend's mother instead. "Do you have your special permit to be out after curfew?"

"Yes." Alie patted her evening purse.

At the hotel, lights of the chandeliers sparkled. The grand ballroom had been decorated with large bouquets of mums and asters. A huge portrait of the Führer adorned one wall, flanked by flags of the Third Reich.

Janke's eyes grew bright when she saw the gowns, the sparkling necklaces and glittering earrings on some of the women. She wondered if the higher ranking military had even let their wives or girlfriends come over from Germany. Frantically, her eyes searched the room for Dinie.

"I can't believe this," Alie whispered. "Looking at this you'd never know there was a war going on."

The orchestra had assembled. Men in funny-looking leather shorts called lederhosen and felt hats with feathers, and girls in traditional dresses, took to the stage. At exactly eight, the musicians picked up their instruments. They opened with a polka.

"Let's sit down." Alie led her to a table with two other girls who they'd gone to school with. They all looked a little intimidated by the glitter and glamor. It didn't take long for the Germans to choose dance partners. Janke spotted her grandparents' neighbors, Tine and Jeltsje. Both were wearing low-cut dresses. They smoked cigarettes and were busy flirting with a couple of handsome soldiers.

"I don't care. I'm going to dance," Alie announced as she rose from her chair after a handsome young man in an immaculate uniform asked her.

Janke turned down two eager young men, while she kept her eye out for Dinie and Helmut. What would she tell Alie about Helmut? But Alie was already caught up in the whirling dancers.

"Janke." An all-too-familiar voice made her turn in her seat. Behind her stood Helmut, his hair still wet and combed to one side. His eyes, shining, looked at her with admiration. She rose and turned towards him.

"Helmut." She blushed.

"I was worried you would turn me down as you did those ahead of me." His smile held her eyes.

Her heart sang as he lead her to the dance floor.

"I'm not very good," Janke whispered.

Helmut placed his arm around her waist.

"Neither am I," he laughed, "but you asked me to go to this ball because," and his face came close, "you said you wanted to dance with me."

Janke smiled up at him. "I did practice with my friend because we want to be ready when the war is over." Her face grew serious.

"Who were you planning to dance with?" His question surprised her.

Janke looked in his eyes. "It's not important anymore."

"Yes. It is very important." His arm tightened around her waist. "I want this war to be over, too."

Janke nodded. "I can't meet you anymore behind the boat house. It is too dangerous."

"I know." He pulled her close, his face touching her forehead.

Her feet got confused as the orchestra played a waltz. She needed to concentrate and focus on her counting. "One, two three. One, two, three."

"I am glad you are keeping track of the meter." Helmut smiled again. His hand at the small of her back held her steady. Her right hand lay in his. She felt so perfect, but at the same time she realized this couldn't last. Helmut and Janke they were not to be.

"I still have your books," he said close to her ear. "I liked very much to read the same books you read when you were a little girl. I feel I know a little bit about you."

Janke felt sad. She couldn't even tell him about herself or her family. She didn't know what to say. Helmut didn't say anything more. They danced. Janke savored every second in his arms because she decided she couldn't dance with him again. She couldn't hide her feelings any longer, not from Helmut and not from the rest of the world. The music slowed to a foxtrot. Their legs didn't find the rhythm. Helmut pressed her closer. His cheek touched hers. Janke's eyes filled. She stumbled. They both lost their balance and crashed into another couple.

"Damn. Can't you look out!"

Janke gasped. They had run into none other than Dinie and her officer. Janke recognized the man from the Mercedes at the train station in Leeuwarden.

"Sorry," Janke and Helmut apologized in unison.

"Oh, hi, Janke." Dinie looked at her with surprise. "I didn't expect to see you here."

"I really wanted to dance tonight." Janke's face felt ablaze. Her shoe had come off. Helmut found it for her and slipped it on her foot. His hand gently brushed her ankle. Shivers ran up her spine. Dinie and her partner composed themselves quickly. Janke watched how they spun around the room. The perfect couple, she thought. The crash had brought her out of her dreamland and into the real world where her assignment was to spy on Dinie.

"Do you know the girl?" Helmut followed her gaze.

"Yes," Janke nodded. She couldn't tell him that they were in the same line of work and both made the mistake of dancing with the wrong people.

"Did you want to sit down for a while?" Helmut placed his arm around her.

"No. I'm okay. We can keep dancing until the orchestra takes a break. Unless . . . you don't want to dance with a clumsy girl?"

He laughed again and held her closer. "To make sure you do not stumble again." His eyes twinkled. She looked up into his face. The sadness had vanished. He looked . . . She couldn't tell. He wasn't handsome like some of the others. But . . . Stop, Janke thought. I have to keep an eye on Dinie. She pushed Helmut in the direction of the couple who were now twirling down the other side of the ballroom.

Janke's mind worked. Perhaps she could ask Helmut.

"They are a handsome couple," Janke said. "Do you know him?"

"Yes. I know him from my hometown. He is very rich from a . . . .wealthy family. This family are important for the Nazis."

"What's his name?" She almost immediately regretted the question.

Helmut looked puzzled. "Why do you want to know?"

Janke blushed. "Oh, just curious."

Helmut stayed quiet for a while. His eyes never left her face.

"Is your interest in German officers the real reason you came to this ball?"

Janke's face burned. She avoided his eyes. She didn't answer him, but instead focussed on her feet and the music. Every now and then she shot a glance at the couple who waltzed effortlessly across the floor.

"His name is Friedrich von Rosenthal. And those two are inseparable." Helmut watched her looking at the couple. Janke didn't respond. She felt awful about the way she'd obtained the information.

"Let us not talk," Helmut said. "I just want to dance with you."

Janke agreed. There were too many topics they couldn't discuss and she had all the information she needed. For now, she wanted to savor the moments in Helmut's arms, because there could never be anything more between them. They were enemies. She couldn't act like Dinie. For it was clear to Janke that Dinie played a very dangerous game. The resistance was not going to like the information Janke would bring it. The part that worried her most was that Dinie knew too much about the underground movement. Janke had to report her to the leaders of the resistance. The thought made her feel uncomfortable.

Helmut pulled her close. Her face touched his. His skin felt warm against hers. A warm feeling travelled up her spine. Butterflies danced in her stomach. Oh, if only time could stop now, she thought. If they could just dance out of this war.

"Janke." His voice was serious. "If something happens to me, or I cannot meet you when the war is over, I want you to memorize my uncle's address in Canada. His name is Hans Grün. He lives at 17 Market Street in Waterloo, Ontario."

"Is your last name the same?"

Helmut nodded.

A dark feeling came over Janke. She pulled his head down. "Don't say I won't see you again," she said.

"Repeat the address." His words were firm.

Janke repeated it without making a mistake.

"Good."

As the final notes of the music faded, he kissed her lips.

"Be careful, Janke. Meet me in Canada."

Janke didn't understand. Was he leaving?

"I will try to see you." He pulled away. "But you have to be careful. The Gestapo is clamping down on your movement."

Shocked, Janke watched him disappear into the dancers. He knew. He knew all about her. The feeling made her sick. She stumbled back to the table where Alie watched her with concern in her eyes.

"Janke. You look like you've danced with a ghost."

"I did." Janke slumped onto a chair that Alie held out for her. "I'm not feeling well." Janke touched her forehead.

"Oh, Janke. You should've never danced with that German!"

"No." Janke nodded. She looked at her best friend and wished she could share her secret about her love for Helmut, but she couldn't. She looked behind her, but the crowd had absorbed him.

"I'll walk home with you."

Janke read the disappointment in Alie's eyes.

"Don't worry about me." Janke put her hand on Alie's arm. "I'll be alright. I'll take the back alleys and cross the cemetery to your house. The fresh air will help me feel better."

They had decided that Janke was going to stay the night, instead of biking all the way to the Jansma farm.

"I don't like it." Alie sat down and held Janke's hand.

"You stay! And that's my final word." Janke took her purse and jacket and hurried out of the ballroom. She didn't see Helmut. Janke composed herself. She held her head high as she greeted some German officers who were standing in the large entrance. One of them gallantly opened the large front door of the hotel for her.

For a moment, Janke stood on the steps and inhaled the night air. The ballroom had been hazy with cigarette smoke and it felt good to feel the cool air on her face. She hoped it would also clear her mind. She was totally confused after Helmut's revelation.

Quickly, Janke turned onto the main road and then found her way down the alleys. After the brightly lit ballroom, the night seemed pitch-black. She tripped once and heard her skirt rip. The sound tore at her. The memory of wearing this pretty dress and dancing in Helmut's arms would always be locked in her heart.

25.

The bell echoed though the hallway of the doctor's house. Janke's heart beat in her throat. She hoped Dinie was home. A smiling Mrs. de Wit welcomed her inside.

"Good to see you, Janke. What brings you here on this sunny afternoon?"

"Good afternoon, Mrs. de Wit. I need to see Dinie. It is urgent," she added.

"Oh, I'm sorry, she isn't here. How urgent? I mean, is it a matter of life and death?"

Janke nodded. She had to meet with members of the resistance at the butcher's at seven that evening. She wanted to speak to Dinie before then.

"I can call her. Follow me."

Janke entered the doctor's office, which smelled of antiseptic. The shelves on either side of a large, Gothic window were lined with bottles and jars. Mrs. de Wit dialled a number while Janke waited.

"Yes, good afternoon. This is Mrs. de Wit speaking. Can I please talk to Dinie?" She waited.

"Yes, Dinie. There is someone here who needs to speak to you and it is urgent." Mrs. de Wit motioned for Janke to come close and handed her the receiver.

"This is Janke Visser speaking." Janke took a deep breath. "Can I meet you somewhere?"

"When?" Dinie asked.

"As soon as possible." Janke worried that Dinie wouldn't want to meet her.

"How about the park at the north bastion?"

"Yes," Janke said. "What time will I meet you?"

"Is two alright?"

"Yes. I'll wait at the bench near the statue of the Missionary. Goodbye, Dinie." The receiver clicked as Janke hung it in its place.

"Thank you, Mrs. de Wit."

"I hope Dinie is alright. She has been such a great help to us." Mrs. de Wit frowned.

"Yes, she will be." Janke left the doctor's house in a hurry. She was glad she had taken her bicycle from the parsonage that afternoon. She had told Alie's family that she was going back to the Jansma farm. Alie had been tired from last night's dance and had gone for a nap.

Janke had slept little. She lay awake, her mind spinning. Now that Helmut knew about her work in the resistance, she didn't know what to think. Might he betray her to his uncle? But he must have known for a while. Janke couldn't figure it out.

Her second worry was Dinie. She soon had to report what she learned at the dance. That had been her assignment, but she felt she couldn't. She was worried that others would decide Dinie's fate. Perhaps Dinie was in a position similar to her own, working for the resistance but seeing a German. That was so wrong, Janke knew, but she could at least understand the girl's predicament. So long as Dinie wasn't working for both sides. If she had told Friedrich what she knew about the resistance movement and the people who worked for it, they were all in grave danger. But then again, her relationship with the officer had been going on for a long time and nothing had happened. By early morning she had decided to warn Dinie.

As the time for their meeting drew near, a bleak sun shone through the clouds, Janke pulled the hood of her jacket over her head. She walked her bike through the park. When she approached the statue, she saw Dinie sitting on a bench dressed in a light tweed coat with matching hat.

"Hello, Janke. I heard concern in your voice and figured that what you had to tell me must be serious."

Janke nodded. She leaned her bike against the back of the bench and sat down beside Dinie.

"Does it have anything to do with last night?" Dinie frowned and she studied Janke.

"Yes." Janke clasped her hands together. Now that she was here, she wasn't sure how to tell Dinie. "The resistance wants to know the name of the officer you are seeing."

Dinie paled. "Did you get his name? Did you tell them?"

"Yes, I have his name, but I didn't tell. I will have to, tonight."

"Oh. What should I do?" The girl, who'd seemed so sure of herself before, faltered.

"Have you heard of 'the Veemgericht'?" Janke looked at her intently.

"Yes," Dinie said softly. "I was part of one once when members of the resistance decided an individual who had endangered the lives of others had to be eliminated. It was the worst thing I've ever done in my life." Dinie stared at a sparrow pecking in the grass at their feet.

"I suspect that's what the meeting is tonight," Janke said. "A Veemgericht."

They sat silent for a while.

"I suggest you pack and leave as soon as possible." Janke stood up from the bench. "Go into hiding for a while."

"Yes, you're right." Dinie rose from the bench as well. "Why did you warn me, Janke?"

"I believe you haven't done anything wrong, except for meeting the wrong man."

"I haven't betrayed anybody, if that's your concern." Her sharp voice shocked Janke. "I want to stay with Friedrich, but I also want to work for the movement."

"You can't." Janke sighed. "Believe me, that doesn't work."

"I . . . I'm in love with Friedrich. I . . ."

"If you want to stay alive, leave now." Janke took her bike.

She shivered in her worn coat. The two girls stared at each other. Janke broke the tension. "I want to know where Irene is. The little girl, remember?"

"She is safe." Dinie fumbled with the buttons of her coat. "I would never betray her."

"Did you tell Friedrich about the little girl? And all the others?"

"No," Dinie said in a calm voice. She looked straight at Janke. "And I never will tell him."

"I knew you wouldn't," Janke said softly. "But the other members might not see it like that. Goodbye, Dinie." Janke stuck out her hand. "Be safe."

Dinie took her outstretched hand. "Goodbye, Janke. Thanks."

Janke pushed her bicycle briskly through the park. She longed to do something normal, so she visited her parents and drank tea with them. Mother was up, her face pale, her clothes hanging from her thin body.

"I'm so glad to see you." Father sounded pleased.

Mother started plucking her sweater. "We have news from Jan," she said with a smile.

"Oh, please tell me." For the first time that day Janke felt hope.

"He has escaped through the German lines." Her father's eyes lit up. "He's staying in the southern part, in North Brabant, which has been liberated. Did you know that Allied troops have landed just south of the three main rivers?"

"Yes." Janke had heard the news, first from Douwe and later from Alie's father.

"He has signed up with the NBS, the Dutch Interior Army."

Janke felt a weight slide from her shoulders. Alie would be so happy to know that, she thought.

"They'll soon come to liberate us." Father patted her on the shoulder.

"I'll stay the night," she said, " but I have one errand to run after the evening meal."

Before going to the butcher's house, Janke went to the parsonage to tell Alie the news about Jan. Her friend's eyes filled and she hugged Janke and twirled her around in the hallway.

"Do you have to leave so soon?" Alie's voice conveyed disappointment.

"Yes." Janke was sorry to leave, too, because she dreaded her next mission.

The kitchen at the butcher's house had filled with smoke and stench from homegrown tobacco. Mr. and Mrs. Dijkstra, Harm, and two men Janke only knew as Bauke and Kees sat at the kitchen table. Janke had told them what she had learned at the dance.

"I don't want to believe it!" Harm's voice shrieked with emotion. "She wouldn't betray us!"

"She has to be eliminated," Kees said.

Janke twisted her hands in her lap. She hoped that Dinie had followed her suggestion to leave. This meeting was a Veemgericht, just what she had feared.

"No!" Harm sprang up. His hands gripped the back of the chair. "She has worked for the movement since the beginning of the war. She's risked her life a thousand times and she gets orders directly from Leeuwarden." His voice quivered. Janke read despair in his eyes. Beads of sweat formed on his forehead.

"She knows too much," Kees said. "If the Germans ever make her talk, or if the boyfriend weasels names of members, or hiding places of divers and weapons out of her, we're all in danger. I say there is only one solution."

His face red, Harm grabbed Kees by the arm. "We can't do that! She has done so much. She's saved many people, especially children."

"Harm. Sit down." Mr. Dijkstra took his pipe and filled it with crushed, green leaves. The kitchen fell quiet. A sickening feeling grew in Janke's stomach.

"I won't be taking part in this." Harm stood up. "If you decide to murder Dinie, I'll resign from the movement."

"You're wrong. You forget something very important, Harm."

Kees breathed heavily. "If you vote not to eliminate her, all of us are at risk."

"If she has been seeing this man for a long time, she could have given him names already." As he spoke, Harm clenched his fists.

"I don't believe we can make this decision here. This has to go to Leeuwarden," Bauke said calmly.

"You shouldn't get carried away by personal feelings, Harm. They are going to get in the way." Mr. Dijkstra looked at Harm. "Especially when it involves the lives of others."

"If she had wanted to, she would have betrayed us already." Harm sagged onto his chair.

"The Nazi could put pressure on her to tell him what she's up to when she's not spending time with him." Kees looked at Harm. "Don't be fooled by a pretty face, Harm."

Harm's face colored. "Prove to me that she has done something wrong!" His eyes shot fire at Kees.

"Let's stay calm." The butcher pointed his pipe at both men. "If she worked for the Nazis, we would have known by now. Dinie has done many jobs and they all were successful."

"I don't agree." Kees's face had turned red. "Our lives are at stake."

Bauke suggested, "We'll write a letter explaining the situation and Janke can deliver it tomorrow morning in Leeuwarden, as early as possible." He looked around the table. "The responsibility of eliminating someone is far too much for this group." His voice was calm.

Kees stood up to protest, but Bauke motioned him to sit down. "We should vote. Leave the decision of what to do about Dinie with Leeuwarden or eliminate her. All in favor of Leeuwarden, put up your hand."

Except for Kees, everyone else in the kitchen agreed that Dinie had worked well for the movement and that Janke should take a letter to Leeuwarden. Janke felt relief that Kees had been out-voted. Their decision would buy Dinie some time to get away.

26.

Before heading back to the farm the next morning, Janke delivered the letter to a house on Willem's Quay. Two days later, when she was back in town, she visited Doctor de Wit and asked for Dinie.

"Dinie has returned to Amsterdam," Mrs. de Wit reported. "Her grandmother has taken ill and Dinie was asked to help take care of her. We miss her."

As Janke biked back to the Jansma farm, she wondered what decision the leaders in Leeuwarden had made regarding Dinie's fate.

November turned into December. Janke biked to Amsterdam to pick up large sums of money which had to be distributed to all families whose husbands were in hiding or arrested and who had no other income. Money could still be used on the black market, while stores only used ration coupons. It was, in fact, forbidden to carry money. Janke hid what she carried in pockets sewn on the insides of her camisole.

Janke was exhausted when she finally arrived at the last checkpoint in Leeuwarden. The trip from Amsterdam had taken all her strength. Wet snow plastered her clothes to her body and made her numb with cold. She felt dizzy and thought she was going to faint, but a friendly German guided her through and let her rest in his little guardhouse. He even offered her hot coffee from a thermos. She gratefully drank it and felt better. She thanked the soldier with her best smile before she went on her way.

Just north of Leeuwarden, the rumbling of an engine sounded

behind her. She moved to the side to let a military truck pass. The truck slowed. Janke's head pounded. What now?

"Hang on!" a voice yelled from the rolled-down window. Startled, Janke looked at the driver. She didn't recognize him. There were no other soldiers in the truck. She placed her hand on the tailgate of the truck. The driver waved at her and the truck slowly picked up speed, while Janke wheeled freely behind it. After half an hour, close to their town, the truck slowed down. Janke let go. She waved at the driver. He smiled back, honked his horn and drove away. Once the truck was out of sight, she steered into the lane to the Jansma farm.

She parked the bike in the barn and hurried inside Afke's warm kitchen. To her surprise, Alie sat at the kitchen table. Her face was all swollen and red, her eyes puffy.

"Take off your wet clothes." Afke bustled by the stove. Annie played with her new doll. "Come on, dear. I need some help with the calves." She took Annie's hand. Together, they disappeared.

Janke threw her wet coat and hat over the clothesline above the stove.

"Alie, what's wrong?" Janke hardly recognized her friend. "Is it Freerk?" Janke sank down on a chair beside her. "The people you're hiding? Your parents?"

Alie shook her head. "Dinie. It's Dinie."

"What!" A chill struck Janke. Had Dinie betrayed everybody? She started to tremble.

"Dinie's dead."

Janke stared at her best friend.

"She was shot," Alie added softly.

"The resistance? Why . . . why did they kill her? Did she talk?"

Alie shook her head. "The resistance didn't kill her. The Gestapo did."

"I don't get it."

Janke thought that if anybody would have killed Dinie it would have been the resistance.

"The Germans suspected her of spying on them and taking information back to us." Alie had composed herself. "Right after the dance, she disappeared and left Bishopville. No one knows why." Alie looked up at Janke. "About two weeks ago, she was arrested."

"Did they interrogate her?" Janke felt cold sweat run down her spine.

Alie nodded. "She didn't talk, or we wouldn't be sitting here. She knew too many people."

"But why did the Nazis kill her?"

"From what my father heard, the order to kill her was never given. One of her interrogators from the Security Police had become obsessed with her. When she didn't appreciate his advances, he . . ."

Alie looked away.

"What about Friedrich?"

"You knew her boyfriend?"

"No." Janke's face colored. "But that was my mission the night of the ball. To find out his name."

"Oh." Alie nodded. "That makes sense. I always wondered what your job was and why you were so upset when you left in a hurry."

"Couldn't Friedrich protect her?" Janke had difficulty breathing. "He was an important Nazi," she said, repeating Helmut's words. The whole thing with Dinie didn't make sense at all.

"Friedrich was sent to the Eastern front because the SS accused him of working for us as well. Once he was out of the way, they assumed Dinie would be more cooperative."

Janke wrung her hands together. Her eyes filled. Had she made the wrong decision, warning Dinie?

"Dinie and another resistance fighter were taken outside the city." Alie blew her nose in a large, red handkerchief. "They were both shot and their bodies thrown into the canal. Dinie was shot thirteen times." Both girls sat silent. Janke was stunned by the news.

"Someone tipped off the resistance and they found her body

last Friday. Doctor de Wit and his wife were very concerned after Dinie had disappeared. That's how my father found out."

Janke squeezed her hands together in her lap. She realized what happened when you got involved with a German. A sharp pain stabbed her heart and the image of Helmut's face came to mind. To be shot, just like that. Tears ran down her face.

"This can happen to us, too, you know," Alie whispered. "I was stopped at a checkpoint last week. I carried a revolver in my brassiere. They checked all my papers, my saddlebags and my purse. If . . . they'd found the weapon, I would've been dead by now too."

Janke placed her arm around Alie's shoulders. "Some days I feel I can't do this much longer," Janke broke the silence. "I'm so tired. My legs ache when I bike long distances. Today I almost fainted in the arms of the soldier who checked my identity card."

"Oh, no." Alie looked frightened. "What did you have on you?"

"Money. Lots of money." Janke patted her chest.

Alie nodded. The girls sat quietly, each of them contemplating the gruesome incident with Dinie. In her mind, Janke added that event to the others. She felt her hatred for the enemy build in her chest to mountainous heights. If the war didn't come to an end soon, her chest would burst.

The days after the news of Dinie's murder went by in a haze. Janke took more risks, defying the enemy more openly.

One Thursday afternoon, she biked along the road at a time Helmut was due to arrive from Leeuwarden. She needed to see him, she told herself, even if it was just a glimpse. Now that she knew he wouldn't betray her, she missed him terribly.

As a black car approached, Janke dismounted. "Janke. I cannot stay." Helmut stood in front of her, studying her face. "Have you heard about Dinie and Friedrich?" His hands were on her shoulders. "That can happen to us, too." Janke's eyes filled.

Helmut pressed her close. "It will not be long now. You remember the address in Canada?"

"Yes," Janke smiled through her tears.

"I will see you in Canada when the war is over." His kiss was hard and final, Janke thought. Before she knew it, he was back in the car, speeding away.

The weather turned cold and wet and the Allied troops who were supposed to have liberated them by now were held up at the three rivers. The German armies were strong despite the fact that they were losing on the eastern fronts and in Italy. France had been liberated. In the province of Sealand, the Canadian armies fought hard, but the casualties were high and the progress slow. Evacuees from Sealand and the two southern provinces, North Brabant and Limburg, flooded into Friesland, a province already crowded with divers.

On December the eighth, members of the resistance raided the House of Detention in Leeuwarden and freed fifty political prisoners without any bloodshed. It was an event that gave people hope.

Rain turned to snow. People pulling small wagons, riding bicycles or pushing baby carriages crowded the roads. On her biking trips, Janke met long processions of people dressed in rags. They all came from the big cities in the western part of the Netherlands, which were dealing with tremendous food shortages. It hurt her to see such hunger, such sadness. They all came for food. Some had walked for days, with children dragging behind them, their faces hollow, their bodies lethargic.

The Jansma farm became a place where people were never turned away. Afke made shelters in the barn. She made sure there was always enough milk to feed the visitors. She listened to their stories. Amsterdam, Haarlem and other cities had long been robbed of food by the Germans. Out of despair, people had eaten their pets, mice and rats, and whatever else they could find. Janke cringed when she heard the stories of people dying in the streets.

An abundance of onions had been harvested this fall and Afke concocted large pots of soup. Some of the children touched Afke's heartstrings. She often offered to keep the children until the end of the war. The Allied troops were so close. As soon as they could cross the rivers at Arnhem, they would come to liberate the north. It could be any day.

Just before Christmas, the Nazis decided to cut the electricity. After enduring shortages of coal and wood, an electric heater had been their only source of warmth. Now that, too, was gone. For Janke and her fellow citizens the lack of electricity made the world even more dark. The days were already short, and daylight hours often came without sun.

The Sunday night before Christmas, Janke and her parents were sitting around the kitchen table by the light of two floaters. Her mother had placed two shallow bowls filled with oil on the table. In each bowl floated a piece of wick, which, when lit, spread a soft, yellow glow around.

A loud pounding on the back door startled them. Her mother panicked and fled upstairs. Her father answered the door. Janke heard his voice and that of another man. She crept to the door and listened.

"You have to leave immediately, Jaap," Janke heard the man say. "The Nazis raided the office tonight. They found the equipment to falsify identity papers. They know the men and women who work at the distribution office. You must leave immediately."

Janke heard the door close. She moved away from the door as it opened.

"You heard."

Janke nodded. "Go, Father. Don't waste any time. I'll deal with Mother."

His face looked grim. He walked past her and up the stairs. She heard the protest of her mother's shrill, high-pitched voice. A soft feeling entered her heart. Then her father was back in the hallway. He grabbed his winter coat, hat and mittens.

Janke tried hard to think of what to give him, but they had eaten the last of the soggy bread for their evening meal and there was nothing else in the pantry. Two big hands grabbed her shoulders. Janke flung her arms around her father.

"Please, be careful," she pleaded.

"I'll send word as soon as I can," he said with much effort. "I'm sorry I have to leave you to look after your mother."

Janke placed her finger on her lips. "Ssh. I'll take her to her parents."

"I'm proud . . . " He couldn't finish, and left quickly through the back door. Janke followed him outside. She stood in the dark night and looked up at the stars. Within seconds her father had been dissolved in the blackness of the night. Janke wondered if she would ever see him again.

She hurried back into the house. She listened for cars, German cars.

Her mother sat on the chair in front of the bed. Her hands were twisted in her lap and the skin on her face looked ghostlike, with thin, dark lines of veins mapping her cheeks. Using a flashlight, Janke grabbed a suitcase. She emptied drawers of warm sweaters and underwear. Hastily, she folded and packed skirts and blouses, all the while listening for outside sounds. Once the suitcase snapped shut, Janke reached for her mother's hand.

"Come," she said softly. "It's time to go. The Nazis could arrive any time now."

As if she were dressing a rag doll, Janke struggled to get her mother into her winter coat. This reminded Janke of a time when she had been a little girl and her mother had tried to wrestle her into a new coat. A coat Janke didn't like. She had wanted her old coat. Mother had screamed that Janke would never listen to her and that it made her sick. In the end, Mother had slapped her and won. This time her mother whimpered like a little girl, while Janke firmly persuaded her to put the coat on.

Janke made sure everything was turned off before she locked the door. She carried the suitcase in one hand. With her other, she propelled her mother ahead of her, through the back lane, behind the houses. At the end of the lane, they stopped. The rumble of oncoming motors hung in the air. Which way were they going? The sound came nearer. Janke felt her mother's body stiffen.

"We'll cross over and then follow the back alleys."

They waited. They couldn't cross School Street.

"Down!" Janke hid the suitcase, then pulled her mother gently behind the house.

On their knees, they watched as German trucks thundered down the road in the direction of their house or maybe the school.

"Two and a car," Janke said.

All this time her mother hadn't said a word. Janke tugged at her mother's sleeve. "Let's go before they comb the neighborhood with their dogs."

Half an hour later, Janke led her mother into her grandparents' home. She calmed down somewhat when Grandmother Janke comforted her with warm milk and a hot water bottle for her feet. Janke watched as the color returned to her mother's face. She would be in good hands. She wouldn't have to worry anymore about the daily stress of how to get food or heat. Janke's grandparents were managing alright.

"I'll see Marie tomorrow and ask her to look after the house," Janke said.

"We don't want the Nazis to move in." Both grandparents followed her to the door.

"I'll make sure you get extra ration coupons." Janke kissed her grandparents and left.

27.

"Get up for Christmas Day! Hip, hip, hurray!" Annie's voice sang right by Janke's ear. "That rhymes!"

Janke groaned.

"Aunt Afke said we can light the candles."

"Oh, yes." Now Janke remembered. She wiped the sleep from her face. Last night they had decorated some linden tree branches that Douwe had cut and put in a bucket with water. Annie and Janke had found a box of decorations in the attic. Together they had tied shiny birds and silver bells and several red balls onto the branches with string from Afke's sewing basket. Bert had sat quietly at the table, watching the girls.

To finish decorating their "tree," Janke had clipped the holders in strategic places on the branches so the candles would stand straight and not burn any of the decorations. They had drank hot milk with anise seed, and Janke had taught Annie a song about shepherds watching their sheep before she went to bed.

Now the little girl danced ahead of Janke, opening the door to the kitchen where Afke already busied herself with breakfast on the stove.

"When do we burn the candles, Aunt Afke?" Annie climbed on her chair.

"As soon as Uncle Douwe and Bert are here." Afke smiled and looked at the girl with so much tenderness, it warmed Janke's heart.

"Oh, I hear them coming!" In an instant she slid off her chair and opened the door for the men.

"Good morning. Something special must be going on." Douwe chuckled and walked over to the sink to wash his hands. Bert followed quietly behind him. The men smelled of cows and hay — a smell Janke had come to love. Annie stood clapping and dancing beside the tree.

"This is my third time having Christmas," she said happily.

Afke wiped her eyes. "I can't believe it's been three years. I know your parents didn't celebrate Christmas, Annie. We don't know much about your holidays, or Bert's." She placed her arm around the boy's shoulders.

"That's alright, Aunt Afke." His face looked very serious.

"I will have the honor of lighting the candles." Douwe took the matches from the counter.

"We will burn them for half an hour now and half an hour tonight." Douwe lit the candles one by one. Every lit candle brought back a Christmas memory for Janke. Christmases at her grandparents' home, the big Christmas tree in their own front room and last year's Christmas when she had received the letter from Helmut. Janke's heart was filled with warmth for these two people who had opened their home and their hearts to her and to so many others.

Just before noon, Janke biked to her grandparents' house. The streets were empty. Most people sought the meager warmth of their stoves. For the first time in her life, Janke did not attend the Christmas service. She didn't want to be seen by the Nazis, and she couldn't bear the thought of Helmut being among them. She parked her bicycle behind the house and slipped inside through the shed, hoping the Tolsmas hadn't seen her. Grandfather Pieter opened the door to the kitchen.

"Oh, Janke. I am glad to see you." His eyes glistened and the white, bushy eyebrows twitched. "We were just saying this Christmas is too quiet." Grandfather pulled her inside the kitchen.

Her grandmother hugged her next. Janke looked beyond her grandmother to her mother, standing in the doorway. In two strides, she reached her.

"Mother." She held her tight. "Are you alright?"

"No. I'm not. I'm sick with worry about your father. We haven't heard anything."

"No news is good news, remember?"

Janke took off her coat. It struck her that whatever was simmering in a big pot on the stove smelled like something she hadn't had for a long time.

"We were just about to have our Christmas dinner." Grandmother took the pot from the stove. "We have no heat in the front room, so we'll have dinner in the kitchen."

While her grandmother set the table with plates and cutlery, Janke watched her mother place the embroidered Christmas napkins beside each plate setting. Just like before, Janke thought. Except there would have been two more place settings. Father and Jan would have been here as well. A lump stuck in her throat when she thought about how she missed both of them. Where would they be hiding? And what kind of food, if any, would they eat tonight?

Grandfather placed the steaming pot on the table. Proudly, he told of the hare he'd snared two days ago. Besides the succulent hare, there were potatoes and rutabagas from the garden.

Her mother pecked at the food on her plate. Janke noticed a change in her mother. She didn't have the fear in her eyes that she'd had before. She didn't jump at every noise that invaded the house from outside.

After the meal, Janke helped her grandmother with the dishes. When her mother and grandmother went for a nap, she played checkers with Grandfather Pieter. They hadn't played for a long time, and for the first two games, Janke lost badly, but the tide turned and she made up for it after that. She beat her grandfather several times. The afternoon passed quickly and soon it was time to pull down the blackout curtains.

Then Janke felt restless. All day her thoughts had wandered to Helmut and she wanted to be busy. She couldn't sit any longer. Then as she took the drying towel into the shed, she heard it. Music. Music from a piano.

"Listen," Janke called. Everyone followed her into the shed and out the door to the back yard. Now the music sounded more clearly. Grandfather handed out winter coats. Through the open garden doors of the house next door they could see a man playing the piano by candlelight, his body swaying gently to the melody of "Oh come all ye faithful." Bright yellow stars flickering across the sky completed the scene.

"Mr. Hagedoorn used to play in the symphony," Grandmother said.

Janke remembered the tall, dark man who seemed somewhat eccentric and kept to himself. Now the cold, frosty night didn't bother her. The well-known tunes overcame her feelings of despair and loneliness. She hooked her arm through her mother's.

"It's beautiful," Mother whispered. "If only we could have peace."

"I know. We will." She felt the need to reassure her mother.

The pianist then played "Silent night." Janke stood mesmerized by the sounds and the memories they held.

Suddenly a rustling in the bushes nearby startled her. She turned. Two dark figures approached. Janke was frozen, unable to move.

"Ssh." The first man wrapped his arms around her and her mother.

"Els, Janke." Her father's voice shook. The next pair of arms went around all three of them.

"Jan," she smothered a cry.

Her grandparents quickly joined in the enormous hug. In silence, they reunited in a giant embrace. Tears flowed while the lonely piano player across the yard played "Peace on Earth."

When it ended, the doors of the garden room closed. The night turned silent.

When the family finally gathered around the kitchen table, a true feeling of Christmas and hope engulfed Janke. The candles cast shadows across the visitors' faces. How thin Jan looked, Janke thought. How much he looked like Father.

"We've both signed up for the Dutch Interior Army." Father looked around the circle of familiar faces. "We're fighting side by side with the Allied forces."

Mother gasped. "Oh, no! You'll both get killed!"

Father put his arm around her shoulders. "Don't worry, Els; it won't be long now. You have to hang in for a little while longer. The war is almost over."

Jan nodded in agreement. "It could be four to six weeks. Two months at the most."

Janke grabbed his sleeve. Her eyes filled when she looked with pride at her big brother. He patted her hand.

"You look so grown-up, Sis. Except that you're skin and bones."

Janke laughed. "You're one to talk."

After a second meal, which her grandmother magically concocted from the leftovers, the men had to leave.

"We'll see you when the war is over." Father held her close. "You be careful, Janke."

When Father and Jan left, Mother cried with long sobs. Janke felt helpless. She wanted to go to her mother, but something held her back. Instead of crying, her mother should've been grateful for the fact that Father and Jan were both still alive. She should be proud of them, proud that they were going to fight for the liberation of their country. She would never understand her mother's actions.

"You go back to the farm now." Grandfather pushed her into the shed. "Your grandmother and I will take care of your mother."

Sleep did not come easily for Janke that night. Thoughts of her mother's inability to cope with the events of these terrible times mixed with her fear for the safety of her father and brother. What would happen when the war was over? Would they be a normal family again? Could everyone pick up where they had left off? Could her father return to being headmaster? Could she and her brother continue their education? Janke tossed and tangled with her sheets and her thoughts. Her last thoughts went to Helmut. Would he survive these last days of a war his side could not win?

28.

January brought more cold weather, evacuees and divers.

Most of the pumping stations that kept the sea at bay throughout the country required coal to run their engines. Since the Nazis had taken all the coal they could get their hands on to Germany, low-lying areas in the southern part of Friesland were flooded. The freezing temperatures turned these areas into an enormous skating rink. On sunny days, everyone who could find skates risked venturing out on the smooth surface. Divers, tired of being locked up for too long, took the chance and skated across frozen lands. Roundups by the Gestapo were more frequent than ever, and a record number of divers and resistance members lost their lives.

Early one morning a little girl, about twelve years old, biked down the lane to the Jansma farm.

Out of breath, she called, "Hide the divers! They're searching every farm in the area. Janke has to take all her belongings and go to Harm Bosma's farm. They need help!"

Afke made sure the girl had a glass of milk before she set off to warn the next farm. Janke and Annie cleared all evidence of divers from the house. Bert took up his spot in the attic from which he had a great view of all traffic to and from town.

Janke dressed in her nurse's uniform, took her medical bag and the few clothes she owned, hugged Annie and Afke and headed out the door. On the road to Harm's farm, she met four German trucks. Several citizens rode in the back of one of them. Men of all ages. Janke shivered.

Harm sat on a crate in the barn behind the farm buildings. She remembered when Dinie had taken little Irene. She shivered and a lump stuck in her throat. Harm stayed seated. His body slumped, his face looked defeated, as if he had lost his war.

Dinie, Janke thought. He was in love with her.

"I have information." Harm didn't look at her. "The Security Police is looking for Janke Visser."

Janke froze. She knew this would be coming. She had waited for this. For an instant she wondered if Helmut . . . No, she knew he would never betray her.

"You have to go into hiding until you have new papers and a new look."

Janke gasped. "How . . . Where do I go?"

"You stay here for a few days. We're working on your papers. This afternoon someone will come to take your picture. My mother will dye your hair and change the style." Harm stood up. "Come to the kitchen with me."

Janke followed silently. A long time ago her heart would have jumped at the prospect of staying at Harm's farm. Now she didn't feel anything, except for a dull ache when she saw the sadness in Harm's eyes. He'd aged many years in the last little while. Hadn't they all?

Janke became Margaretha van Dam with short, blond hair. Mrs. Bosma even bleached her eyebrows with a solution of water and peroxide. Janke looked at a strange girl in the mirror. Later that afternoon she had her picture taken, and the following day her new identity card arrived.

"You better go." Harm's mother gave her the address, which from now on would be her base.

When Janke went to get her bike, she found Harm outside, smoking a cigarette. She'd packed all her belongings in the saddlebags. Harm watched her. It looked like all interest in life had left him.

"You look different," he said flatly.

Janke looked up at his handsome face. "I'm so sorry about Dinie."

"Yes." Harm nodded. "I had no chance. She was in love with the Nazi. But I trusted her, Janke." His voice rose. "She didn't betray anybody. I've heard that even when they interrogated her . . . she didn't give them any names." Pain and anger twisted his face. Janke placed her hand on his arm.

"She was very brave."

Harm's eyes filled. "She fell for the wrong man."

Janke turned and left. She biked down the lane to the main road. Harm's words echoed in her head. She fell for the wrong man. She fell for the wrong man. And so had she. Another sad face came to mind, and it wasn't Harm's. Tears ran freely as she pushed the pedals toward her new home. The pain in her chest increased. She wasn't going to end up like Dinie. She couldn't. But had she already given too much of her heart to Helmut?

The small house with its pointed gable stood behind a warehouse on a quiet street in Dikeside, a fishing village on the north coast of the Wadden Sea. Once, a long time ago, the house had green-and-yellow-painted shutters. Along the side of the house stretched a clothesline. Shirts, pants and socks moved in the wind, stiff with frost. The wind bit through Janke's coat. She blew on her hands before she knocked the rapper. A young woman, in her early twenties, her hair tied in a ponytail, opened the door.

"Good afternoon." Janke looked into a thin face with worried eyes.

"Margaretha van Dam?" the woman asked in a tired voice. "I'm Sietske. Come in."

Janke followed Sietske up the stairs.

"Your room's on the right. It isn't very big, but at least it has a washstand. The bathroom is outside."

Sietske opened the door to the bedroom. Light fell through a small skylight in the angled roof. A single bed with pale blue blankets stood along the wall. A chair and bedside table were the only furnishings.

"Under the bed is a rug, and under the rug is a door which opens down." Sietske bent down and lifted a woven rug off the floor. "If you ever need to, you can climb in there. The hiding place is between the floor and the ceiling. There is a chamber pot, and some crackers."

Janke looked at Sietske with terror in her eyes.

"You have to be very quiet. The floor squeaks."

"Did you have many . . . ?" Janke didn't complete her sentence.

"Yes. A few times." Sietske's voice was strained. "Once you're settled, come downstairs. I have some real tea."

In the following days, it became clear to Janke that Sietske played a major role in the underground movement. She'd lost her young husband during the first few days of the war. His picture, showing a handsome soldier with laughter-filled eyes, stood on the mantel.

Tucked away behind the warehouses, Sietske's home went unnoticed by anyone who wasn't familiar with the area. A maze of alleys made it possible for divers to escape easily. The warehouses looked closed for business, their windows boarded up. At night Sietske went out into one of the buildings. With two other women, she had set up a small press. All night the women worked on newspapers with news from the BBC, Radio Orange and the Dutch government in exile. Sietske came home at around four. She slept until ten. After a quick breakfast, she went on her way to distribute packages of newspapers.

Soon Janke became involved in the distribution of papers as well. Frequently, she biked to her hometown and had to deliver close to her grandparents' street. So often she felt the urge to go and visit them, to find out how Mother was coping and if they'd heard anything from Jan or Father. By showing up, she could jeopardize her family's safety. Instead, Janke cycled back to the small fishing town, where she found Sietske waiting for her with a new assignment.

One night she took a British spy to a safe address thirty-six kilometers away. The following weeks seemed like a long string of assignments. In heavy snowfall Janke delivered information, people and weapons. Rumors continued that the war would end soon, and a new determination settled inside her. By the middle of March the underground movement was concentrating all its efforts on sabotage.

"It's only a matter of time before the Allied forces will liberate us," Sietske told Janke. "They have finally crossed the River Rhine."

Janke wanted to believe her, but she had mixed feelings about the end of the war and what would happen to Helmut.

"We have to carry these explosives to one of the bridges on the road to Leeuwarden," Sietske said as she unloaded a large burlap bag of dynamite onto the kitchen table.

Janke's eyes grew wide. "How will we transport them?"

Sietske ignored her question. "The Germans are taking more and more supplies, especially horses and cattle, to Germany. We have to take out the bridges to slow down these transports."

Janke shivered. This assignment made her feel deadly cold.

"You better wear your nurse's uniform." Sietske tied a string of sticks of dynamite around her waist. She handed Janke the second string. "Tie your white apron over the sticks." She helped Janke fasten the strings.

Sietske looked at the rest of the explosives still lying on the table.

Janke wormed her arms into her coat, which she could hardly do up. A slight bulging in the waist was noticeable.

"We look pregnant." Sietske forced a smile. Her eyes travelled to the photograph on the mantel of the handsome young man in uniform, his smile frozen in time.

"I'll put half the sticks in my saddlebags." Janke fastened on the navy blue headdress. "Do you have some towels?" Janke watched Sietske struggle with the buttons of her coat. "We could wrap them."

"Good idea." Sietske opened the closet in the hallway and took out two white bedsheets and some hand towels. "Place the sheet on top." Sietske closed the door behind them. Their bikes stood parked in the shed.

"I'll bike ahead of you." Sietske fastened the buckles of her saddlebags. "Don't trail too far behind."

Janke nodded. She secured her saddlebags. The weight around her waist bothered her. She waited a few minutes in the alley beside the house until she knew Sietske was a safe distance ahead of her.

The sky, a clear blue with powdery, white clouds, produced a brisk sharp wind which made Janke shiver in her threadbare coat. She watched the figure on the bike ahead of her, pushing the pedals against the wind. The sticks of dynamite squeezed her ribs every time her feet turned the pedals. Janke didn't think beyond her focus on Sietske. They had to travel through Bishopville and she hoped they wouldn't be stopped at a roadblock. Two church steeples ahead served as beacons against the blue sky.

As they approached the town, Janke saw several German trucks parked along the roadside.

"Shoot." She clenched her jaws. Janke slowed down to give Sietske time to pass first. A sigh of relief escaped when she saw that, after showing her papers, Sietske was waved through. As Janke neared the checkpoint, she repeated with every turn of the pedals, "Stay calm. Don't say a word. You don't know anything. You don't know any names."

"Stop! Dismount!" The sharp voice of the Nazi stopped Janke.

"Identity card!"

With trembling hands, Janke handed him her card. The soldier looked at her. Looked at her picture.

"Heinz! Come here!"

A second soldier came running.

Janke stared at the soldiers. Their rifles ready. A sinking feeling gripped her stomach. They would execute her. She knew. But before . . . Janke bit her lip. They would try to get names from her. Names of people in the resistance. The tip of a rifle touched her arm.

"You are Margaretha van Dam?" The soldier's eyes penetrated hers.

Janke nodded.

"And you also go by the name Janke Visser?"

"No." Janke looked at him. She felt numb.

One of the soldiers had already grabbed her bike. The other one, the one who'd asked her the questions, seized her arm. "Come with me!"

The soldier forced Janke into the back of one of the trucks. At that moment a black Mercedes arrived at the scene. The chauffeur got out and opened the door to the passenger seat for a high-ranking officer of the SS. The man saluted the soldiers with "Heil Hitler." Janke cringed. She recognized the chauffeur. It was Helmut. She didn't want him to see her like this. Caught by his comrades. Humiliated in front of him. The officer walked toward the truck. He barked something to the soldiers. They motioned for her to get out.

"Schnell! Schnell!"

Hindered by the explosives, she scrambled out of the truck and jumped onto the road. She walked past Helmut, her head down. The officer told her to walk to the Mercedes. One of the soldiers opened the door and pushed her into the back seat. After a brief moment, Helmut and the officer took their places in front of her. Doors slammed. The engine revved, reversed, then sped in the direction of town.

Janke looked out the window. She didn't dare look at the driver of the car. They passed a young woman on a bike. Janke didn't move. The woman turned to look at the car. Horror filled her eyes as she recognized Janke as the passenger in the back seat. Janke felt dizzy. The pain in her chest was excruciating. She had trouble breathing.

Before long, the car pulled up in front of the police station. The door opened. The officer ushered her into the building. Helmut followed at a distance. They entered a small room. He closed the door behind them. For an instant Janke felt relieved that Helmut hadn't followed them into the room, but her fear returned as she looked at the man in front of her.

"Take off your clothes!" the officer ordered.

Janke took off her coat, her headdress and her apron. She untied the string of explosives and placed them on the table. She paused.

"Schnell!" He paced the room. A room that smelled of leather and cigar smoke.

Janke pulled the nurse's dress over her head. Embarrassed, she stood before the officer.

"That's enough!" he thundered. "You have something to tell me!" His eyes gleamed with satisfaction as he picked up the sticks of dynamite. He'd made a great catch, Janke thought. He'd probably get another medal to add to the ones gleaming on his chest. The officer nodded at her clothes and left the room. She heard the lock turn. Janke looked at the one small window, but it was barred with heavy iron rods.

She quickly dressed and sat down on the wooden chair. Frantically, she tried to calm herself, but her heart beat like a wild drum. Her head spun. Was Helmut still in the building? This man who had humiliated her was his uncle, the commandant, she realized with a shock.

Janke already knew her sentence. And even if Helmut wanted to, he couldn't help her. Footsteps came to the door and a key turned. Janke's hands clasped together under the table. Now the interrogation would begin, she thought. The commandant marched in, followed by another soldier with a clipboard. They both sat down across from Janke.

"Where did you get the explosives?" He puffed on a big cigar.

Janke looked at him. His face was almost handsome. His dark eyes looked her over. He was overweight and she remembered Helmut saying that he was lazy. One moment she hoped he would be too lazy to question her and she would be put against the wall right away. She tried to focus on his cigar, from which the smoke curled up in tiny ringlets.

"Who gave you the explosives?"

Janke didn't answer.

"Where did you come from?"

She tried to blank all thoughts from her mind.

"We know you were going to blow up the bridge, so you might as well tell me the whole story."

Janke stared.

"It will be a lot less painful for everybody if you tell me now!" His voice rose. He stood up and strode to the window. Janke stared at the table in front of her. He walked back and halted beside her chair. "We want names."

Janke didn't move.

"If you tell me who you get your orders from, I'll let you go, I promise."

Only a fool would believe that, Janke thought.

The officer pulled a photograph from his pocket. He threw it in front of her.

"Who is this?" he continued.

Janke's breath caught. The man in the picture was Mr. Dijkstra, the butcher.

"Who is this?" His voice barked like a bulldog. His cigar wobbled. "I know you know this man."

Janke felt beads of cold sweat trickle down her spine.

"If you help us by telling where he lives and who works for him, maybe I'll let you go this minute."

Janke blinked. Her jaw stayed locked. She didn't believe him.

"Do not deny it. We know you know him. You work for him." The officer moved closer. His breath smelled of alcohol. A wave of nausea gripped her, and she grabbed onto the edge of the table.

"You would be smart to cooperate, fraulein. Pretty girls like you should not get involved in sabotaging our regime." He shifted impatiently. "Who do you work for?" Now he stood right beside her. "Answer me! We don't want to harm you, but you must cooperate!"

He grabbed her chair and turned her to face him. His now red face was close to hers. Janke tried not to think, not to look at him.

SLAP! His hand hit her right cheek. It caught Janke off guard; the blow made her sway in her seat. For an instant, she felt nothing; then a sharp, stinging pain burned her face. Only once before had she been hit like that. The image of Mother's panic-stricken face and raised hand flashed before her. Anger replaced her fear.

Janke looked the officer straight in his eyes. She felt an urge to jump on him and scratch his eyes out. Instead, she swallowed hard to get rid of the tears.

"You stupid girl. You are wasting my time." His fist hit the table. He swore and turned to the soldier with the clipboard. "Tomorrow morning, she will go to Leeuwarden to the House of Detention." He pivoted on his heel and stood once more in front of Janke. With his finger, he lifted her chin and forced her to look at him. "They know how to make little girls talk." He smiled.

He reached in his pockets and threw a pair of handcuffs on the table. "Lock her up!" he barked. "No food tonight! Perhaps the little girl will talk in the morning after a hungry night."

The soldier pulled her arms behind her. He closed the handcuffs around her wrists and turned her toward the door. Janke stared at the floor. The soldier marched her down the hall of the police station. They passed the office at the entrance. Two soldiers were sitting at a desk. There was no sign of Helmut. At the end of the hall were two empty holding cells. Janke was forced into the one on the right. The door closed. The key turned. She was surrounded by brick walls that at one time had been painted white. The heavy steel door had a small, barred window at eye level. On the opposite side, a tiny window with iron bars let in some light. It was too high for Janke to reach. From the ceiling dangled a single lightbulb. Along one side stood a small bunk with a dirty mattress. A pail, to be used as a toilet, and a wooden chair stood along the other wall.

Janke wondered how she could use the pail while her hands were cuffed behind her back. Her pride told her she wouldn't give them satisfaction by asking.

Defeated, she sat down on the bed. Her wrists hurt from the

metal cutting into her skin. But this pain would probably be nothing compared to the pain they would inflict on her tomorrow when the real interrogation would begin. She'd heard stories about the Nazis pulling out fingernails to make their prisoners talk. Or holding their prisoners underwater, not quite long enough to drown. Her stomach churned. The end would be the same. Blindfolded, against the wall. Just like the three girls in the concentration camp. Would she be brave enough to sing the national anthem when they aimed their rifles at her? She didn't think so. She thought of her parents and Jan and Alie. Tears filled her eyes and ran down her face. She was unable to wipe them.

Later, Janke stood up from the mattress. She looked at the window. All she could see was the sky and the clouds in a now-fading light. Tomorrow might be her last day alive.

Soon darkness entered the cell as it had entered her soul. In her mind she saw Helmut's face. A deep pain carved at her heart. Janke kept staring at the night sky. Staring at her own darkness.

29.

A key turning in the lock woke Janke. She didn't bother to turn around. The door closed again. Suddenly aware of the presence of another person in her cell, she turned and almost cried out when she felt two hands touching her shoulders.

"Janke! Do not say a word! I am getting you out!"

Helmut. Her knees buckled. She must be dreaming.

"Quick. We have no time." By the small beam of a flashlight, he unlocked her handcuffs. Janke rubbed her aching wrists. Helmut opened the cell door. He looked down the hall and pulled her behind him. They tiptoed to a side door and entered the washroom. Helmut opened the window.

"If you crawl through the bushes outside, you get to a gate. Go on your stomach until you reach a brick wall. You can disappear easily behind the houses." He pressed a kiss on top of her head.

Janke grabbed his arms. "But you're risking your life!"

"Do not speak." He hugged her tight. "Just go to the North Bridge."

Janke clung to him.

"Wait for me. I will meet you there."

Without another word, he opened the window. He supported her while she climbed through. The opening was barely large enough. She jumped down. The branches scratched her legs and arms. The window clicked closed. Janke breathed the cold night air. She couldn't think, but mechanically followed Helmut's orders and crawled on her stomach until she reached the brick wall.

She listened. Her knees still felt weak, but a new surge of energy fuelled her. Now she was an outlaw. They could shoot her in flight, like a duck in the fall hunt. Once more she crept behind houses and through dark alleys. How many times had she done this? This time was different. Dangerously different. When would they discover what Helmut had done? Would he get away? Would he meet her at the North Bridge?

Hope kept her going while she stumbled through the darkness. She banged into a wooden shelf sticking out from behind a shed. A sharp pain shot through her hip, but it didn't matter. She had to hurry.

The road to the bridge looked clear. She listened before she dashed across. Like a frightened hare, she leaped into the reeds of the canal bank. As quietly as possible, she crept towards the bridge. The reeds rustled, but she couldn't avoid the noise. She could flatten herself against the slope if a car passed.

Out of breath, she reached the bridge. Janke found a spot between two pillars. Sheltered from the wind, she sat down on the ground. The reeds scratched her legs, but she didn't mind. She shivered in her thin coat. But she was alive.

Why was she waiting? Should she get herself to a safe address instead of waiting for Helmut? If she got to the other side of the bridge, she could cross the meadows and find Bass Lake. From there she could reach the houseboat. What was she waiting for? Helmut had helped her escape. Her heart made her stay. Helmut had risked his life to save hers. Comfort and fear entered her chest at the same time.

Janke waited. Numb with cold. Weak from hunger. Exhausted from the tension. The darkness created monsters out of every little sound. A rustling behind her made her jump.

"Ssh." Helmut closed his arms around her. Tears filled her eyes. Helmut had come for her.

"We have to leave. Quick. Where can we hide?"

"I know." Janke took his hand. "Follow me. First we have to cross the bridge."

They crept to the other side of the bridge and jumped a ditch. One of Janke's feet sank into the clay. Helmut bent and retrieved her shoe. Grabbing his hand, she ran beside him. The fields were bumpy, with clumps of grass sticking up. The night air shrouded them in its hazy coldness. She stumbled several times, but Helmut's support kept her on her feet. A wooden gate separated one meadow from another.

"Where are we going?" Helmut panted.

"We have to follow . . . the lake . . . and find a small . . . houseboat." She didn't stop, but pulled him with her.

Janke followed the shoreline. She walked now, her eyes searching until she spotted what she was looking for. They waited in the long reeds beside the boat, sheltered by hawthorn, willow and alder bushes. The night was quiet except for their uneven breathing. Her heart pounded.

The outline of the boat was nothing more than a dark shadow. Janke crept closer. Near the window she whistled "It's a Long Way to Tipperary." Again she waited. Nothing. She whistled a second time. Still no reaction.

She opened the hatch of the boat, halted in the opening. A musty smell welcomed her. Apart from the pounding of her heart, she couldn't hear any breathing. No Allied pilot, spy or diver was in here. Carefully, she climbed into the cabin. She listened. She trod the five steps down into the hold. Not a sound. The hold was darker than night.

Retracing her steps, she stuck her head out of the hatch.

"Helmut."

A few seconds later she heard him stumbling along the side of the boat onto the gangplank. Janke held out her hand and pulled him inside the cabin. Darkness enveloped them as she closed the hatch. Helmut's arms went around her. He pulled her close and rested his head on hers. She stood, barely breathing, barely alive.

Their breathing finally slowed, matched in even rhythm. Janke was the first to pull away from the embrace. "We have to go down five steps."

Helmut followed her down. In the darkness she felt for the table where she had found matches and a lamp the last time. The glow of the oil lamp filled the hold. Helmut watched while Janke opened the cupboards and discovered two cans of beans, a can opener and a metal pot.

"You have been here before?" Helmut stared at her.

Janke nodded. She lit the single burner and heated up the beans. She found two enamel plates and two spoons. Janke couldn't speak. Her mind went round and round while she stirred the beans. Her thoughts jumped from relief to fear.

"Why? Why did you save me?" Her hands shook and she dropped the spoon on the table. Helmut turned down the burner and grabbed her shoulders.

"They'll execute you," she said. The shaking travelled up her arms to the rest of her body. Janke gasped, long sobs tore from her throat. Helmut pulled her close. He didn't speak, but simply stroked her shoulders, her hair. Part of Janke wanted to struggle out of his arms, but his soothing hands calmed her. The warmth of his body slowly quieted her. He led her over to the bed and gently lowered her onto the mattress. Helmut placed the oil lamp on the floor in front of them.

"You wanted to know why I saved you." Helmut spoke slowly. His face was serious, his eyes held hers.

"You wanted to go to Canada," Janke said softly. "And now you have thrown that opportunity away by rescuing me. Don't you understand? We are outlaws of the worst kind." Janke grabbed his hands. "The Nazis and the resistance will both kill you, and if the resistance discovers me with a Nazi, they'll think I'm a traitor."

"Sh!" He stared at the lamp. "I often wanted to ask you to take me to a hiding place, but I was not sure if you trusted me. So often I saw doubt in your eyes." His eyes bored into hers.

Janke shifted on the mattress. A feeling of guilt enveloped her. "I sometimes told myself I couldn't trust you, but I did."

They sat silently. The tension built around them.

"Tonight we might be safe." Helmut turned to face her. "Tomorrow we have to think of a plan to go somewhere."

"There is no place to go." Panic rose inside Janke again.

"But the war will be over soon."

Janke shook her head. They could never be safe.

"I admired you so much. You were good for your fatherland." He touched her hands with his lips. Janke shivered. The warmth of his lips travelled up her arms and down her spine.

"How did you know that I worked for the underground movement?"

"I saw you more often than you saw me. You went to the train station in Leeuwarden many times. You are cold. Let's put the blanket around you."

Helmut draped the blanket around her shoulders. "It did not take me long to find out what your job was."

"Was it obvious?"

"No. Only to me because I always looked for you. Many times I saw you turn in at a farm lane."

"The Jansma farm," Janke said.

"And I found out where you lived. The house beside the school."

"When did the SS start looking for me?"

"I do not know. I found out this afternoon when my uncle told me the resistance was going to blow up the bridge to Leeuwarden and he knew who carried the explosives."

"I didn't like your uncle. He slapped me."

"I know. I saw your face."

He pressed a kiss on Janke's right cheek.

In the quiet of the small hold, they sat on the bed with the blanket covering both of them. Janke felt his warmth. She smelled his scent, sweat from running. She snuggled closer. Helmut tightened his arm across her shoulders.

"I was lucky. I saw you often. I was proud of what you did for your people. But I was scared. I was afraid you would be caught and I would not be able to help you."

"You haven't told me how you managed to get me out of the cell."

"After my uncle took you for questioning, I searched my brain."

Janke smiled. How she loved the way he spoke her language.

"My mind went crazy to find a way to get you out. My chance came when the guard became sick. I volunteered. When I let you escape, I went back to the desk. When the night guard came at eleven, I told him you were in the cell, that I had just checked up on you and that you were asleep. Then I went to the bridge."

Janke clenched his hand. Her voice shook. "I was sure I would be tortured and then executed."

"I know what they do to political prisoners, Janke. You could not have taken it. They would have killed you in the end. I could not let them do that to you."

They sat quietly, listening to the water gently splashing against the bottom of the boat, until Janke's stomach started to make gurgling sounds.

"You are hungry."

"We can heat up the beans." Janke got up from the bed and relit the burner under the pot.

Janke stirred. Helmut watched her. Helmut carried the steaming plates over to the bed. The smell of the food made Janke's stomach grumble and reminded her of the soggy bread she and Sietske had eaten centuries ago. The warm beans satisfied their hunger. The ticking of metal spoons on metal plates echoed in the small space.

Helmut placed the empty plates on the floor beside the lamp and grasped Janke's hand. He turned down the oil lamp. "To save fuel."

Janke smiled.

"And I will never forget the ball," he said close to her ear. "You looked like a princess."

In the dark, she felt his smile. Janke touched his face. He captured her hand in his.

"I'll never forget the ball either." She stroked his fingers. "It felt so good when we danced together. I wanted to dance forever."

"Yes." His lips brushed her fingers. "When you left, I wondered if I had dreamt of holding you in my arms."

"I was at the ball because of a job I had to do," Janke admitted.

"You used me when you asked about Friedrich."

Janke's cheeks burned. "I felt ashamed after."

"It was bad what happened to Friedrich and the girl."

"Yes." Janke nodded in the darkness. "So often I wondered if I hadn't informed the resistance about Dinie and Friedrich, if Dinie would still be alive." And it will happen to us next, she thought. We will both be dead.

She moved closer. She was afraid to think of tomorrow. Janke's body trembled. Her mouth felt dry. She clung to Helmut. His arms went around her and he pulled her down with him on the bed. Janke stretched out beside him. Helmut pulled the blanket over them.

The coarse wool of the cover caressed Janke's skin. Her hands found Helmut's face. Her fingers stroked his hair, his eyes, his lips. Her lips followed her fingers. Helmut returned her kisses, caressed her face, her neck. Janke shivered, but not from cold. Her body tingled under his touch. Their kisses grew longer, deeper.

Outside the wind picked up and hurled branches against the sides of the boat. The waves became stronger and rocked the small craft. Inside, Janke and Helmut liberated themselves from the war that had separated them since their first meeting. They soared like birds toward peace. In the end they cried in each other's arms for a life together that could never be.

The morning songs of birds woke them. Janke smiled while her hand found his. No words were needed to begin the new day. She tensed. A great search would soon begin for them; perhaps it already had.

30.

All day they listened, watched and held each other. Janke shared stories about her youth, her parents and her brother with Helmut. They sat in the grass against the trunk of an alder. The branches, their buds swelled with spring, hung over them like an umbrella. The earth smelled of hope and new life. Janke leaned against his chest. Helmut's arms held her safe.

Helmut told her about growing up in Germany before the war. "I had to take part in the Hitler Jugend, an organization that brainwashed children." His fingers travelled over her arms. "We had to believe that Jews, Gypsies, homosexuals and mentally handicapped people were all evil. They were the cause of the destruction of Germany. We all had to help get rid of that evil." A sigh escaped his lips. Janke turned to look at him. Again, she caught the sadness in his eyes.

"My father and uncle told me that Hitler was evil. My mother did not agree. I am not going back to her." Helmut stared along the shore of the lake. Janke didn't answer. She didn't think he would. She couldn't even imagine they would make it out of here alive.

In the afternoon, they caught a small pike with a fishing rod they found in the houseboat. Helmut cooked it with a bit of water in the pot on the single-burner stove. Janke added a few leaves from dandelions and meadow daisies. They feasted on their simple meal. Enjoying their closeness, Janke noticed the small blond hairs on the top of his fingers, his eyebrows curved like bananas. She wanted to take in as much as she could during their time together.

Quietly, they sat that night on the edge of the bed with the blanket wrapped tightly around them. This time they waited. Waited for things to happen.

"Some people know this hiding place." Janke watched Helmut tuck the blanket more tightly around them.

"Do you think someone will come here?"

Janke nodded.

The sound of "It's a Long Way to Tipperary" being whistled outside the houseboat startled them both.

"You stay here." Janke went to open the hatch. Her heart drummed wildly. Her chest tightened. This was the end, she thought. Whoever it was would snatch their time together away. She climbed through the hatch. In the dark night stood the shadow of a man.

"Janke?"

"Harm. Are . . . Are you alone?"

"Yes. Are you alright? Is he . . . ?" He pointed at the boat. Harm drew a revolver from his coat pocket.

"No!" Janke threw herself against him. "Don't," she cried. "He does no harm. He rescued me and now they're after him, too. You have to help me save him."

"Janke! I don't believe you. He's a Nazi!"

"No, Harm, he is not a Nazi. Hear me out, please." Janke held onto his arms. Her face was close to his, her breathing fast. "He's a boy from another country who was put into a situation he never chose. Hitler made him act like one of them. Helmut knew of my involvement with the resistance, but he never betrayed me. He risked his life to save me."

Harm shook his head. "Are you sure we can trust him? He might just use you because they're losing the war."

"No!" Janke's voice rose. "I've known him for a long time. More than a year. He put his life on the line for me!"

Harm stood silent. A bird screeched. The branches whispered.

"Okay, let's go inside. Does he have a weapon?"

"No."

"I better meet this fellow who has captured your heart."

Janke blushed. "You have to promise to help him get away first, Harm." She placed her hand on his chest.

He looked at her. "You fell for the wrong boy, Janke."

Janke nodded. Her eyes filled. She swallowed. She didn't want to cry in front of Harm. She pounded her fists on his chest. "Please, Harm!" Her voice shook. "It's the only favor I'll ever ask of you."

Harm sighed. He held her hands and looked at her. "I know how you feel, Janke. I lost someone, too, remember. She chose someone from the wrong side and you know what happened to her."

Janke couldn't speak. Harm's words were true. Helmut had no chance.

"I'll do my best." Harm walked toward the gangplank. "As long as the war is still on, I can't guarantee you that he will be safe."

Harm followed Janke inside. They sat on opposite sides of the table. Helmut didn't say much. He looked intimidated by the tall, strong farmboy. The shoe was now on the other foot. Harm was the predator and Helmut the victim.

"It's all over town." Harm looked at his opponent. "Rumors are flying and the manhunt is on. They must have searched every house in the area." Harm looked beyond them. "They'll now start searching every farm. Who knows what they will find if it isn't you." Harm's face twisted.

Helmut shifted in his chair.

"You have put your superior to shame. He is furious. If the Gestapo get their hands on you, there will be no mercy." Harm's words stung.

Helmut nodded. His face lost its color. He looked at Janke. She held his gaze for a moment.

"But I'm thankful you saved Janke." Harm's eyes searched Helmut's face. "I owe you."

Helmut turned his eyes to Harm.

"I knew of this boat," Harm continued. "I hoped Janke had escaped and come here. I just didn't know what the situation with the Naz . . . with you was."

"Helmut is not a Nazi," Janke repeated.

A tense silence returned to the small room. The wind had picked up. Janke listened for a moment to the branches scratching the roof. A peaceful sound, she thought, yet the hold was filled with tension, war. She felt it. Harm hated every German, good or bad. Janke had too . . . but now . . . since last night . . . some of the hate had left her.

"I'll be back early in the morning, before curfew ends." Harm's words jolted her thoughts. "I'll bring clothes, food and a camera. You both need your picture taken for your new identity cards."

Janke crossed to Helmut. She placed her hand on his shoulder. Her eyes filled. She looked at Harm. "Thank you."

"I said before, I can't guarantee anything."

"Thank you, Harm." Helmut took Janke's hand.

"I'll bring scissors, so we can cut your hair." Harm laughed. "There must be about three centimeters of dark and the rest is frizzled and yellow from the bleach my mother used."

That night, Helmut and Janke both felt restless.

"If we get away alive," Helmut held her close, "will you come to Canada with me?"

Janke didn't answer. She hadn't thought of the future.

"It will be hard for you." His voice tensed. "You have to choose between your family and me."

Janke turned to face him. "First, we have to get you to safety." Her voice rose. "How can you even think of going to Canada?" She swallowed hard. They didn't have a future together. It would never work out.

"I want you to be safe." Helmut pulled her close. "And I want to be with you."

"You are with me tonight." Janke turned off the oil lamp and pulled Helmut into her embrace.

The familiar tune woke them early the next morning.

Quickly, Janke dressed and opened the hatch. Harm greeted her, dragging two large bags inside the boat.

"Helmut, you get dressed in this. I'm taking you with me."

Janke's eyes grew wide with concern.

"Don't worry. I'll do my best to get him, no, I should say her, away."

Helmut reluctantly dressed in a skirt and blouse, a blue cardigan and a gray wig, which was tied in a bun. A triangular scarf with blue cornflowers had to be tied to keep the wig in place and to hide his chin which, after two days, showed the shadow of a beard. The outfit didn't match that well, but at this stage of the war, no one was able to follow the latest fashion.

"Sorry, Janke." Harm looked at her worried face. "You have to stay for now. We haven't figured out how to get you away from here yet."

Helmut pulled her to him. His eyes told her he didn't want to leave her.

"A long time ago, I had a crush on Janke," Harm smiled. "But she was my best friend's little sister."

Helmut insisted he be the one to cut Janke's hair.

Harm laughed. "You could pass for a fifteen-year-old boy with that mop of dark curls."

Helmut turned her to face him. He smiled at the new Janke.

"Let me take your picture before we leave," Harm said. "This new hairdo might save your life."

Janke couldn't resist smiling. With her last identity change she'd still been female. Now even her gender had changed.

"We have to get away before it becomes too light," Harm said in a rush. "We need the darkness to protect us."

"We will meet in Canada." Helmut kissed her. "Write to me through my Uncle Hans in Canada. Please, Janke. Hans Grün, 17 Market Street, Waterloo, Ontario."

Janke nodded, unable to speak, unsure what she was agreeing to.

For a brief moment she wrapped her arms around him. Then

Janke stood alone in the wet grass, long after the two young men had been enveloped by the darkness.

The day dragged by for Janke. She worried about Helmut, despite her doubts, hoping he would be alright. Her eyes and ears stayed alert for every sound, every squeak of the old boat. She tidied, ate some bread that Harm had left for her, watched the lake and went back inside. All day she kept the blackout curtains drawn. Overcome by loneliness and a feeling of oblivion, she felt as if she were in mourning. With Helmut gone, her heart had darkened. That night she huddled under the blanket in the empty bed and missed Helmut's arms.

The familiar whistle woke her. Harm had come to fetch her. He'd brought her boy's clothes. A cap, shirt, blue oversized milking pants and a jacket.

"They were mine," he smiled. "We're running out of civilian clothes. Now we have more uniforms than we can use."

"How's Helmut?" The question burned her lips.

"So far so good. He went on a farmer's wagon to the market. From there, someone is taking him to the next safe address."

Janke knew that was the end of Harm's knowledge. Now Helmut's safety was in the hands of other people. Janke followed Harm through the fields.

"Harm," her chest tightened, "what happened to the butcher?"

"He and his wife are both in hiding. The shop is closed. We got a tip that someone had informed the Nazis. That's probably how they found out about you, too. The Dijkstras got away just in time, but for you . . . " He paused to look at her. "We didn't find out about you until Sietske told us."

"And the bridge?" Janke hoped Sietske's mission hadn't been for nothing.

"We couldn't blow it up. There were too many Germans all over the place."

Janke pondered what would've happened if she and Sietske hadn't set out with the explosives. Would the Germans have caught her anyway?

"I'll take you to a farm that has been searched twice in the last few days. The farmer and his wife moved their weapons and divers just in time. You'll be their new farmhand."

Albert and Martje were an older couple in their late sixties. Their farm was half dairy, half agriculture. High above sea level on a manmade hill, close to the sea dike, the farm was set off by itself, isolated and therefore safe. It didn't take long for Janke to pick up the routine of the farm chores. One day passed into another, as the three of them worked long hours. At night they listened to the encouraging voices of BBC Radio and Radio Orange.

"It won't be long now." Albert smoked his pipe. Martje knitted socks with homespun wool and Janke mended the knees of a pair of work pants. The grandfather clock ticked and Herta, the big German shepherd, lay in her basket beside the stove.

Janke's thoughts wandered to her family. Had Father and Jan joined the Allied armies? But, most of all, where was Helmut?

31.

A meadowlark sang with all its might as Janke walked through the fields. It was the middle of April. She found some solace in walking among the pastures with their multicolored carpets of flowers. Plovers and warblers entertained her with song. In the distance she could hear the breakers of the Wadden Sea. Oh, how she longed for the sea. She often wandered here after the midday meal, when Albert and Martje took a nap. Soon they would be sowing grain, and new potatoes had to be planted. There wouldn't be any time for walks. Work was the best medicine to push away thoughts of family and worries about Helmut.

As the days turned into weeks, Janke began to accept that she would never see Helmut again. She wished she could hide here forever, tucked away at Albert and Martje's farm for the rest of her life. The air was clear, the sky a deep blue dotted with soft, puffy clouds. She turned and her eyes followed the dike. Along the coast she saw the proud steeples of the villages of Dikeside and Small Port. Further inland she could see the tall smokestack of the milk factory and the steeples of the two churches of her hometown. She was so close and yet so far from her family and Alie.

Suddenly, she stopped. What was hanging from the steeples? It looked like . . . No. It couldn't be . . . Flags? She shielded her eyes from the midday sun and squinted . . . Flags! They were flying the flag! She looked to the west. From the steeple of every little town dotted along the coast, she could see the national flag flying proudly and free!

Janke ran toward the farm through the plowed fields. She jumped the last ditch. When she neared the farm buildings, she started hollering, war cries, high-pitched screams. She yanked open the door to the stable.

"What the devil . . . ?" Albert grabbed the door frame, just before Janke ran into him.

"It's over!" Janke screamed.

"What do you mean?"

"Look." Janke dragged the farmer outside and pointed to the west, to the nearest village, then to the east, to Bishopville.

"Look at the steeples."

"Oh, my God." Tears ran down his leathery face.

Janke pressed his hands and ran inside. She found Martje in the kitchen, busy with the afternoon tea.

"Come outside, Martje." Janke took her by the arm. "The war is over!"

Later that afternoon, the couple sent her home on an old bike. The tires were so bad she had a hard time turning the pedals, but it didn't matter. The war was over. Everywhere in the streets, Janke met dancing and singing people. Some just stood on the street waving the Dutch flag. Flags that had been hidden for five long years. Children had tied flags onto their bicycles. Allied military trucks, jeeps and tanks greeted her on the way home. Young girls had climbed atop army tanks. Canadian and Dutch flags decorated the fronts of the tanks.

"Janke! Is that you?" A familiar voice shouted from one of the big vehicles.

Alie stood on top of one of the tanks. A Canadian soldier had his arm draped around her shoulder. Janke waved.

"What's with your hair? Come on up!" Alie motioned her to climb up. Janke didn't move. She just stood there and watched. A wave of emotions flooded her.

"I'm going home!" she shouted at Alie. She needed to find out if her mother was back in their house. Perhaps Father and Jan had returned home.

Just before she turned on Main Street, another procession met her. Three men were paraded on a wagon, dressed in burlap sacks, with their hands tied. People stood along the road, chanting, "Kill them! Kill the traitors! Kill them!"

Janke stood still. Five years of war had sown so much hate in people's hearts that the time had come for payback. Janke's heart felt numb.

At home, she was greeted briefly by her mother. Chairs, carpets and curtains had all been dragged outside. The back yard was littered with household items.

"You have to help me get the bedding down the stairs."

Janke looked at her mother with an open mouth.

"Don't just stand there." Her mother pushed her in the direction of the stairs. Stunned, Janke helped bring the mattresses and blankets down and spread them all over the lawn. Her mother's eyes gleamed. She looked younger than when Janke had visited at Christmas.

Feverishly, as if she were washing away the whole war, Mother scrubbed and cleaned. Janke smiled. This was her mother's way of celebrating.

At dinnertime, Janke quietly buttered some bread and poured two glasses of cold milk. She found her mother upstairs, washing floors. In silence they ate their bread. Had Mother not heard about her arrest and her rescue? Did she not want to ask Janke how she was and where she had been hiding?

"Take down all the blackout curtains. I don't want to be a prisoner in my own house any longer." Mother stood up from the table, a hurried look in her eyes. "Did you know there isn't one German left at the school?"

Janke could have guessed.

Alie saved Janke by visiting at eight o'clock.

"No curfew tonight," she sang. "There is a dance at the hotel tonight. Go change. Let's go."

Janke hesitated. Dancing? Not at the hotel where the memories of dancing in Helmut's arms still hung in the air. But she went with Alie all over town. It was great to walk openly down the main roads and see people laughing and singing. No more fear of German boots and rifles. But Janke couldn't sing; her chest ached with another fear.

Music and singing drew the girls to the square in front of the Catholic church. A band had assembled for a parade. Two wagons pulled by a team of horses stood ready to follow. The horses, nervous with the crowds and the noise, became skittish. Foam lathered around their mouths. On top of the wagons, tied together, were six or seven girls. Their heads had been shaved. Two men poured thick, black goo from a bucket over their bald heads and then stuck feathers on the sticky substance.

"Tarred and feathered!" Alie shouted. "That's what they deserve, those Moffen whores." She grabbed Janke's hand and started running toward the wagon.

"Whores! Whores!" Alie screamed at the top of her lungs. The crowd, hyped up by the hysteria, joined in. Janke recognized Jeltsje and Tine, her grandparents' neighbors.

Slowly, the procession got moving. A woman threw an egg at the girls. It hit Tine's forehead, broke, and the gooey yolk ran down her face. The crowd roared. In shock, Janke watched the people. They acted like beasts. She didn't recognize Alie. Janke felt as if she was someone else, following this crowd. Alie pulled her. Her feet moved without her knowing. Alie screamed and ran until her voice was hoarse. The parade went on, but Alie took Janke towards the hotel.

Canadian and Dutch flags decorated the front entrance. Janke heard a band playing inside. She pulled away from Alie.

"Janke. What's wrong?" Her eyes were large and blue. "You promised me we would dance when the war was over. The war is over!"

Janke's mouth went dry. She looked at Alie. "I . . . can't."

"Janke, is it because of the Nazi who saved you? You have to tell me the whole story, but not tonight. Tonight, I want to celebrate. I have just one question. Rumors say that you stayed for one whole night in the boat with him." Alie took a step toward her. "Did you?"

Janke nodded. Something tight coiled inside her. She didn't recognize the strange light in Alie's eyes. She wanted to scream, He saved me. He risked his life. But the words stuck.

"Did you?" Alie's voice squeaked. "I have to know, Janke. I need to know what you did in that boat." A frightening distance grew in Alie's eyes. Janke backed away from her best friend. But Alie closed the gap.

"Tell me!" she screamed as loud as her hoarse voice would allow.

"The rumors are wrong," Janke whispered.

"I'm glad." Alie almost smiled. "I knew you wouldn't spend the night with a Nazi. I knew . . . "

"I spent two nights with him. And I don't regret it." Janke's words were sharp. The look of disbelief on Alie's face made Janke back away.

"You . . . " Alie's face turned crimson. "You are no better than those . . . "

Janke stood facing her friend. Should she be ashamed of being alive? Should she be ashamed of what she had shared that night with Helmut? A deep feeling settled in her heart. She would never be ashamed of their love. She was no whore. Janke realized she could never share her experience with Alie. She didn't want to. In those two nights, Janke and Helmut had soared beyond this world, beyond these people so full of hate, including her best friend. She turned away from Alie and started to run. She never looked back at Alie or the hotel.

Later that night, when Janke had joined her mother in making the beds, there was a loud commotion at the back door. They ran downstairs to find two tired and dirty-looking men — Father and Jan. The reunion became festive as they presented food, drinks, chocolate and real Canadian cigarettes that they had brought.

It almost felt like the old days. Janke looked around the table. Mother smiled. They all had stories to tell. Proudly they told about fleeing Germans, some carrying their boots instead of wearing them.

"You'll never guess who joined us today?" Jan's eyes were big. Janke shook her head.

"Freerk. Freerk, who escaped to Sweden, travelled to England and then joined the troops in Belgium to move up north."

Janke was grateful that Freerk had made it. When she finally had a chance to talk about her heroic rescue by the German soldier, the kitchen fell silent. Father didn't look at her. Jan pretended to study the tablecloth. Mother wiped her eyes. Panic engulfed Janke.

"Aren't you happy that he saved me?" Her eyes travelled from one face to another, but no one met hers. She pushed away from the table. "Would you have felt better if the Germans had tortured and executed me?"

Father didn't answer. His eyes briefly met hers. In his expression, Janke read a distance she didn't recognize. Her voice came out shrill.

"It would have been a heroic death. Right? Now how are we going to explain my rescue? What are the people of Bishopville going to say about the headmaster's daughter?"

"The rumors are flying already." Jan spoke first. "I can't believe you took him to the boat, Janke."

"Where else could we go?" Janke clenched her fists. Did she have to defend herself for being alive?

"You are a disgrace to our family," Mother added.

Janke's eyes filled. Her arms dropped limp against her body. No one wanted Helmut to be the hero. Father, Jan and Mother, and even Alie were so full of hate they couldn't allow one exception, not even for a gentle boy. Not even for her.

Later, she lay in her own bed for the first time in a long time, but sleep didn't come and take her away. She slept only fitfully.

The next morning her mother said, "You have to get some bread for us." She took two ration coupons from her apron pocket. "Go quickly. The men are hungry."

As usual, there was a lineup at the bakery. When there were five people ahead of her, Mrs. de Beer spotted her. Janke saw the change in her expression.

In a loud voice Mrs. de Beer said, "Did everyone see the parade of Moffen whores last night? Those girls should have been shot. They fooled around with the enemy and thought they could get away with it."

The people in the store agreed.

"And then there is Janke Visser," she continued while she pulled two soggy loaves from the shelves. "She was rescued by a handsome Nazi. Now I wonder how she paid for her freedom?"

The faces turned to look at her. Janke's mouth dropped open. Mrs. de Beer's words stabbed her heart. Everyone stared at her as if she had some strange disease.

"Get out!" Mrs. de Beer yelled. "Get out of my store, you whore!"

In a trance, she walked home.

"Where's the bread?" Her mother had come in from the living room.

"There was none," Janke said flatly and tossed the coupons on the table.

Janke walked up the stairs and closed the door to her room. She lay on the bed and stared at the ceiling. Her thoughts wandered back to the girls on the wagons. Moffen whore, Mrs. de Beer had called her. Would they get her next and parade her round town, tarred and feathered?

She got up and packed her few clothes in a pillowcase. In a drawer she found the teddy bear from the little Schumacher girl. Janke thought of the Jewish people in the death camps. She shivered and pressed the little bear against her face before she added it to the pillowcase.

The door opened. Her mother stood on the threshold, her eyes wide as if she were a chased doe.

"You have shamed our family!" The bedroom door slammed shut.

Janke stayed in her room until after the evening meal. Quietly, she walked down the stairs. The pillowcase hugged to her chest, she stood in front of her family.

"I'm leaving," she said softly.

Her father didn't say a word. His face was white. The muscles in his jaws and cheeks clamped shut tight, as if they were springs. He turned and left the house.

Jan shook his head. "You don't make sense." He looked at his sister with a strange gleam in his eyes. Suddenly, Janke wasn't his innocent "little Sis" anymore, the sister whom he needed to protect from the big, bad world. Janke realized it would have been easier for her family if she had been executed.

"It's best if you go away for a while. You have nothing to be proud of." Jan went upstairs.

Janke trudged out of the house. Leaning against the shed, smoking a cigarette, stood her father. He turned toward her. Pain flooded his eyes. Janke's chest filled with love for her father. A love she couldn't express. She took her bicycle from the shed. Father looked at her. His lips never moved.

For the last time, Janke biked down the lane behind the houses.

She had considered the Jansma farm, but decided to bike to Harm's farm. In the evening shadows, a lonesome figure sat on the fence. He jumped when he heard her come near.

"Harm, it's me, Janke."

He took the bike from her hands.

"I came to ask if you know where Helmut is and . . . if he's still alive?"

"Yes. He is in England."

A sigh escaped her. At least he was alive.

"All I know is that he landed safely there. I have no address."

Tears burned her eyes. She didn't look at Harm.

"I have no place to go." Janke gazed at the shadow of the barn.

He touched her cheek. "They don't like how you were rescued?"

Janke nodded.

"I'll help you."

Janke felt tired. She hung onto the fence as if it was her last stronghold.

"Will you go to Helmut?"

Janke shrugged her shoulders. "I don't know . . . My family . . . "

"Come with me." Harm draped his arm around her. "I have a good hiding place in one of the barns. That's where you'll stay tonight. You will have all night to think about your future."

32.

They sat at the kitchen table.

"I understand your parents' reaction." Aunt Anna looked at Janke over black-rimmed glasses. "You have nothing to be proud of."

The words from her aunt wounded Janke's heart. "It would have been better if the Germans had shot me." Janke blew her nose.

"It would have been much more heroic." Aunt Anna looked away.

Janke's hands twisted the handkerchief in her lap. What had she expected? That Aunt Anna would praise Helmut? Aunt Anna who'd lost her son. Whose husband had not been heard from since he was sent to a concentration camp. Who had seen so much misery in the last five years.

"You can help me here, for a while at least. I'll pay you. You will need the money if you want to find your Helmut." Her aunt got up from the table. "There's much work to be done before this country is rebuilt and cleaned up."

"I won't take any money." Janke took her few belongings to her room.

Soon she fell into a routine of daily duties. She was in charge of housework, while Aunt Anna helped the people who returned from slave labor in Germany. They all needed clothing, ration coupons and sometimes a place to stay. There was room enough in the mansion since two of the women had returned to their homes.

Janke's days were too busy, but at night, in the quiet of her room, she thought of Helmut. Would he still be in England or would he have made it to his uncle in Canada? Often, Janke felt an urge to write him, to tell him that she would come to Canada. But her words never made it to the paper. It wasn't that she didn't believe in his love for her or her feelings for him, but she didn't want to leave her family like this. Every day Janke hoped for word from her family. Every night, before she went to her room, she checked the road for a familiar cyclist, hoping her father would come and ask her to come home with him.

Slowly, groups of war prisoners returned from concentration camps. Janke shivered as she watched the moving skeletons dressed in rags. They looked like death, their eyes staring into nothing, their stillness eerie as they passed. In the following weeks, full of hope, Aunt Anna and Janke watched the groups of prisoners. But her uncle was never among them.

Three weeks later, on May 5, 1945, while the whole country celebrated the liberation, Aunt Anna received a letter from the Red Cross, informing her that her husband had died of pneumonia on January 17. Aunt Anna worked even harder. Janke noticed how thin she looked. The features in her aunt's face grew tight and determined. She hardly spoke. Janke began avoiding the woman she loved so much, but who had become hard and unforgiving.

One evening at the end of May, Janke's father arrived. Janke invited him inside, but he refused.

"Let's go for a walk," he said.

They took a path through the orchard. Apple blossoms snowed the last of their pink petals, making a soft path for them.

"How's Mother?" Janke hardly knew where to begin.

"She's doing a little better." Father didn't look at her, and Janke sensed that her mother probably wasn't better at all. Janke could imagine that her mother would not go out because of the gossip in town about the daughter who had brought shame to their family.

"I'm hoping to open the school next week. Jan has helped me fix everything up. They left quite a mess. The classrooms were lined with bunk beds; it was a big job."

"And Grandmother Janke and Grandfather Pieter?" Janke realized how much she missed them.

"They're fine. They seem to be busy helping people out."

They walked on in silence to the end of the orchard. A wooden fence separated the property from a farmer's pastures. Father leaned on the fence. He found his tobacco and rolled a cigarette. Janke glanced sideways. He looked thin. She stared at the grazing cattle, their tails swishing in unison.

"You look pale." Father turned to her. "Does Aunt Anna have enough food?"

"Yes," Janke nodded. "We have enough food."

"Were you thinking of coming home?"

It was the question she had been waiting for, but the tone her father used made her hesitate.

"Are they ready for me to come home?" Her face was hot.

"No."

Janke bit her trembling lip. She fought hard not to cry.

"I'm going to Canada." She had made up her mind. All she had needed was that last push to make the choice for her.

"What will you do in Canada?"

"I will marry Helmut."

"That's his name." Father blew out the smoke of his cigarette in a billowing cloud. "How long have you known him?"

"A year and a half."

"You met him on Sunday afternoons?"

"Yes, at the harbor."

"I knew it." He turned to face her. "We are not ready for this, Janke. Not after everything the Germans have done. You must understand."

Janke nodded. Her throat was thick with tears.

"You took a terrible risk." He sighed. "And now you have to live with the consequences."

"If I hadn't known Helmut, I would be dead." Tears streamed down her face.

Father pulled her close. He rested his head on hers. "We need time, Janke. We need a lot of time to come to terms with these five horrible years."

Janke wiped her face on the sleeve of her cardigan.

"It could take twenty years or more before we can even look at a person from Germany and not see a Nazi."

"Helmut wasn't a Nazi. He never wanted to be in the war."

"No one will understand that now, Janke. People have this collective hate against Germans, men, women and children." He offered his handkerchief. Janke blew her nose. As she looked up, she noticed the glistening in her father's eyes.

"There is so much hate, Janke. Can you blame the people?"

"No." She couldn't. She had heard, seen and experienced too much cruelty herself.

"We better go back." He turned and took her hand. "I'll say hi to Aunt Anna and then I have a four-hour bike ride."

Janke knew. She'd made the trip many times.

"How will you pay for your trip to Canada?"

"I can borrow money from Aunt Anna."

"Are you sure this is what you want to do?"

Janke nodded. She was sure. "I can't stay with Aunt Anna for the rest of my life." Now that she had said the words out loud, she felt determined to go.

Janke waited outside while her father went to say goodbye to his sister. Ten minutes later the door opened and he came out alone. He took his bike from where it stood against the wall of the house.

"Do the best you can," he said softly. "You have a future ahead of you in a land they say has many opportunities." He swallowed hard. Janke threw her arms around her father. She could find no words to express her feelings. He patted her shoulder. Without a word, he mounted his bicycle. Janke watched as he pedalled off. He never turned. He never waved. She stood and watched until she couldn't see him anymore.

In her room, Janke reached for pen and paper and wrote the words that had been locked in her heart for the past weeks. She wrote the address of Helmut's Uncle Hans on the front of the envelope. As she closed the flap, she hoped with all her heart that Helmut had made it to his uncle's bakery in Waterloo, Ontario.

Aunt Anna helped Janke apply for permission to travel to England. The documents arrived the first week of August. Through her connections with the underground movement, her aunt was also able to find her a place to stay in Liverpool. Janke planned to work there until she had enough money to book her passage to Canada.

The wind blew through her short curls. She grabbed onto the railing as the trawler's engines started up. Large cranes and big ships lined the quays in the damaged harbor of Rotterdam. Much of the city was gone from the Nazi bombardment at the beginning of the war, a bombardment designed to bring the Dutch government to its knees. Blackened ruins along the quay stood as silent witnesses of war.

Slowly, the boat inched its way out of the port, maneuvering around other fishing boats, its bag-like fishing net rigged high up, the Dutch flag flying proudly at the top of the mast. The crew busied themselves below deck. The skipper's face peered from the wheelhouse. His hand went up to acknowledge her.

Janke had never been outside the Netherlands, and now she was on her way to England. Hopefully soon she would be crossing the Atlantic Ocean to Canada.

Janke blinked as the boat slowly made its way into the North Sea, carrying her to a new life. She watched the buildings and cranes become smaller and smaller. Her tears ran freely as the long, winding ribbon of coastline slowly faded from view. She heard the splashing of the waves against the bow of the boat. Gripping the railing, she wondered if she would ever see her homeland again. She wondered about Annie and Bert. She would have to write Douwe and Afke once she had settled in England.

She thought of her parents and her brother Jan and her grandparents. She thought of Alie, Freerk, and Reverend and Mrs. Bergman. She remembered the pain of Alie's last words, the loathing in Jan's eyes and her mother's stinging remarks. "We all need time," her father had said. But there had been pain in his eyes. The pain that she brought. Janke stood at the rail and cried.

But after some time the tears stopped flowing from her eyes, her chest stopped heaving. The wind slowly dried her face. An emptiness greater than anything she'd ever felt engulfed her and chilled her body. She stood entirely alone, gazing out over the sea but seeing nothing.

Finally Janke turned away from the view of what she was leaving behind. She walked to the other side of the ship and looked toward her future. What would it be like in Canada? She didn't know anything about the country except that it was many times larger than the Netherlands. How would she survive? Nothing had prepared her for this loneliness that threatened to swallow her whole.

Then her thoughts moved to Helmut, his gentle voice, his kindness. Her heart fluttered when she remembered the ball, dancing and the feel of his arms, the rescue and their time in the boat. Her heart told her that Helmut had somehow made his way to Canada. All she had was his uncle's address and faith that Helmut was waiting for her. Her new mission mustn't fail. Her whole life depended on the choice she had made.

Janke wiped her eyes. She took a deep breath. The sea air filled her lungs. She watched seagulls dive in and out of the water in a dance for food. Her arms stretched out to embrace the earth and sky. In the distance, the masts of a tall ship moved in slow motion from south to north. Soft winds brushed her face, played with her hair. She was free. Not free from the past, but free to look ahead, beyond the horizon, to her future with Helmut.

Author's Note

When the War Is Over is a work of fiction based on real events that occurred during World War II. The character of Janke represents the many brave women and girls who risked their lives working for the resistance.

On Friday, May 10, 1940, as part of Hitler's Blitzkrieg (Lightning War), German troops invaded the Netherlands. Heavy bombardments quickly destroyed the seaport of Rotterdam, and the Germans threatened to bomb other major cities. Though the Dutch armies fought bravely, the government was forced to surrender after only four days. The royal family and the Dutch government fled to England.

The Nazi government instituted many new laws and regulations in the Netherlands. Jewish people were rounded up and forced to live in the ghetto in Amsterdam. Trains transported them to the concentration camp at Westerbork, and from there many were sent to the death camps in Germany and Poland. Many Jews went into hiding, as did many others (students, musicians, physicians and political opponents of the Third Reich).

The resistance grew quickly in the Netherlands. It began with the printing of illegal newspapers, which were distributed mostly by women and children. Falsifying identity cards and printing food ration coupons also became a major operation for the movement. Young girls and women played a major role in the resistance throughout the course of the war. Many were arrested, brutally interrogated, sent to concentration camps and, in some cases, executed by the SS.

After reading several personal accounts by women who had worked for the resistance during World War II, I felt inspired by their courage and determination to fight the enemy.

For more information on the couriers and background information on World War II, please visit my web site at www.marthaattema.com

martha attema

Acknowledgments

The author would like to thank the following people whose support has made this book possible.

Fokke Wagenaar, archivist of the Resistance Museum of War in Leeuwarden, Friesland, who helped me find research material on the couriers.

Kit Pearson, Jo Bannatyn-Cugnet, Cathy Beveridge, Norma Charles, Kathy Cook-Waldron and Sheena Koops, who, during the Sage Hill Writing Experience in the summer of 1999, helped me reduce the interesting, historical background material while leaving the story intact.

Margaret Geurtsen-Dekker, for remembering what it was like during the war.

Marla Hayes, for her friendship, patience and invaluable editorial advice.

The members of the Children's Writers' Group of North Bay, for their constructive criticism and support.

My publisher and editor Bob Tyrrell, for believing in this story.

Romkje and Rikst, for their honest criticism.

Sjoerd, for his love and encouragement.

Albert, for putting up with my frustrations, and for always being there for me.

When the War Is Over is martha attema's third teen novel set in the Netherlands. *A Time to Choose* (Orca, 1995) won the Blue Heron Book Award and was a finalist for both the Arthur Ellis Award and the Geoffrey Bilson Award for Historical Fiction. *A Light in the Dunes* (Orca, 1997) was an American Library Association "Quick Pick for Reluctant Readers" and made the New York Public Library Books for the Teen Age list. martha attema lives in Corbeil, Ontario.

www.marthaattema.com